THE LONG HUNTER

A NOVEL BY
DON McNAIR

Illustrations by James Tampa

Palladium Imprint
Medallion Press, Inc.
Printed in USA

Dedication:

*I dedicate this book to the loving memory
of my father-in-law, Dr. William Moore Hadley.*

My friend, my mentor, my very own Noah Dandridge.

Published 2006 by Medallion Press, Inc.
The MEDALLION PRESS LOGO
is a registered tradmark of Medallion Press, Inc.

Printed in the United States of America

Library of Congress Cataloging-in-Publication Data

McNair, Don, 1938-
  The long hunter / Don McNair.
    p. cm.
  Summary: After Indians kill his parents and kidnap his sister, fourteen-
  year-old Matt searches for her, gaining along the way survival skills
  from his experiences and a yearning for a true home and family.
    ISBN-13: 978-1-932815-51-1
  [1. Frontier and pioneer life--Virginia--Fiction. 2. Coming of age
  --Fiction. 3. Survival--Fiction. 4. Indians of North America--Fiction.
  5. Shawnee Indians--Fiction. 6. Indian captivities--Fiction. 7. Brothers
  and sisters--Fiction. 8. Virgina--History--Colonial period, ca. 1600-1775
  --Fiction.] I. Title.
PZ7.M478792868Lo 2006
[Fic]--dc22

                                             2006009098

10 9 8 7 6 5 4 3 2 1
First Edition

THE LONG HUNTER

A NOVEL BY
DON McNAIR

Illustrations by James Tampa

CHAPTER 1

THE BITTER NORTH WIND STRENGTHENED THIS NOVEMBER day in 1770 as it squeezed southward between the Virginia Valley's Allegheny and Blue Ridge mountains. It had started in Pennsylvania, in land peopled by real neighbors, clapboard houses and steepled churches, but now slipped its cold fingers through mostly untouched wilderness. It whined along the James River, and swirled around a stark log inn perched alone in a cluttered clearing.

Young Matt McLaren stared out an inn window and watched an old man approach from the south, squinting against the wind. The man tugged his jerkin tighter at the neck and leaned forward, stumbled and regained his footing. He reached the building, sighed, and elbowed the plank door open. Matt turned to the door.

The man looked away from the bright flickering fireplace at one end of the long room and stared instead at the rough-plank bar at the other end where several drinking men with glowing yellow faces watched him. The bartender eyed him as he leaned on the counter.

"Dandridge." The bartender nodded and held the gaze. "Well, shut the damned door."

"Struthers." The old man stomped to dislodge dirt from his moccasins, and slammed the door tightly against the chill.

"I s'pose you want to sit. We're pretty filled up."

The bartender glanced about the murmuring crowd sitting at the room's four long, split-log tables. His bulging eyes spotted Matt leaning against one cluttered table, a bucket dangling from a limp arm. Struthers slapped his rag against the bar.

"You! Get back to work! We got people what want to sit down."

Matt straightened and sloshed his wash rag into the greasy water. He wrung it out, dark liquid oozing between his fingers, its odor stinging his nostrils. He gagged, turned away, and wiped more table scraps into the bucket. Sweat dropped onto his chin, more prominent now than when he'd arrived two weeks ago, before he'd lost the weight.

Struthers glared at Matt as he poured a shot of whiskey. Beaded sweat glistened on his bald head in the low light thrown from beef-tallow candles, which dripped foul-smelling waste down the chinked log walls.

Matt wiped the table with jerky motions, and the old man sat down. Sounds of clinking tankards and murmuring voices softened. Matt fought off vomiting, balanced his load of dirty trenchers in his thin hands, and glanced at the twisting path to the kitchen. He gathered his strength and sidestepped among the farmers and tradesmen dressed in animal skin caps, deerskin jerkins, moccasins and home-pegged boots, sipping their nightly pints and whiskey. Two wore frayed frock coats left from earlier days in the north, or in Tidewater towns across the Blue Ridge Mountains.

Matt knew more stragglers would arrive before nightfall. The inn was an island of civilization on the lonely rutted Great Road that snaked through the Virginia Valley's rolling, tree-choked terrain. It laid just a stone's throw south of the James River's Cherry Bottom ford, where the forest opened to a wedge of brush and grass next to the river's swift waters.

When Matt's own family moved down from Pennsylvania two summers ago, they had no choice but to sleep upriver under a sailcloth tent. But those who could afford it were glad to pay six pennies for a bed upstairs with reasonably clean sheets, or four pennies if they'd sleep two or more to a bed. The single room was full every night he'd been there. The travelers pulled their cots close to the fireplace and buried their deerskin valises and traveling trunks under them for protection. Some paid another shilling to eat a warm meal with meat downstairs, then wash it down with beer or whiskey. He cleaned up after it all while they slept.

Matt reached the small lean-to kitchen and set the dirty trenchers and utensils beside the wash tub. The black slave woman, as thin as he but a head taller, dried her bony hands on her tattered grey gown and felt his forehead. He welcomed the coldness of her touch. She frowned.

"You be sick," she said. "You got no business doin' this kinda work."

He looked into her black face and shrugged.

"I means it." She felt his forehead again. "You just a child, no bigger'n a tadpole. A bitty thing like you, and him working you to death. You ain't fit to be out of bed."

He stretched tall, arms back, trying to loosen his aching muscles. The dizziness came back. He steadied against the wall and blinked to refocus his eyes.

"You needs some air, boy." The woman grabbed a huge wooden pail of scraps and thrust it at him. "Here. Slop them hogs, and stay out there a while. 'Fore you keel right over."

He grasped the bucket's frayed rope handle with both hands and duck-walked out the door and down the dirt path past the stable. Foul garbage sloshed onto his home-spun trousers and bare feet with each step. He upended the bucket and watched the slop spill over the bottom fence rail into the pig trough.

Matt leaned against the fence and glanced around. He'd started before dawn, after Struthers shook him out of his feverish sleep, to feed the fire. The sun broke over the Blue Ridge Mountains as he set out breakfast things, melting the frost around the inn and its stable, where he slept. It was high overhead when he chopped the kindling just before the noon meal. Now, it was almost dark.

He glanced north into the cold wind, toward where he'd lived until two weeks before, then turned west. A big red sun was setting over the Allegheny Mountains. He fought back the wind's chill and the memories, concentrated instead on the sun. He could actually see it sinking when he looked at where its round edge touched the treetops. Actually moving down, taking with it the light, then the color from around him. Just now, the tree colors were changing from blue and green and brown to purple, a deep purple that washed over the landscape as if a giant hand brushed it on.

An owl hooted to his left, a bobcat screeched. Matt stood still. What lay on the other side of the mountain besides the Indians? The Virginia province claimed all that land, clear to where an ocean might stop it. But King George forbade his subjects from settling there, on what the Shawnee Indians called the Can-Tuc-Kee land, although he did allow French and Indian War soldiers to claim homesteads there as pay. None had moved yet, as far as Matt knew.

But some men did go there to hunt. People called them the long hunters because they stayed a long time before returning with their hides and stories. His closest neighbor, Paul Tatum, had gone the year before. He'd harvested his crops, then set out with a hatchet, a hunting knife, and a shot-pouch on his belt, and his long black rifle in the crook of his arm. He'd led two pack horses past the McLaren farm and waved to Matt. When he returned earlier this spring, his horses loaded with pelts, he told exciting tales. There were big buffalo herds, he said, and elk and other game, all easy targets on the salt lick trails.

Matt looked south, down the valley. A few had settled down there, in Cherokee country. They didn't have to fight the mountains. They just walked down the valley, forded the rivers, and started a new life in the forbidden wilderness.

Heavy footsteps. Matt turned as somebody grabbed his arm.

Struthers!

"What the hell you doin'?" The man jerked him back to the inn. "You finish them damned tables."

Struthers' broad hand shoved Matt at the inn's door. Matt stumbled, caught his balance and glanced back toward the disappearing sun. The purple was gone now. In its place were black and gray, and jagged edges. He went inside and got his wash bucket from the kitchen and returned to the dirty tables, then realized he'd left his cleaning rag behind.

"Use this one." Struthers, now behind the bar, tossed a soggy rag at him.

Mat missed. It hit a plate and knocked pork scraps onto the table's uneven surface.

Struthers shook his head.

"You ain't worth a bucket of warm spit."

A bar customer laughed and Struthers grinned. The laughing young man wore a leather jacket and a tomahawk hung at his side. A white scar angled across his whiskered cheek.

"He ain't worth nothin' now, but I'll learn him," Struthers said. "Though prob'ly I should'a left him out there with the Indians, that's what I should'a done."

Matt's stomach churned. He wiped another section of table top, next to where the farmer called Dandridge was sitting. The old man frowned at him.

"You don't look too good," he said. "You all right?"

Matt nodded. His eyes blurred when he glanced back at Struthers. Horrible pictures flashed in his mind's eye. Images of the burned-out cabin, of what happened at the Indian camp. Struthers told the story at least once a night.

The innkeeper leaned back, his fat belly pushed against the bar. His stubby fingers grasped its edge as if for support to launch the story once again. He licked his uneven teeth and grinned at the man who'd laughed. He gurgled fresh whiskey into his glass.

"On the house, sir." He leaned back, beaming. "Like your looks. Want to hear a hell of a story?"

The young man nodded and sipped his whiskey. He set the glass aside and hunkered down on the bar, peering at Struthers over crossed forearms.

"Well, it's hard to believe." Struthers sighed and pulled another towel from under the bar. He slowly wiped the surface, worried a small spot into submission. "You'd think this here valley was gettin' civilized. Hell, we been living here a while, at least up in the north part. But it ain't civilized at all, no siree."

He bent forward and squinted hard at Matt. The crowd quieted. Struthers' gaze drifted from Matt to his bar customers. He let the silence build, as if he enjoyed the attention. Finally he spoke.

"Well, I was standin' right here, and that there boy come runnin' in," he said. "He must be . . . what, fourteen, fifteen years old? But he was cryin' like a baby. Said the Indians killed his daddy and run off with his mama and sister. Next morning some militia took him back up there and found the Indian camp up on the Jackson River, 'fore it and the Cow Pasture form the James."

His voice rose during the story's telling, and the crowd quieted more. Matt gathered three trenchers and carried them down the table, dodging among staring patrons. His ears burned, his face was hot. Struthers now stood erect, palms planted solidly on the bare bar before him, boring his gaze into Matt's soul.

"Them Indians was already gone," Struthers said. "But they found the boy's mama. She was layin' there deader'n hell, stripped naked."

Matt felt every eye in the room on him. That farmer watched, too. But he looked different now, like he had a question. The old man glanced at his rough, weathered hands, sighed, and set his whiskey down. He turned to Struthers.

"You have to talk about it in front of the boy?" He shot a critical glance at Matt.

The innkeeper eyed the farmer, his eyebrows raised. He flicked his rag at something on the bar.

"Hell, Dandridge, it's a good story. And this here young man ain't heard it yet."

He wiped the now-polished bar surface, shrugged and turned back to the stranger.

"His ma's head was skinned completely bald. I hear they peeled her scalp off just like a rabbit hide. The militia laid her 'tween two rocks and piled more on top to keep the animals out, they did, then chased after them damned Indians. And you know what? It looked like they might've been Cherokee, from the south, not Shawnees like you'd think. Could'a been up here on a raidin' party, I s'pose. Then again, mebbe it was Shawnees."

Struthers slowly poured more whiskey into the stranger's glass. He frowned, then looked up and beamed. "Why, by God! Maybe they *was* Shawnees. 'Member when that stranger shot that Shawnee kid a month back? Not five miles from here. The one that got too close to his camp? Why, that was a Shawnee, he showed me the scalp! I 'spect they killed this boy's mama and daddy to get even."

The room was silent. Tears rolled down Matt's cheeks. His own mother, naked and scalped, had laid there for all to see. He turned toward the wall to hide his shame. And his tears.

"I said that'll be enough!"

It was Dandridge. He stood, staggered slightly and pushed his bench back, making scraping sounds on the puncheon floor. He was tall, even lanky, yet looked muscular across the chest. His long white-speckled brown hair shook as he slammed his empty tankard down onto the table and turned to Struthers. The two men stared at each other for several seconds. Dandridge's body sagged.

"I think that'll be enough," he said, softer this time. He motioned to Matt. "Don't you see the boy don't feel good? Why torment him?"

Struthers stared at Dandridge. He threw his rag down and stomped around the bar, stopped in front of Dandridge with a tight-lipped glare. What had earlier seemed like fat now looked like solid muscle, tensed and ready to explode. His right hand hid something behind him, and Matt knew it was the pistol the man had played with two nights before while telling a customer how he'd shot someone trying to rob him last winter.

"This here's my bar," he said. "I can say what I want."

"But you don't have to be mean to the boy," Dandridge said. "Common courtesy, that's all I ask."

The old man's hand inched down to his mug and he wrapped gnarled fingers around its handle. He seemed unsteady. Matt realized he'd started drinking long before he came into the tavern.

"What rights you got to this boy, anyhow?" Dandridge said. "He ain't yours."

"You're drunk again. Every time I see you you're drunk."

"Who the hell is he? He ain't your boy."

"I aim to get him bound out to me, if it's any of your business," Struthers said. "My indentured boy run away."

Dandridge waved Matt over and Matt felt a chill. He paused and set his load down. Two trenchers crashed to the floor, slopping food on a man's boots. He walked slowly to Dandridge and stood there, staring at his own bare feet.

"How about it, boy. You want to stay with Struthers?"

Dandridge's whiskey breath hit Matt's face in a long sigh. Matt glanced at the stiffened innkeeper, back to the floor.

"Well?" Dandridge stumbled sideways, caught himself.

"I guess."

"What's that? I couldn't hear . . ."

"I said I guess. I don't have no place else to go."

Struthers relaxed. "There, you see? Now, you go on back to your drinkin'. Just sit there and get sloshed, like you usually do. And you, boy, clean that mess up off the floor!"

Matt started to turn. Dandridge touched his shoulder and Matt paused to peer into the old man's face. He appeared to be about Granddad McLaren's age when he died three years ago up in Pennsylvania. Wrinkles moved at the corners of his puffy red eyes. He cupped his rough fingers under Matt's chin.

"Son, you look terrible. How long you been like this?"

Matt tried not to move. Dandridge shook his head, then dropped his hand and turned to Struthers.

"This boy's sick," he said. "I'm taking him with me."

Struther's mouth dropped open. "You're . . . you're what?"

"The boy's coming with me. He ain't goin' to be your draft horse."

Struthers stepped back. His face looked like somebody had rubbed flour on it. He fingered the pistol and waved it at Dandridge.

"You ain't goin' to talk to me like that," he said. "A little work won't hurt him none. Besides, I seen him first."

The inn was quiet. Matt stared at the floor and wished he could disappear. When he looked up Dandridge's soft face worked slowly, then stopped.

"What's your name, son?"

"Matthew McLaren."

"Well, Matthew — Matt — it's up to you."

Matt glanced at Struthers. He looked mad enough to pop a blood vessel. Then he looked at Dandridge. He knew what he wanted to do.

"I'll go with you," he said, quietly.

"Fine. Then let's get out of here."

The innkeeper stepped forward. "Now, just hold on. I don't want to have to use this gun! 'Sides, how's a drunk like you goin' to take care of that boy?"

Dandridge peered at the other man with sad eyes. "Look. I'm too old to worry about gettin' shot. You do what you have to do. I suspect, though, that not everybody here'd want you to shoot us."

Struthers' face got blood red. He leaned toward Dandridge until their noses almost touched. "You're a dead man," he breathed, too softly for anybody but Dandridge and Matt to hear. "I'm goin' to kill you for this."

Dandridge's hand guided Matt to the door. He stumbled, and Matt felt his weight as they stepped outside. The cold wind hit him, and he shivered as he tried to fight his chilling sickness. He walked rigidly, braced for a bullet.

He heard a click, then a pop behind him. The stars swirled, and he hit the ground.

CHAPTER 2

Pipe smoke, liquor, musty clothing. Warm flesh touched Matt's arm, something cold pressed his chest. He flinched, groaned, peeped through swollen eyelids. Two forms loomed over him. The cold thing went away, the warm pressure moved to his forehead.

"He's bad off." A strange, deep voice. The pressure dabbed at his forehead, slid down his cheek. "It's lung fever. He's real bad off."

"Been like that two days, Doc." Another voice. Where'd he heard it before? "I'd thought he'd get better by now, but . . ."

"Barefoot, you say? And living in the stables?"

"That's what he was doin' when I found him. Struthers worked him 'most to death, then put him out'n the stable at night like a horse."

Struthers! Matt shivered, jerked away. His eyes squeezed shut.

"He's tryin' to come out of it, Doc. You think?"

The soft pressure rubbed along Matt's arm. "It's a

wonder he's not dead. He mumbled the name 'Mandy.' Know her?"

"Nope. Said it all last night, too. He'd say, 'Mandy, I'm sorry.' Over and over."

"Well, we've got to build up his strength. Hand me that bag, Dandridge."

Dandridge!

Matt's eyelids popped open. Two hovering bodies came into focus. The farmer from the inn, his face lit by the flickering fireplace flames, stared into Matt's face. He smelled of whiskey. The deep-voiced stranger on the bench behind him rummaged through a small black satchel.

"Let's see. Antimony, cinchona, jalap, paregoric . . . ah! Mercury." He pulled out a little container and opened it. "Triturated mercury. We'll rub some into his arms and thighs, then give him twenty to forty grains by clyster, twice that by mouth. I'll leave you some for tomorrow."

Matt lay on his side and watched the doctor rub the medication on him. The man pulled a foot-long pewter syringe from his bag and fingered a wooden plunger sticking out its end.

"We'll need some water," he said. He worked the plunger loose from the cylinder.

Dandridge swigged from a jug and set it on the table. He disappeared and returned with a noggin of water, and the fireplace again threw flickering light onto his face. No question. It was the man who'd stood up to Struthers at the inn.

The doctor tapped mercury into the cylinder, poured in some water, replaced the plunger and shook the mixture.

"Well, let's get his britches down."

Matt felt the old man's hands pushing into his armpits. He lifted, grunting. Matt moaned, tried to stand, went limp. The farmer grunted and dropped him face down across the doctor's knees. Matt struggled — tried to, at least, but knew he hadn't really moved much — then felt his trousers slide down his legs. A cold object slipped inside Matt's rear end. The old man's jug gurgled.

"You can see how I'm doing it, Dandridge. That's all there is to it."

"Bet that don't feel good," Dandridge said, softly.

"I expect not. But it may help him get well. There, now."

The tube left Matt's body. He struggled, again felt Dandridge's strong hands under his arms. Dandridge laid him on the pallet and covered him up.

The doctor coughed. "Don't you think we need a chamber pot about now?"

"Oh, my God!" Dandridge bounded out of Matt's vision and returned with a pot. He placed it on the floor, picked Matt up and plunked him down on it like a sack of flour. Sweat sparkled on Dandridge's face. He looked ready to leap — in what direction, Matt couldn't tell. The old man stared around with wide eyes and grabbed the pallet blanket. He wiped his face with one corner, then wrapped it around Matt. Dandridge upended his jug and drained it empty. He scrunched his eyes closed, gritted his teeth and set the jug back on the table.

The doctor shook more mercury onto a small square of paper and folded it into an envelope. "I'll leave the syringe here. Pick it up in a couple days."

"Well . . . well, all right. If you think I can handle things."

Matt felt the doctor's gaze, saw him out of the corners of his eyes. The doctor took hold of Dandridge's arm and walked him to the cabin door. His voice dropped, and Matt strained to hear his whispers.

"Struthers is fit to be tied," the doctor said.

"I don't doubt it."

"You've made a real enemy. You probably saved the boy's life, but Struthers takes it personally. Says you belittled him in front of his friends and customers."

"Customers, maybe," Dandridge said. "I doubt he's got any friends in that group." He fingered the clay pipe dangling from a leather thong around his neck.

"I'm sure you're right. He's killed two men I know of, and only one could be considered justified. Murdered the other one, but they couldn't prove it."

"I'll watch myself."

"Yes, well . . . take care. Think you can handle things?"

The room was quiet a few moments, then Dandridge spoke slowly. "If the boy can live through his folks' murders and all, I suppose I can live through giving him a clyster. Didn't look all that complicated to me."

"Fine. Fine. I'll look in on the boy in a couple days." He opened the door and left.

Matt coned the blanket around himself, his head stuck out the top, and stared at Dandridge. The farmer looked away and busied himself cleaning the cabin. He dragged the bench back to the table, took a soiled trencher and the noggin of water outside. Presently he returned, wiping the wet plate with his sleeve. He set it on the table and picked up the whiskey jug and turned it up. Nothing came out.

"Be back in a little," he said. He went outside again and soon Matt heard bumping on the cabin wall behind him. Probably a lean-to storage room. More silence, then Dandridge returned. He guzzled from a full jug, corked it and set it on the table.

Matt was sitting in the same position as before. He'd tried to move once, but dizziness stopped him. It was impolite to stare, but he didn't have the strength to look away from the farmer as he moved about the cabin. He picked up dirty clothes, wiped table crumbs to the floor with them, threw them into a corner with some others. Finally he stopped in front of Matt.

"Mornin'," he said. "Feelin' better?"

Matt nodded. Then he remembered. "Am I shot?"

"What?"

"Did . . . did Mr. Struthers shoot me?"

"Oh, at the inn? No, just shot in the air. Tryin' to scare us."

He peered into Matt's face. "You're pale as a ghost. You look terrible, for a fact."

"You think Mr. Struthers'll do something?"

"Now, don't you worry about that man." A callused hand touched Matt's face. "You just get well."

Dandridge glanced around and apparently saw nothing else that needed doing. He sat on the bench, hummed, finally looked back at Matt.

"Who's Mandy? Don't mean to pry, mind you. Just curious, that's all."

"She's my little sister. The Indians took her."

"Oh. Just wonderin'. Well, I'd best get on with the chores."

He went outside. The sun flooded in through the open door and struck Matt in his blanket covering. He watched Dandridge stride out to a huge oak whose budding branches threw stark shadows onto the front yard. Dandridge pinched tobacco from a small pouch and stuffed it into his pipe and glanced back toward the cabin where the fire was. He shrugged, leaned against the tree and puffed the unlit pipe.

Cooling liquid poured over Matt. Something touched his forehead. Sunlight from the lone window crawled down the cabin wall two, three times, separating days from flickering darkness. Snapping logs, more cool liquid. The odor of tobacco, whiskey.

Play with me, Matt. Oh, Matt, look at my dolly sleep. Hold my dolly, Matt. Please?

Curly blond hair, blue eyes.

Can I go to the woods with you, Matt? I'll be quiet, honest I will.

Coolness again. The cold metal tube. Light, dark, a horse's whinny.

Matt awoke and wrapped the blanket tighter. He sat up.

Dandridge stirred something in a fireplace kettle, beyond a high sun's rectangular light patch on the dirt floor.

"I'm sure hungry," Matt said.

Dandridge jumped. "God, you scared me. You awake?"

"This your place?" Matt tried to get to his knees, but fell back.

"Now, you take it easy. You been layin' there four days, wouldn't take more'n a cup of soup all that time. No wonder you're weak."

"I'm hungry now."

"Well, I'd imagine." Dandridge ladled some of the kettle's mixture into a wooden bowl. "This here'll be good for you. Got both bear and deer meat in it, don't remember what all else."

He handed the bowl and a wooden spoon to Matt. "Careful now, it's hot. Sure you can handle it?"

Matt tasted it. "It's awful good." He ate quickly, turned the bowl up and drained the last liquid, then lay back.

"Want some more? Here, I'll fill it up again. Got plenty, and you're sure . . ."

The sounds and light went away.

Matt woke to the sound of chopping. The sun streamed through the window at a sharp angle. Mid-morning. He must have slept almost around the clock. He pulled a leg under him and stood, fell against the wall, grabbed it for balance and waited for the room to stop spinning. He hobbled to the table, got a bowl and went to the kettle to dip up some food. He slumped onto the bench and ate his second meal since leaving Struthers' inn.

Chopping continued outside. Matt wrapped the blanket around himself and stepped out into sunlight that warmed his face. It flashed off Dandridge's swinging ax by a small clearing down the hill, past the oak tree, next to a harnessed roan horse. The man looked up the hill, lay the ax down, and came to the cabin.

"You up? Well, that's good. You oughta be sittin' down, weak as you got to be."

"I'm all right. What you doin'?"

"Here, sit on the splittin' stump. There, that's good. Been wantin' to clear more corn land this year. Thought I'd get started."

Four fresh stumps poked up next to the patch of the old cleared land, where Dandridge had started a burn pile for the branches. He'd already dragged the smaller logs to the woodpile.

"That's hard work," Matt said. "I can help you."

"Now, don't be talkin' like that. You got to get well."

"I mean it. I like to work. Helped my daddy some, and Struthers . . ." The innkeeper's face flashed in Matt's mind, and he shuddered.

"Well, you got to get well 'fore you do anything. Then if you really want to help . . . " Dandridge looked south, down the hill, and Matt followed his gaze. It was pretty land. The Blue Ridge Mountains and the Alleghenies formed a valley his daddy said had the finest farmland God ever made.

Some parts of it, up north where his family had come from, were up to seventy miles wide. Down here the ridges were closer, and the land rolled more. But the soil was just as good, maybe better.

"I cleared that little spot the first year Martha and me was here," Dandridge said, pointing. "Right 'fore she died. Still grow a little corn for my whiskey, and to trade for provisions."

"We could put in more," Matt said. "I can help you."

"Well, that's nice, but you don't owe me nothin'. Stay as long as you want, though, glad for the company."

They sat for several minutes, feeling the warm sun. Dandridge loaded his pipe and dry-smoked it, looked out over his land. The silence sat heavy on Matt, and he searched for something to say.

"What would you grow, if you was to start farming again?" Matt asked.

"Hemp. That's what I'd raise, if I ever got the ground ready. England buys it for navy rope. Why, I heard the county proved certificates for more than a hundred twenty thousand pounds of hemp last year. And it's not even settled yet! A man could make a good livin', growin' hemp."

"I could help you," Matt said.

"Well, guess I'm just dreamin'. Takes money to farm right. Some, at least."

He got up, went into the cabin, came out moments later puffing his pipe. He sat and blew a long sigh of blue smoke that curled in the still air.

" 'Course, we could plant corn this spring. The best time is when the dogwood is in bloom, or —" he looked up into the oak tree — "or when them there buds are the size of squirrel ears. Won't be long now."

He leaned forward, a smile on his wrinkled face. "By golly, we could sell that corn next fall and buy a well-broken young horse. A good one, not like ol' Benjie there. We'd have to get twenty, thirty pounds Sterling together to do it. If we could make thirty, thirty-five bushels an acre and get a shilling a bushel . . . why, with my savings, it might be enough. We could clear more land this next summer and fall, and maybe the next year we *could* plant that hemp."

"I bet we could," Matt said. He stood and the world started to move. He fell back to the stump and touched his head.

Dandridge jumped up. "Son, you get back inside. Damned if I wasn't thinking of doing what Struthers done! Get a poor helpless boy good and sick, then work the tar out of him. C'mon inside, now."

"I'm all right, Mr. Dandridge. Just a little dizzy."

"Noah, that's my name. Call me Noah."

"All right Mr. . . . Noah."

"Inside, now. I'm ashamed, that's what I am. What's the difference between you clearin' tables at an inn and clearing timber at a farm? The work here'd be even harder. You all right?"

Matt nodded and held onto the old man's shoulder. They walked slowly into the cabin, and Matt lay on the pallet. He looked up at Noah.

"That's a good idea you got," he said. "Hemp'd be a good crop, looks like. I get my strength back and we'll do it, sure enough."

CHAPTER 3

MATT TOUCHED HIS FIERY BRANCH TO THE DEAD OAK leaves, and crackling blue smoke curled toward his face. He tossed the torch into another leaf pile and shinnied up onto the fallen oak's trunk.

He looked down the hill. The yellow river of dried grass, kept out until the previous spring by the trees' sun-blocking foliage, seemed to flow down the hill and disappear over the next rise, carrying vine-bound trunks toward the evergreen-blotched gray ridge that shimmered through heat rising from the fires. The clearing's edges were straight and true for plowing.

A crisp breeze brushed Matt's neck, raised bold goose bumps on his bare arms. He rubbed them idly, leaving pale streaks in dark caked dirt. A cold bite in the late afternoon November air hinted of snow to come. He'd already seen two vees of geese flying south that morning. He smiled. He was thankful for the brief break, yet working among the fires with his friend Noah raised a sweat that somehow felt good.

The work itself felt good. His daddy had often left their

cabin with an ax on his shoulder and a smile on his sun-tanned face, returned later dirty and sweaty, but with his smile intact. "There's nothing like opening up new land," Matt heard him tell his mother once. "Nothing like it back in Scotland, or Ireland, or anywhere else. We're doing something good here."

Matt stiffened. Dark memories tumbled over themselves as the fires, crackling and snapping around him, awakened the horrible nightmare of his life. He grasped the rough bark beneath him for support and closed his eyes. He could almost see that day, that terrible day, when his daddy returned early from his own clearing work for the last time. Matt and Mandy were in the poplar grove south of the cabin when he heard a big gobbler in the bushes. He sent her home for his daddy's gun so he could shoot it, and waited a long time for her to come back. The gobbler finally spotted him and scrambled off, and Matt stalked back to the cabin thinking mean thoughts about his sister.

He flinched and dug his fingernails deeper into the bark as his mind's eye saw the smoke billow from the direction of the cabin. He'd run blindly through the thickets toward it, and stopped at the clearing edge. Fire shot up a hundred feet from the cabin's dry logs, laid lovingly by his daddy and their neighbors. It twisted and flickered in the wind, formed a black plume that darkened the sky. He saw a fallen object in the cabin yard, and felt a thousand needle pricks as he stumbled toward it. It was his daddy, lying dead, face down. Moist, dark red blood covered his skull where his scalp once was. His mother and sister were gone.

"No! No!"

Startled by his own voice, Matt looked up. Noah's ax was thunking echoes into the valley as he cut limbs to push back the forest walls. He stopped abruptly and glanced in Matt's direction, then quickly returned to his work. Matt felt ashamed, then thankful that the old man said nothing. Usually Matt cried out only at night, when the dreams overtook him in his sleep in the cabin they shared.

Matt returned to work. There was a lot to do before they could plant hemp next spring. The fires would burn the limbs and part of the trunks, but they'd still have to borrow an ox team to pile the heavier charred logs and set them on fire again. Then they'd have to grub the stumps out. Or maybe they'd just plant around them.

"Hello, the house!"

Matt cocked his head toward the voice. It came from near the cabin, on a rise two hundred feet to the north. Charred logs lay between him and the voice, the near ones still smoldering, those farthest away cold markers of time. Beyond was the clearing Noah and his wife had made, long before Matt even came to the county. Brown, ear-laden corn stalks leaned every which way, their brittle dead leaves clicking in the breeze. He and Noah would pick that corn when the burning was done, then shell it together before the fireplace.

A man on a horse came into view next to the cabin. He dismounted and tied the reins to a bush and stared at the doorway. It was a stranger, for sure. He was the only visitor they'd had since the doctor last came calling.

"Hello!" Matt yelled, waving at the figure. "Down here!"

The chopping stopped behind him. Noah shaded his eyes and shrugged. He studied the fires, pulled a burning branch away from the forest and into the grass still soaked from the morning rain. He shouldered his ax and limped toward Matt. A log had fallen on his right leg last week, but he'd never mentioned the injury. Sometimes, though, when Noah thought he was alone, Matt saw him flexing his badly bruised thigh.

The stranger, hands on his hips, turned slowly and squinted down at them. He approached through the corn, taking pains to plant his feet firmly between the rows where Matt and Noah had trod it smooth during their hoeing. He was a stern man, judging from the way he frowned. His clothes appeared stern, too: black, tight-fitting trousers and vest pulled across his pot belly, buckleless dark shoes. He reached them and removed his black tri-cornered hat and nodded to Noah. His nose was long and hooked, his bushy eyebrows knitted together. He glanced at Matt, then away quickly.

"Noah Dandridge?"

The man paused by Matt's tree. He seemed not to notice that the shifting breeze swirled smoke in their direction.

"Am I speaking to Noah Dandridge?"

"That's me," Noah said, reaching a hand out. "And you are —"

"Reverend Ashbrooke."

The man grasped Noah's hand with his fingertips, then rubbed them on his pants leg.

"Christopher Ashbrooke. I am this parish's church

warden."

"I see. And to what do we owe the honor?"

Noah set the ax head on the ground and leaned on its handle. He wiped a sweat-stained forearm across his brow.

"I take it this boy is Matthew McLaren," Ashbrooke said. The visitor's dull gray eyes studied him from top to bottom. It was hard to look into them, more comfortable to focus on Noah's ax handle.

"That's right," Noah said. "Matt McLaren. May I ask what your interest is?"

"I'll be brief, Mr. Dandridge. Samuel Struthers is concerned about this boy's welfare."

Matt shivered. Memories of Struthers flooded back. The stranger's gaze bore into him, inspected his torn linen shirt, his too-tight pants, the rough moccasins Noah made him.

"Concerned for him?" Noah lifted the ax, banged it down again. "Why, that lying fool. If you'd seen Matt at Struthers' inn almost a year ago, you'd have had plenty of reason to be concerned about his welfare!"

Matt knew he was right. He'd been sick and weak, but since then he'd developed the muscles of a full-grown man. He was a good three inches taller from growth spurred by the big appetite his work had given him and the abundant wild game he and Noah took from the forest.

"Struthers is concerned?" Noah repeated. "Pardon me, sir, I don't follow what you're saying. Struthers was *killing* the boy. That's why I took him away from there!"

"Well, the boy was working for his keep, of course," the man said. "Helping Mr. Struthers clean tables and such.

Apparently, you've got him working here, too."

"Well, yes . . ."

Ashbrooke raised a hand. "I must consider the boy's future. Mr. Struthers wants Matthew bound out to him so he can raise him proper and train him in the inn-keeping business."

That's ridiculous," Noah said. "Hell, I can train him better to be a good farmer. That mean bastard . . ." He swung the ax into the ground.

"Mr. Dandridge!" The church warden's nervous feet jumped back from the ax. His face reddened. "There's no need for profanity."

"Matt's learnin' a lot here. He's got good instincts. He'll make a fine farmer."

Matt blushed at Noah's praise. Noah had never said that before. But there had been lots of encouragement. *That's the way . . . you're getting the hang of it . . . you learn quick . . .*

"You can't just keep somebody like this," Ashbrooke said. "This is new country, but we're still civilized. The boy has to be bound out, legal and proper."

"Struthers already has one boy bound out. How many does he need?"

"That other boy's a runaway, Mr. Dandridge. He left last spring. They caught him and he ran away again a few days ago. Mr. Struthers has given up on him, and he's making room for Matt here."

"I'd have had Matt bound out myself, if I knowed I could," Noah said. "I didn't figure they'd let an old widower like me do it. But Struthers ain't married, either. How come you let *him* do it?"

Matt felt light-headed. He looked at Ashbrooke, who shifted his feet and frowned again.

"I had hoped I wouldn't have to get into this. But your way of living is a big concern. Mr. Struthers told me you're a drunk. Matthew, get your things. Come along, now."

The stranger strode toward the cabin, but soon apparently sensed he was walking alone. He stopped and turned.

"Come along?" Matt called, still standing there. "Where to?"

"You'll have meals and a warm bed with a good family until the court date in two weeks," the stranger said. "After that I expect you'll be living at the inn."

"I ain't no drunk," Noah said. "I take an occasional drink, but who doesn't?"

"I don't," Ashbrooke said.

"I've already got meals and a warm bed, Mister." Matt looked at Noah. It appeared as if he had a hangover, but he didn't. He hadn't drunk since they began clearing the land.

"Hey, Mister! Can't you see he's hurt? His leg's real bad, and he needs me. I got to help him here!"

"Son, you may have a few minutes to say good-bye, and get your things. And then —"

"I don't want to go!"

Matt didn't feel the tears until they were halfway down his cheeks. He couldn't find the words to make the man go away. He peered into Noah's moist eyes for help.

Noah looked just like he did when Sam Struthers

threatened them with his pistol. He looked defeated, dejected — but in the next breath he'd almost dared the inn-keeper to shoot. And they walked out free.

"You'll have to go, Matt," Noah said. "Go wash up."

"But . . ."

"Get goin' now." Noah pushed him gently toward the cabin.

Matt hesitated. Then he shuffled up the hill, between two corn rows. He barely felt the scratchy leaves brush his arms. What he did feel was the hurt from Noah's rejection. Saying those nice things about him, then telling him to *get goin'.* He'd stood up to a tough-talking Struthers, but now gave in to a smooth-talking stranger. Matt walked faster. Well, if Noah was giving up on him without raising a finger, maybe it *was* time to clear out.

He stormed into the small cabin and slammed the plank door. It bounced open again on its leather hinges, letting daylight into the dark room. He dipped a rag into the water bucket and washed the grime from his face and arms in long, quick strokes. The man didn't even care! They'd worked side by side all these months, hunted together, eaten together — and now — well, Noah might just as well have said *the hell with you!*

Matt scanned the room. What did he have to take? Damned little. A pair of Noah's hand-me-down trousers, a little bird he'd whittled with the pocket knife the old man had given him. He picked up the bird and rolled it in his fingers. It didn't look too bad, really. They'd whittled to-gether for a whole week, the old man sharing little tricks.

He'd taught Matt how to sharpen the knife at the grinding wheel, then they sharpened the scythe, the ax, and the foot adze they'd use later to square up timbers for the barn they were planning. Matt hadn't realized it at the time, but Noah taught him important things farmers needed to know, just like he'd told the Reverend. And Matt could have learned plenty more from the old man, even enjoyed the learning.

But not now. Not if he was going to wait tables and scrub floors! Tears blurred his vision, and he couldn't blink them back. Thoughts of Struthers hounding his days and nights were more than he could bear.

A crash sounded outside, from the rear of the cabin.

Then another.

Matt dropped the wooden bird and rushed outside. A grunt, another smashing noise. He rounded the corner. Something flashed in the lean-to. Ashbrooke, clinging wild-eyed to a post, didn't see him approach. The man recoiled as wet blotches landed on his pants and knee stockings.

Noah swung his ax, again and again. Jug after jug shattered and sprayed liquor everywhere. An inch of whiskey soon soaked the dirt floor. Thick streams flowed from the main puddle, sloshing debris in their paths. Noah was drenched with the liquid, surrounded by piles of broken crockery. Stunned, Matt and Ashbrooke watched the old man destroy his precious corn whiskey supply.

Noah didn't stop until he'd broken his last jug. He panted, leaned on his ax handle.

"Suppose I could of just dumped it out," he heaved, "and saved the jugs . . . but I got mad . . . and I couldn't take it out

. . . on a man of the cloth."

His gaze landed on the still itself. With a mighty lunge he buried the ax head deep into its side, splitting the seam. He glanced around once more, tossed the ax into the corner, and faced Ashbrooke.

"I s'pose I should get back to the burnin'," he said. "We're gettin' some wind, and that grass'll dry out quick."

"Yes, I suppose so," Ashbrooke said. He'd not moved from his spot, but stood there staring at the old man.

" 'Course, if those fires was to flare up, I don't think I could handle it by myself. If they was to spread to the trees, well . . . I really could use some help."

He looked at Ashbrooke, then at Matt.

"Matt here knows what to do. He'd be a big help."

Another pause. Matt studied Noah, then Ashbrooke, who still stood like a statue.

"I suppose he would be," the church warden finally said. He shuddered, as if shaking himself out of a daze. He looked at Matt, then at Noah.

"If I let him stay, can you have him at Fincastle court two weeks from Monday?"

"I guarantee it."

"I should take him with me, but . . . I'm counting on you to be there." He adjusted his coat and smoothed its wrinkled front, as if he had personally done the chopping.

"Well, I'd better go. I can count on you? Two o'clock Monday afternoon?"

"I guarantee it." Noah got his ax and limped from the lean-to and led the way around the cabin to Ashbrooke's horse. Ashbrooke mounted it. He regarded Matt and Noah a moment, then wheeled around and spurred the animal into a trot. For several seconds the only sounds were from the disappearing horse and the flapping corn leaves.

"Guess we'd better tend to the fires," Noah finally said. "You coming?"

He shifted his ax to his other hand and limped down the hill. Matt caught up with him. There was enough daylight left to finish the fire-tending. Matt knew all along Noah exaggerated the danger of fire. But he liked him all the more for it.

If he wasn't too tired come night, he might whittle another bird. A bigger one this time, with its wings spread. Maybe he'd have a really pretty one done by the time they went to Fincastle.

No. There were more important things to do before that.

He looked to Noah. "I'll help you clean up the jugs," he said. "If you want me to."

CHAPTER 4

JUST ENOUGH RAIN FELL DURING THE NEXT TWO WEEKS TO let Noah and Matt complete their burn safely. Each morning they awoke before dawn and were working among the felled trees as light and color came into the eastern sky. They returned to the cabin at dark, stirred the fireplace ashes, and added logs to keep the colder night temperatures outside.

The first week they ate their boiled potatoes and jerked venison, then sat before the fire and repaired clothing and tools. That done, Matt went back to whittling, and Noah worked with a large piece of dressed deerskin. He cut out long shapes and threaded leather thongs through their edges with his awl. They worked steadily, talking about unimportant things. Sometimes Noah told about living in Northern Ireland. Occasionally he gave Matt whittling tips.

"That'll split if you cut down the grain that way," he said once. Matt studied the piece, saw the grain swirl around an unseen knot. He turned the block and cut from a different angle. He worked slowly, deliberately. It was like Noah said. A good job was more important than a quick one.

Neither mentioned the upcoming court date, but it haunted Matt just the same. Three days after Ashbrooke's visit, he made a calendar stick. Each evening he fetched the stick from its hiding place behind the cabin, cut another notch, and ran his finger along the stick to count the notches. Ten, eleven, twelve — when he counted thirteen he stared into the bright moonlit sky toward the southeast, where Fincastle lay. He heard a snap and realized he'd broken the stick.

Matt flung the pieces into the dark woods and went inside. Noah looked up from his usual place on the bench, where he was whittling on a fresh piece of wood. Lying next to him was a new pair of leather breeches. Matt sat next to them and stared into the fire. Neither spoke for several minutes.

"Well, better get to bed," Noah said. "We're leavin' well before dawn."

Matt nodded. He looked down, saw the breeches again, but said nothing.

Noah cleared his throat. He, too, looked at the breeches, then off toward the wall. "It's getting cold. Put those on in the mornin'."

"Yessir."

Noah stood. He went to the corner and picked a tow sack off the floor. "Better get your things together tonight," he said, tossing it to Matt. "Here, put them into this."

Matt caught it. He stood and quickly looked away so Noah couldn't see his tears. He walked around the little room, gathering his belongings. When he looked back, Noah was lying on his own pallet, facing the wall. Matt lay down, too, and slipped into a troubled sleep.

Matt felt pressure on his shoulder. He opened his eyes. Darkness filled the room, except for lines of moonlight cast through cracks in the lone window's shutters. The lines ran across his blanket's rough contours and fluttered on Noah's moving body. Matt rose and dressed quickly in the chilly room. The new breeches were cold and stiff against his legs.

Noah laid green wood onto the fire's glowing embers, then banked it under ash. It would smolder for many hours and be alive when Noah returned. The old man got jerky from a covered box and handed Matt a piece. He put more into a sack and stuffed it into his jerkin. They stepped outside into the November blackness, where Noah's saddled horse snorted fog into the frost-bit air.

"You ride first," Noah said.

Matt mounted, and the old man took the reins. He led the horse around the cabin, and headed down the trace that wound eastward through the forest. The moon blinked through trees as they traveled past bright pairs of eyes that reflected its light, past the small, still lake where they'd often caught bluegills and bass to add variety to their diets. Matt saw its mirrored surface through the brush, could almost hear the now-hibernating frogs and crickets, whose chorus had kept them company many a summer evening.

They came out on the Great Road and turned right, south toward Fincastle, some eighteen miles away. Matt glanced behind him. Two miles up that way, at the James River's Cherry Bottom ford, was Struthers' Inn.

After another hour, they exchanged places. Matt walked faster than usual, trying to match the horse's pace. The three-rut road, formed by wagon wheels and hooves of oxen and horses, stretched endlessly toward Fincastle and beyond.

He'd never been farther south than this point. But Paul Tatum, who had traveled this way on his long hunts, said the Great Road forked into three directions after Fincastle. Tatum took the west fork through a mountain pass into the land they called Can-tuc-kee. The east branch eventually wound east into the North Carolina province, and the center one followed the Virginia Valley south into Cherokee country, where few white men had gone.

The Cherokee were down there. Was Mandy there with them? Or was she with the Shawnee, over to the northwest beyond the mountains? He didn't know. But either place, his heart cried out for her. Someday — someday he'd find her, and he'd take care of her the rest of her life. Matt heard the horse snort ahead, and ran to catch up.

CHAPTER 5

MATT STOOD IN THE STABLE DOORWAY AND STARED ACROSS the road, at the log courthouse. It looked new, like it had been built that very morning. It measured maybe twenty by twenty-four feet, not counting a lean-to at each end. Flanking it were a lumber store, a saddler's shop, a blacksmith shop, and a tailor shop. Some of the houses lined up beyond the stores, also made of logs, were as small as twelve feet by twelve feet.

The jail, which shared the courthouse commons, was the largest building Matt could see. It looked about forty feet long and sixteen feet wide, including the jailer's quarters. On the way in they'd passed a public ducking stool in the mill, and now he saw a set of stocks in front of the jail. They sure knew how to punish a person around here.

A boy younger than he herded a dozen grazing cattle on the commons. Matt watched him, then looked up and down the busy street. Several backwoodsmen leaned against trees and building fronts, talking and laughing. Three young men raced by on galloping horses, whipping their mounts, yelling.

There wasn't even a town here five years ago. Matt's daddy said Fincastle, like Martinsburg up north near the Potomac, was settled mainly to help defend the settlers against the Indians. They reasoned the closeness of civilized activity would warn the savages to leave the white people alone. That theory must work in general, because there was now little Indian activity.

But it hadn't worked for his own family.

Noah finished with the stable keeper and they crossed to the oak-planked courthouse door. Noah put a rough hand on the latch.

"Well, here goes nothing. You ready?"

Matt nodded and Noah opened the door. Large double doors loomed across the small entry foyer, and single doors stood in each side wall. The foyer was empty except for a polished wood desk, where a young man busily scribbled with a scratching quill pen. Noah walked up to him, his steps echoing loudly.

"We're here for the . . . the McLaren case," he whispered. "Matt . . . Matthew McLaren. This is him right here."

The man glanced at Matt, thumbed through papers before him.

"It'll be at least an hour, but go on in. Judge Berkley dislikes tardiness."

He scratched some more with his quill. Noah stood waiting, hands folded together. The clerk looked up.

"Beggin' your pardon, but where do we go?"

"In there." The young man waved his quill toward the double doors behind him

"Thank you, sir."

Noah and Matt walked to the doors and quietly opened them. A scattering of people sat in spindle-backed chairs facing the room's long south wall. A yellow sunlight blotch glowed on the oak puncheon floor, divided by the shadow of a polished rail that separated spectators from an elevated bench. An old man sat at the bench, his wadded-leather face peering from under a white wig. He turned toward a tall man in a bright green suit, who was talking in official words, then glanced at the white-haired Negro standing before him. Several other men, in white wigs and patterned coats and vests, whispered at two big tables near the bench. Matt's heart quickened. Christopher Ashbrooke, in his black clothing, was with them.

Matt and Noah tiptoed to empty chairs. As Matt started to sit, he glanced across the aisle and froze. His knuckles whitened on the chair back. Noah turned to see what had caught his attention.

Samuel Struthers.

The man was barely recognizable. His usual grease-stained clothing was replaced by clean, dark pants buckled just below his knees. A fine white linen blouse peeped from under a dark buttoned coat that squeezed his upper bulk. He spotted Matt and grinned.

Matt shivered. He shot a glance at Judge Berkley, who peered over rimless glasses at the Negro.

"You plead guilty to stealing four guns and a hog," the judge said. "Anything to say before I pass sentence?"

The black man's Adam's apple bobbed.

"Nothin', suh. "Nothin' I ain't already said."

"Then I sentence you to be hanged by the neck until dead. I order the Sheriff to cause execution of this judgment on Saturday the twenty-second day of this month between the hours of nine and twelve in the forenoon."

Matt clasped a hand over his mouth to cut off a squeal. Two guards went for the black man. The taller guard dragged him past other people lining the east wall, and the other opened the side door and pushed him through it.

The judge turned to someone writing in a big book. "Enter into the record that the court values the said slave at ninety pounds."

Matt cupped a hand to Noah's ear. "Are they really going to *hang* him?" he whispered.

Noah nodded, shifted in his chair.

The judge looked toward the guards. "Come now, gentlemen. We have a busy morning!"

The short guard brought the next defendant forward. He was a thin, balding man with a black eye, tattered vest, and shredded sleeves.

As proceedings droned on, Matt pictured the indentured manservant's story. He'd run away from a local merchant's house nine months before. When they found him they dragged him back behind a horse to teach him a lesson! The judge ordered him to spend an extra two hundred eighty-six days at the merchant's house — the time he'd been away — and to either pay or work off the expense of capturing him, plus court fees.

A slave, a runaway servant — himself, about to be

bound out to Struthers — how really did they differ? They were all brought here against their will. Matt hadn't been chained, at least not yet. But they'd probably do it the first time he tried to escape from that awful place. They all were at the mercy of this mean-faced judge now motioning for the next case.

Matt grew more sickened as each person was taken away. Nobody was set free. The judge ignored the prisoner's side. Try to speak up, and a person got a gavel banged in his face and was told to be quiet.

If the judge refused to believe grown men, what chance would he have? Anybody could see the judge was in cahoots with the people who wore fancy clothes, like Struthers. He always ruled the way they asked him to. They knew courtroom manners, knew how and when to say "if the court please" and "if your honor will allow." The judge would go along with whatever they wanted.

A thin man named William Dunn stood to hear his punishment. For "insulting and abusing his master," he got a whole year tacked onto his time of service. A whole year! But his fat master stood right there beside him, and he didn't have a mark on him! He'd probably just dreamed up the charge so the judge would add penalty time. Dunn would probably never see a day of real freedom. Matt wouldn't, either, once Struthers got hold of him again. All Struthers would have to do was complain, and the judge would order Matt to slop hogs and clean the privy for one more year.

Matt stole another look at Struthers. The man's gaze was fixed forward, his face frozen in a smile. He sat bolt upright, his stomach sucked in, wrists resting on his thighs, pudgy fingertips pressed together between them.

Matt knew he'd leave Struthers the first chance he got. Maybe he'd get caught like these others did. If so, he'd just have to run away again. And again and again, if need be.

Someone said his name and Matt looked up at the bench. The judge stared down at him, gavel poised, waiting.

". . . a petition to have Matthew McLaren bound out to one Samuel Struthers," the man in the suit was saying.

"Will the petitioner rise?"

Struthers stood and moved slowly, almost gracefully, to the railing. He opened the gate.

"That's far enough," the judge said. "What is your occupation?"

"An innkeeper, your honor," he replied. "I run Struthers' Inn up on James River."

"And why do you want this boy bound out to you?"

"Why, I feel sorry for him, your honor. He come to the inn the day the Indians killed his folks and I took him in. I fed him, and tended to him, and —"

"Now, wait just a minute!" Noah jumped up and stalked toward the bar. "That bastard took advantage of this boy!"

The judge glared at Noah. "Sit down! Another word and the bailiff will escort you out of the building."

The judge looked back at the innkeeper. It looked like he started to say something, but Reverend Ashbrooke came over from his table and whispered to him. The judge laid down his gavel and leaned back.

"There is a witness here to testify," he said. "I will

allow it."

The hallway door opened. A young man, about eighteen years old, appeared with the bailiff. He was thin and had a scraggly beard. As he neared, Matt saw he favored his right leg.

"You!" Struthers exclaimed. "Where you been?"

The boy didn't answer. He sat beside the judge's bench and the court clerk swore him in. He didn't look at Struthers. The innkeeper stood red-faced, his eyes bulging, but he kept his jaw clamped shut.

"Your honor, this is Patrick Grant, Struther's current indentured boy," Ashbrooke said. "He ran away not long ago."

"And what is his purpose here?"

"I believe young Mr. Grant can give us a good indication of Mr. Struthers' character," Ashbrooke replied.

Struthers slammed a fist on the bar before him. "He's a runaway, your honor! He ain't no better'n that Negro slave, an' he ought to be strung up, too. Why, he even stole his indenture papers, tore them up, he did, and threw the pieces all over the inn!"

The judge rapped his gavel.

"Beggin' your honor's pardon, sir," Struthers added.

Ashbrooke turned to the young man in the witness chair.

"Mr. Grant, tell the court what you told me. Mr. Struthers paid your passage from Ireland and you were bound out to him for seven years. Why did you run away after only one year?"

The boy kept staring at his folded hands. " 'Cause he beat me. He said I was too slow an' beat me with his club.

But he waited until nobody could see him do it."

"That's a lie!" Struthers raised his hand as if to back-hand Patrick, but scratched his own arm instead. "I treated this boy fine. He's got no complaint about me. He got caught running, and now he's trying to weasel out of our bargain!"

Matt stared at Patrick. He'd seen that club behind the bar! It was a good three feet long, with blood stains on the heavy end. He saw Struthers throw it at a rat one morning.

Ashbrooke touched Patrick's shoulder. "Show the judge your leg," he said.

The boy paused, pulled up his pant leg. Matt caught his breath. Patrick's shin bone was bent! It came down normal to halfway between his knee and foot, then bent out side-ways, where there was a big bump. No wonder he limped!

"He hit me over and over," Patrick said. "He beat me with the club, an' I ran outside. But he kept on. I was on the ground, an' he reared back and clubbed me as hard as he could! He broke my leg. He broke it, he did!"

"My God!" Noah murmured. "He didn't even get it set. Didn't even have a doctor look at it."

"It was an accident," Struthers said. "People have acci-dents. I didn't do nothin' wrong, and you can't prove I did."

"I believe I can," Ashbrooke said. He strode over to the innkeeper, looked unblinking into his eyes. "After I left the Dandridge farm I got to wondering how you treated Matt McLaren. I talked with several people and I can now pro-duce any number of witnesses against your character. I'll do just that if you proceed with this petition."

Struthers stood, all muscles tensed, glowering at Patrick.

The only sounds came from outside, where a wagoner was yelling at his team.

"Your honor, I ask that this man's petition be denied," Ashbrooke said. "I further request that you bind Matt McLaren out to the man he came here with. Mister Noah Dandridge. We could find no worthier person to raise this boy. If you approve, I'll prepare the paperwork today."

Matt turned quickly toward Noah. The old man's hand came up nervously to his throat, and he returned Matt's stare. He stood.

"I'd consider it an honor, Judge. I'll do right by him."

"Well, this is certainly a turn of events," the judge said. He looked at Matt. "Would you be agreeable?"

"Why . . . yes. Yes, sir, I would."

Could it be happening? Could it really be happening?

The judge rapped his gavel. "Then it's done. I order that Matthew McLaren, an orphan of fourteen years age, be bound to . . . " He looked at Ashbrooke.

"Noah Dandridge, your honor."

". . . be bound to Noah Dandridge until his twenty-first year. The said Mr. Dandridge is to teach said orphan to read, write, and cipher as far as the five Common Rules, and to learn him the trade of . . ."

Ashbrooke looked around at Noah. "Farming," he said.

"And to learn him the trade of farming. So ordered. Next case." He tapped his gavel again and looked to the man in the pretty suit.

Struthers glared at Matt and Noah, then whirled and stormed out of the courtroom. Noah touched Matt's arm.

"I guess we won't be going home today," he said. "We got to wait for that paperwork."

Matt nodded. "Yessir, I guess we do. But I . . . I don't mind. I don't mind at all."

He looked toward the door where an angry Struthers had disappeared, and felt a chill. He had a feeling they'd not heard the last of that man.

CHAPTER 6

Light snow sifted down as Matt led Benjie off the Great Road onto the westward path to Noah's farm. He glanced at Noah. *Our* farm, he thought. At least until I'm twenty-one years old. It's *our* farm.

He smiled down at the new flintlock rifle resting in the crook of his right arm, primed and ready to shoot. He felt the barrel's coldness, the stock's smoothness, as he shifted it to his left arm. Noah had bought it for him the day before in Fincastle while they were waiting for the court papers. "Adam Stephen's gunnery made it, and they're the best around," Noah had said, as Matt hefted it in the store. "There's none more accurate."

And probably none heavier, Matt thought, smiling. The long gun stood to Matt's ear. The thick, soft-iron barrel, itself four feet long, was fitted into a short stock with a scooped-out butt. It was made to carry a ball of forty to the pound, rifled to spin that ball and keep it flying straight.

"Most guns east of here are smooth-bored," Noah had said. "But we know how to make them here in the mountains.

Why, that thing could shoot a gnat off a deer's rump."

Maybe so, but it would take a while to get used to its weight and balance. His father's gun had been smaller, smooth-bored. The day of the . . . the fire, and all, it hung on the cabin wall. Matt had used it many times, mostly when out with his father.

He hefted the rifle again. Of course, he could put it on Benjie's backpack, along with the provisions they'd bought. But what if they scared up a deer, or even a bear? By the time he got the gun, loaded it, and aimed it, the animal could run off over the mountains. Now, he could just swing it up and shoot.

The snow came harder. At first it melted into wet specks, but for the past hour it had been sticking. Whiteness covered the dark earth and dead grass in the trail's open areas, changed sharp edges and angles into taffy-like surfaces.

Matt saw a single horse's hoofprints ahead, going in the same direction.

"Company," Noah said behind him. "Probably Ashbrooke. He said he'd be up this way, might stop by if the snow hit."

Matt wasn't surprised Noah noticed the tracks first. He moved like a cat in spite of his age, read sign with the best of them. He'd already taught Matt a lot about tracking and such, but there was much more to learn. Now there'd be time for that.

They followed the trail another hour, watched the hoofprints soften and finally disappear in the falling snow. Ahead, over the trees, dark smoke rose from their fireplace.

They rounded the last bend and the white-roofed cabin stood before them, dark shingles exposed where they touched the warm chimney. A hint of hoofprints went around the cabin, probably to the lean-to. A whinny from behind the building was answered by their own horse. Ashbrooke must have rebuilt the fire. It would have gone out otherwise, after two days of banking.

Matt stopped the horse in front of the cabin and Noah dismounted. As the old man reached up to untie the load, the cabin door swung open. A rifle barrel poked out.

Smoke and fire exploded from it.

Matt heard several distinct sounds as he dived for the snow. The rifle's blast. Noah's grunt. A pistol's pop. A bullet whizzing past his own head. His own rifle firing with a startling boom.

A high-pitched squeal came from the cabin as Matt half rolled, half crawled toward the oak tree.

"Noah!"

The old man's horse whirled away. Noah lay face down in the snow between Matt and the cabin door. He lay still at first, then raised his upper body from the blood-splotched snow. He looked toward Matt and bent a knee under himself to stand. His body shook and he pitched sideways into his own blood.

A man staggered out through the doorway, grasping at his bloody side. He managed one, two steps, fell to his knees. His pistol dropped into the snow. It was Struthers!

"You shot me!"

The man's eyes were open wide. He sat back on his

haunches, stared as his upturned hands dripped blood onto his greasy pants.

"You little bastard, you shot me!"

"You killed Noah!" Matt cried out. "You killed him!"

His sobs trailed off as he grabbed the powder horn hanging around his neck. He fumbled it open and shook powder down the barrel. "Damn you!" Matt squinted at Struthers through tear-blurred eyes. "Damn you to hell!"

Struthers' empty rifle lay back in the doorway. The pistol lay off to his side, out of reach. He stared at Matt, watched him load his rifle.

"You goin' to kill me?"

Matt pulled a ball from its pouch. It dropped into the snow. He retrieved it with trembling fingers, wrapped a wad of buckskin around it, stuffed it down the barrel with his hickory ramrod.

Struthers tried to get up, but couldn't. He grabbed a handful of snow, lifted his shirt and wiped away the blood to inspect the wound.

"Go ahead and shoot, I don't care. Damn you, I'm dead anyways."

Matt slid the ramrod home under the barrel. He poured powder into the pan, shook some on the snow.

Struthers' darting glance found the pistol. He lurched for it, screamed in pain. He reached again, but Matt got there first and kicked out wildly. The gun banged against the door jamb, bounced far out of Struthers' reach. The blood-soaked innkeeper clutched his side and looked up. Matt's rifle barrel trained on his head.

"Well, you goin' to kill me, or not?" he said, almost conversationally. He sat there a few moments, frowning. Then a grin showed his tarnished teeth.

"Hell, you ain't going to shoot. You ain't got the guts. I know you, and you ain't got the guts!"

The barrel lowered. Matt lifted it into Struthers' grinning face and strained to hold it there. The heavy gun again pulled down, wavered when he tried to aim it between Struthers' eyes. It lowered again.

"Damn you!" Matt yelled. He threw the rifle down and raged at the killer with his fists.

"I'll *kill* you, I'll *kill* you, I'll *kill* you!" he screamed in sobs. He drove the words home with fists that smacked the man's head and shoulders.

Struthers tried to ward off the attack with his arms. He clamped Matt's right fist between his huge hands and grinned wider when Matt struggled to pull away, felt his feet slipping in the slush. Struthers pulled harder, then let off pressure so quickly that Matt fell backward.

Matt pulled both knees to his stomach as he went down. He jammed his heels out straight into Struthers' face and felt the man's nose and teeth break. Struthers screamed and let go of Matt's hand. He caught a bloody tooth as it fell from his mouth and stared at it. He looked up, blood streaming from his mouth and nose.

"You had no call to do that."

The innkeeper leaned on his left elbow in the snow, glaring at Matt through bloodshot eyes. Matt sobbed from deep within, almost unable to catch his breath. His daddy, his mama, now Noah. All the people he loved . . .

"And you're still a baby, ain't you," Struthers said. "You're crying like a baby."

He shifted again, his mouth and nose still bleeding, as well as his side. But he appeared not to notice.

"I'll tell you what you're going to do," he said. "You're going to get on that horse and leave this country for good."

Matt sobbed softer. He crawled over next to Noah, pulled the old man's head to his chest, hugged him, smoothed his graying hair. Death stared at him through Noah's eyes.

Struthers was getting weaker. But the sneer was still on his face, in his voice.

"I'm goin' to tell the sheriff you killed him. I come up here and seen you shoot him, and then you shot me. I tried to stop you, but you run away."

Matt tried to understand what he was saying. Struthers was an adult. He knew a lot of people, and they'd probably believe him. He looked around at Noah's horse, still loaded with all the provisions they'd just traded for. His own sack of things was on the horse, too. Everything in the world he owned was on that horse, except his new rifle.

"You ain't got nothing here to stay for," Struthers said. "This ain't your land. Why, they'd just bind you out again. Hell, they might even give you to me!"

Struthers snorted, coughed up blood. It dribbled down his chin onto his shirt. He rubbed it with his hand, looked at it.

He was right. Not about his going to Struthers, but the rest of it was true enough. He had no reason to stay. He looked down at Noah's face and brushed his eyelids closed. He'd leave. But not because Struthers told him to.

The man coughed again. Matt looked up.

"You're going to die," Matt said. "You're going to die, and I'm going to sit here and watch it."

Struthers looked at him, then down at his gut wound. He slipped down from his leaning position until he was lying on his side in the snow. He breathed heavily, spasmodically.

"Can I have some water? I'm thirsty."

Matt said nothing. He hugged Noah's head again, stroked his hair. Occasionally he looked at the innkeeper, whose eyes were half closed. The man's breathing was irregular, labored.

Presently, Struthers looked up again. "Matt, will you . . . will you say some words over my body?"

Matt didn't answer. He watched Struthers' strength ebb, almost felt it enter his own body, his mind. The killer's eyes were closed. He brought in a huge gasp of air and expelled it in a long, rattling sigh.

He was dead. The cabin yard was still. Even the chickadees were quiet.

Matt sat there as the snow fell, finally obliterating the blood patches. The shadows slanted longer, blended into dusk as the sun sank and left a half moon to light the earth.

At last Matt laid Noah's cold head down on the snow covered ground and stood. He went around the cabin to the lean-to and got Noah's shovel, walked down the back path to where the old man had buried his wife next to a rock out-

cropping. He hacked at the frozen soil until he dug a shallow grave, limited by the rocks beneath, and dragged his friend to the site. He covered him with dirt and looked around.

Rocks. He had to put rocks on the grave to keep the animals out, like they did for his mama. He found some, rolled them onto the fresh earth. He bowed his head, but tears didn't come. He didn't know if he'd ever have tears again. But he did have his feelings, and his heart ached. *Good bye, Noah. You'll always be with me.*

Matt went into the cabin and lit a candle. He paused for his eyes to adjust to the darkness, then inspected both his and Noah's blankets. Noah had given him the thickest one. He spread it on the floor and tossed things onto it, starting with the jerky left in the box. It would keep him going until he could kill game. The bullet mold, the lead, and the gunpowder were next.

He moved quietly, looked into and under things, retrieved what might be usable yet easy to carry. The small pile grew to include the knives, extra flints, candles, two pots and a spoon, the tinderbox, Noah's ax and his tomahawk. He added other items, but left some out because of their weight. When he finished, he hitched the blanket corners with a rawhide strip and swung the load over his shoulder.

He stood for a minute, looking around the little cabin he loved. Then he went outside and tied the stuffed blanket onto Noah's horse, across from the things they had bought in Fincastle.

He untied Struthers' horse and led it around the cabin to retrieve his own rifle. As an afterthought he put Struthers' pistol in with the provisions, tied his reins to Struthers' saddle and started to mount, then paused. He walked to Struthers' body, now almost covered with snow, and stood there a long time, looking down.

"May God have mercy on your soul," he mumbled.

Matt mounted the innkeeper's horse and glanced back at his friend's last resting place. He wheeled the horse around and started down the trace, Noah's horse tethered behind.

Mandy. Somehow, he'd find her. He'd spend the rest of his life looking for her, if he had to. She was with the Indians, someplace. He hoped she was, at any rate. The alternative was death. But which Indians? The Cherokees would be easier to get to. He could just keep on going south, ford those rivers, and walk into their camps.

But Struthers seemed to think the Shawnees got her, and that would mean they were in the Can-tuc-kee land. Maybe instead he'd cross the Alleghenies through the Cumberland Gap, as Tatum had, and look for Mandy there. Either way he went, he'd be out of the sheriff's reach.

He glanced one more time back at Noah's quiet cabin, then turned and went down the trail in the dim moonlight. He'd go on through Fincastle and take that middle fork to the Cherokee land, or maybe the right one to Can-tuc-kee, and keep going until he found Mandy, or another reason to stop.

I'm sorry, Mandy. I'm sorry I sent you back to the cabin when we seen the turkeys. I should have gone and got the gun myself. I should have been the one the Indians took.

When he reached the Great Road he turned south.

CHAPTER 7

THE CUMBERLAND GAP LOOKED JUST LIKE PAUL TATUM said it would.

Matt kneed Benjie around and stared back at the almost sheer walls that towered a thousand feet on each side, into a dark blue sky. After several hard days of riding, and of constantly glancing over his shoulder for signs of the sheriff, the night before he'd camped in what another traveler had called Powell's Valley. At dawn he'd brushed the snow off his pack and saddle, hitched up, and entered the shadowy path that squeezed between the walls. The rising sun felt good when he finally broke through.

He turned back west and surveyed the valley. A level, circular forest extended at least five miles out until it hit a ridge. It was as if the whole thing had been pushed down among the mountains, like an oversized coin, and had scooted them away to all sides. The sun glared off creeks and rivers that drained the mountains and must have given life to a million wildflowers in the springtime. Now most trees were bare and the valley was still, as if waiting for something to happen.

"Let's go, Benjie," he said. Matt pulled the reins left, and Noah's old horse turned, Struthers' horse following. They continued west on the Warrior's Path, a wide, winding rut Tatum had said was used by the Cherokees from the south and the Shawnees from the north to raid each other's settlements. No Indians lived in the Can-tuc-kee land itself, but they used it as hunting grounds.

Benjie stumbled, and Matt patted his shoulder. "You just take it easy," he said. Noah had told about the time he had raced the old horse against a neighbor's up in Pennsylvania, about being embarrassed by the whole thing. Benjie was a good plow horse, though. He could pull a log with the best of them, respond to every "gee" and "haw" to keep a plow on track. Matt patted him again, hoping the horse would be able to help plow his own land whenever he had a chance to settle down. He looked back again toward Fincastle. He'd never be able to go back to his parents' home, or to Noah's. But someplace he had to make a home. He needed a place to take Mandy, when he found her.

The sun arced overhead, threw longer and longer shadows at him from the west. The trail turned north, threaded among the ridges. By mid-afternoon a straight, flat ridge stood before him, disappearing in the distance at both ends. It marched closer as the shadows lengthened, its details sharpening. The Cumberland River came in from the right, and Matt followed it through a cut in the ridge.

The river curved ahead, and the path stopped at its edge. He dismounted Benjie and peered across. There was snow on the ground, but no ice on the river.

"Looks like we get a bath," he said to the two horses. He shucked his clothes, piled them on the packhorse, and tied his powder horn to his rifle barrel. Holding the gun high overhead, he stepped in and grunted at the coldness, then splashed forward on the sloping rocky bottom, pulling snorting horses behind. The water crawled up to his knees, his hips, finally his waist. He gasped and plunged ahead, smiled with gritted teeth when the bottom leveled.

"Not much longer, Benjie. God, it's cold!" The water receded, and a wind gust chilled him where he was wet. He jumped out on the other side and stood shivering, jerked his leggings on and pulled his leather shirt over his head. As he slipped on his moccasins he studied the terrain.

The Warrior's Path continued toward the north. Well, he'd follow it tomorrow. He'd already put in a good day's work, gone through two gaps and waded that river. It was time to make camp and warm up.

Matt gathered sticks and dry vines and grass, shivering as he struck flint against iron. The spark caught, and soon he lay next to a roaring fire. He fell asleep amidst thoughts of finding Mandy.

The voice came from the darkness. "You crazy boy! You want us to get killed?"

Matt jumped up from his blankets, felt frantically for his gun. A tall deer-skinned figure emerged from the pitch-black night, waving a long rifle.

"If I was a Injun, you'd be dead right now!" The man stormed over and kicked at the fire, his white-streaked brown beard blowing in the night breeze. "Help me get this out!"

Matt froze in place. "What's going on? What you got against a fire?"

"Damn, kid, you might just as well give 'em a written invite to kill us!" Sparks flew into the blackness as the stranger kicked the glowing logs apart. "Get some water. Move!"

Matt grabbed his cooking pot and dipped it into the river. It hissed and steamed as it sunk and he dragged it full, ran back to the campfire, now in pieces at his feet, splashed the water on and ran back for more. The stranger flung a flaring branch into the river. Then another. In a minute, only one was left.

"Get your things. Where's your horses?" A whinny came from the left. "Pick up that stuff. I'll go get 'em."

The stranger led the hobbled horses up and Matt threw Benjie's saddle on him. The stranger did the same with Struthers' horse, in a startlingly swift motion, and they tied everything on.

"What all the hell you got here?" The stranger fingered a bulge in the pack.

"Just things to hunt with."

The man eyed him. "You going to hunt? Well, you got some learning to do." He jiggled the pack to check it and tied Struthers' horse to Benjie's saddle. "Git up there and sit still. Now! You'd probably get lost down on the ground."

The man flung the last glowing stick into the river. It sizzled, and blackness was complete. Benjie's saddle squeaked as his hooves crunched in rocky soil.

Forms slowly took shape. Ahead, a black peak showed

against a slightly less black background. Muted river ripples reflected light from an unseen source, and dim light points hung in the murky sky. Black tree shapes stretched upward.

Matt could now make out the stranger's shape. They followed the murmuring river until the man led them away into thick woods. Branches grabbed Matt's legs, scraped the packhorse's load. The man stopped.

A glint of light appeared to the right.

"That you, Pa?"

"Yep. You can put that gun down."

"I see you got him. Think the Indians saw it?"

"Hell, who knows?" The man took something from the packhorse. "Get down, boy. Roll up someplace in this."

The thrown blanket hit Matt's chest. He dismounted and removed Benjie's saddle by feel, heard the stranger unload the packhorse. He slipped hobbles around both horses' front legs, felt for a tree, and slid down its side to the ground. Snow-covered leaves rustled under his hands and he stirred them to mix the snow in, opened the blanket and lay on one half, pulling the other half over him.

"G'night," he said. No one answered. Soon snoring came from both sides. Matt stared up at the blackness.

A clinking bridle woke him, and Matt peered out from his cover cocoon. No shadows, just a blanket of gray and tree forms that seemed to sharpen as he watched.

Two men stood next to as many packhorses, adjusting skimpy loads of traps and supplies. The older one, the one who'd doused his campfire, turned toward him.

"Goin' to sleep all day?"

"No, sir. Getting up right now." He threw the cover off and jumped up, felt the morning's nip. "Name's Matt McLaren."

"You ain't a hunter. What're you doing out here?"

"I can hunt. Done it all my life, almost. I hunted a lot with Noah Dandridge up in the Virginia Valley. And before that, with my dad. They're all dead now. Killed." He threw the saddle on Benjie, pulled it tight.

"Killed, you say. How?"

It was the son who spoke. He looked to be about eighteen years old. He was thin and had a quick smile that showed big, crooked teeth.

"Indians. They killed my folks, took my sister. Later a white man killed Noah. I was helping on his farm."

"That's too bad. Pa? You think . . ."

His father held up a hand. "You're awful young to be out here, huntin' or no. Don't have no place to go? No relatives?"

"No, sir. But I'll be all right. I can hunt, I know I can. I done it before, lots of times!"

"Well . . ." The man frowned at Matt's pack, still on the ground. "Well, I guess so."

"What?"

His son grinned. "Pa's saying you can come with us. We're joining James Knox and his hunters out in the Barrens. This here's Meager Hollinger, and I'm Jacob."

"I guess Knox won't mind," Meager Hollinger said slowly. "We cain't just leave the boy here. He'd starve." He tapped his horse and rode down the trail, turned right and was out of sight.

Jacob poked Matt's arm. "Pa's fumin'. We don't want to get crosswise with him, I guarantee."

They mounted, and followed Meager toward the Cumberland. Matt glanced back at his packhorse and pictured it loaded with pelts, just like Paul Tatum's horse was when he'd gotten back from the Can-tuc-kee wilderness. Him, a long hunter! He liked the way it sounded. He'd stay out hunting for the fall and winter, and maybe find Mandy, and they'd go back to Virginia with a load of pelts as tall as a tree. He took one long look east toward Fincastle, wondered if the sheriff had found Struthers' body yet, then shuddered and turned back west.

CHAPTER 8

THEY STAYED CLOSE TO THE RIVER MOST OF THAT DAY, THEN moved north to a westward trail to avoid the river's curves. The second day went faster. When the light faded, Matt figured they'd covered a good thirty miles.

Jacob was just ahead, Meager beyond him. They'd spent both days following single file, dodging branches that stuck out from the overgrown forest. The path widened and Jacob dropped back to Matt's side.

"Gets cold in these trees," he said. "Ever been out here afore?"

"No." Matt had answered that question at least three times, but enjoyed the company.

"Pa says it'll go on like this for another two, three days. Then . . . hell, I ain't going to tell you. It'll be a surprise." He grinned.

Meager Hollinger sat straight on his horse up ahead. He dismounted when they approached.

"We'll stop here," he said. "You two set up camp and get your guns in order. I'll look for sign. Might as well kill us a buck for dinner. Here, take my horse."

He disappeared on foot, and Matt and Jacob pulled off the trail. They unsaddled and unloaded the packhorses, and Matt cleared leaves off a small hill.

"Think it's safe to light a fire?" he said.

"Pa says they won't be no Injuns around here. Too far away from the Warrior's Path. Besides . . ."

Thuds of running feet and cracks of breaking branches shattered the still air. Meager appeared down the trail, head lowered like a bull, feet flying. "Indians!" he said. "Their fire's still burning, and they —"

"God, Pa . . ." Jacob jumped up from his log perch and stared down the trail. Meager slid to a stop, glanced around at the surrounding forest.

"Git those horses!" He checked his rifle. "Your guns loaded?"

"Mine ain't!" Jacob grabbed his gun and powder horn. His hands trembled as he primed his flintlock pan, spilling powder.

"Damn, boy, you got buck ague! Don't know can you fight or not. You there, you loaded?"

"Yes, sir!" Matt said. "I . . . look out!"

Fire and smoke exploded from a log forty yards away, and Matt and the Hollingers dived for the ground. Matt rolled over and swung his rifle up as three Indians appeared, reloading their guns. Two others drew arrows into bows. Matt shot one, saw him double up, fall. His arrow struck the ground.

"Jacob! Hold your fire!" Meager swung his own gun

up and an arrow glanced off it. He recovered and blasted at a running Indian trying to reload. The Indian fell, and his gun bounced out of reach.

"Get your backs together! They's trying to surround us!" Meager shouted.

Matt frantically loaded his gun. His rifle was more accurate than the Indians' cheap non-rifled trade guns, but took longer to load. Was Noah right? Would the Indians use too little powder, not be able to hit anything over fifty yards away? Problem was, they were closer than that!

An Indian swung his gun toward Matt.

"Now, Pa?" A grunt from behind. Two shots sounded, one from the Indians.

A bullet plowed past Matt's cheek, thunked into a tree behind him.

"Damn!" Meager's gun clattered to the ground.

"Where'd he get you?" Matt said. An Indian fell from Jacob's bullet and lay still

One Indian gun left. One bow. Matt finished loading, pulled back the hammer, swung around. The bowman pulled a seated arrow back as powder exploded in Matt's flash pan. The Indian jerked backward.

One more gun.

Jacob stood frozen. Meager was weaponless, holding his upper arm.

The last Indian let out a yip and pointed his gun at Meager. Matt reached into his hunting shirt, brought out Struther's pistol, and fumbled powder into its pan. It belched out a bullet and the Indian dropped his gun, surprise on his face. He fell forward.

Silence. Gun smoke floated like fog in the still air. Matt pulled his hunting knife from its scabbard and inspected each Indian. They all lay still, dead. He put the knife away.

"Gawd dang," Jacob said. He pulled his own knife out, moved to each Indian and kicked with his toe.

"They're all dead," Meager pronounced, and pulled off his shirt to study his wound. A line of blood lay across his arm muscle, the injury superficial. "I'll live. Where'd you get that there pistol?"

"Brung it along," Matt answered. "Loaded it this morning when we broke camp."

"Well, it saved our lives. You was a pretty good shot on them moving targets."

"Gawd dang," Jacob said. He bent over the Indian he'd killed and pulled his head up by its scalp lock, slid his blade around it. In a few seconds he jerked and there was a popping sound. He held his bloody trophy high. "My first scalp! Why, this'll sure look good on the cabin wall!"

Matt turned away. His stomach churned and he felt lightheaded. That's what the Indians had done to his momma. But Jacob did it so quickly, without even giving it a thought, like it was a sport or something. The Indians that killed his momma probably scalped her just like that, too, laughing while they did it. He felt sick.

He gazed toward the other Indians. They were Shawnee, according to descriptions he'd heard. Tall and muscular in life, they seemed small now, as if asleep.

He looked down at one and memorized his features.

Black hair, all cut off except for a long lock in back. Silver rings in his nose, ears cut from the tips two-thirds of the way round and extended with brass wires until they touched his shoulders, thin silver plates hanging from the wires. Hair pulled from his eyebrows and eyelashes, parts of his face painted dark red. He wore white man's clothing, except instead of breeches he wore a girdle around his waist and a piece of cloth drawn through his legs and turned over the girdle before and behind, like a short apron.

Matt felt the pressure of Meager's hand on his shoulder. "Your first one?"

"Well, it's my first . . ." Matt caught himself. "Yes, sir."

It was his first Indian. Of course he'd killed a white man not long before. The sheriff was probably looking for him right now, ready to drag him to court and throw him into jail. Or hang him. No, he could never go back and farm his folks' land, or visit Noah's place again. A white man, three Indians . . . why, at this rate he could kill a thousand people before he died. Was that where he was headed?

"They wasn't your fault," Meager said. "We're far away from that big bonfire of yours. Don't look like they was planning on a fight, does it? Looks like they'd of left their jewelry to home."

The pressure left Matt's shoulder. "Well, let's get going," Meager said. "Let's get some air 'tween us and them." He looked west on the trail. "But we got to be careful. These might just be guards, an' they's a whole passel of Indians up ahead."

CHAPTER 9

RAIN DARKENED THE SKY THAT DAY, AND THE NEXT. ON the third morning the clouds broke up and the sun peeped through. Matt was soaked. He didn't even try to ride around the wet limbs. Jacob dropped back at mid-morning and grinned.

"You look like somethin' a dog drug home."

"You don't look no better," Matt said.

"You just wait. Maybe today you'll see my surprise. I ain't seen it yet either, but Pa hunted here last year and told me all about it."

Meager usually rode only a few feet ahead, but today he seemed anxious. An hour ago he'd trotted out around a bend and soon couldn't even be heard. Now there were sounds of approaching hooves, and a whoop. Meager came into view, bouncing in his saddle.

"It's the Barrens," he shouted. "Get on up here!"

The trail opened up as Matt rode toward him, then closed, and opened again. Bright sunlight hit Matt, and he blinked and stared at the landscape.

"Lookit there, Matt!" Jacob said. "Ever seen anything like it? Bet you never did!"

Ahead, instead of trees, was nothing but rolling, grass-covered hills. Matt hadn't been out of trees his whole life, except where people had cleared land. But here was grass as far as the eye could see! There were hills way out on the horizon, two knobs off to the right, and — he squinted to get a better look — and a bunch of huge dark, animals grazing to the left.

"Buffalo!" he said. "Why, they're big as a house."

"They's a million of 'em out here, I expect," Meager said. "Good eating, too. We killed some last year and ate the best parts, like the tongues."

"Told you I had a surprise!" Jacob said. "Ain't that something?"

Meager waved toward the west. "The river's off there to the right, mebbe fifteen, twenty miles," he said. "Knox and his bunch'll be out straight ahead, 'tween the Big and Little Barren Rivers what come off'n the Green. We'll prob'ly get there sometime tomorrow."

"Didn't I tell you, Matt? Didn't I tell you?" Jacob nudged his horse forward. "Gawd, them buffaloes is big. Just you look at them bushy heads!"

They camped by a stream that night, wrapped in blankets to protect against the chilled western wind that rolled the grass toward them in waves. By daybreak they'd broken camp, and by mid-morning the wind stopped and the sun warmed them. They continued west, and when the sun was overhead Matt spotted a dark line of trees. After a while

it became separate trees he recognized: cottonwood, sycamore, birch, and a lot of cane, fed by a river flowing through
them. They stopped and watered their horses.

"I'm guessing this here's the Little Barren," Meager
said, looking north along the tree line. "I'm going exploring. Be back in an hour or two."

When he returned he looked happy, relieved. "They's
traps up there. I seen footprints and followed them down to
the water. I'm saying we just sit tight and let Knox's people
find us."

"We can hunt while we're waiting," Jacob said. "We
can camp here, and . . . Pa, don't move! They's a deer behind you!"

Meager froze. "How far away?"

"Hundred yards. He's eating."

Meager squatted slowly, turned. The deer hadn't seen
them yet. Matt watched the man's face. Meager had done
all the hunting for food so far; maybe this was Matt's chance.
He picked up his rifle, saw Meager's slight nod.

Matt checked the breeze. Good — he was downwind.
But the deer was out from the trees, and Matt had no cover.
He cocked the rifle and tiptoed forward. Before he'd gone
five steps the deer looked up, saw him, and scampered away.

Matt went back to the others. "I was quiet as could
be, but —"

"You might as well have waved a flag at him," Meager
said.

Matt's face felt hot. "I tiptoed and all, but he looked up
and seen me."

"But by God, he told you he was going to look up. You wasn't watching. He warned you." Meager stood and checked his own gun.

"I don't know how he did that," Matt said. "I —"

"Jacob, stay here. Me and Matt're going to kill that there deer. Or his brother."

He motioned for Matt to follow, and they walked slowly north, along the river. Meager stopped and looked back. "When I hold my hand out like this, you freeze," he said. "When I start walking again, you walk."

Matt nodded and Meager led the way by the river. For ten minutes they crept along the trail, birds jabbering in the river trees.

Meager's hand went up. Matt stopped, focused on a buck nibbling grass a hundred yards ahead. He'd never seen a bigger rack of antlers in his life. The buck looked up, then went back to eating. Meager motioned Matt forward and they hunched over and moved closer. Meager signaled again, and again the buck looked up. He resumed eating and they moved to within fifty yards.

"Take 'em," Meager whispered. Matt aimed, fired, and the buck dropped.

Meager grinned and stood straight. "Let's get him skinned," he said. They jogged over and looked down at the deer. Matt's bullet hole was behind its shoulder.

"Good shot," Meager said. "You might get to be a good hunter at that. You ain't now, though. Not 'til you learn a few things."

Matt knelt and touched the carcass. "But how'd you know

when to move?" he said. "You was right, every time."

"Somethin' you learn," Meager said. "When a deer's goin' to look up, he flicks his tail first. And when he's done lookin' and wants to eat some more, he flicks it again. Hell, you know that, and there ain't nothin' to huntin' deer."

"Well, I'll be damned," Matt said. "I'll just be damned."

CHAPTER 10

THE TRAPPER SHOWED UP THE NEXT DAY. MATT SAW HIM coming, head down, stumbling along the river from the north. He was an old man, dressed in deerskin. Stringy, yellow-tinged white hair hung from beneath his beaver pelt hat.

The trapper tied his packhorse, half loaded with green pelts, to a sapling fifty yards north and disappeared into the tree line. A minute later he came out empty handed, un-hitched his horse, and walked into their camp, still looking down. He glanced up through red-lined eyes that sat above puffy bags, chewed his tobacco wad, and spat.

"Meager. You could at least offer to help me clean these danged pelts," he said, and pointed to his packhorse.

Meager grinned, got up from his log perch. "Long time, Wade Russell. Doing all right?"

"Yep. Who're these folk?"

"This here's my boy Jacob, that's Matt. They sent you out here alone? That don't seem right."

"Well, I ain't usually alone. My partner's so pokey I left

him back at camp." Russell waddled over and leaned his gun on Meager's log. "Guess I'll sit down a minute, take a load off."

A piece of paper was tied to his gun's forward sight. "What's that for?" Matt asked. "That paper?"

"Why, that's so's I can see the sight and aim at a deer or something. I miss sometimes, but I get my share!"

Meager shook his head. "Looks like deer hunting's even easier'n I thought," he said. "Your eyes getting worse?"

The man didn't answer. Matt moved to his pack horse and fingered through the load of pelts. He frowned. "No deerskins," he said, mostly to himself. The old man squinted at him and spat.

"Now, why would I skin a deer this time of the year?" he said. "Their pelts ain't no good this late. Summer and fall's when you want deer. We already got a ton of 'em back at camp, all cleaned and ready to take home."

He shifted forward, elbows on his knees, sparkling watery eyes aimed at the pelts. "But them's the best beaver, otter, and muskrat skins you'd ever find, son. That's what you want in the winter."

While Russell rested, Matt's party packed up their camp. They rode south with him until late afternoon, forded the Little Barren and started up the other side. The old man kept staring down, occasionally turned off to the river. Sometimes he'd just frown at the water's edge where he'd put a trap under an animal run earlier, then back off and continue downriver. But occasionally he found a trapped animal, and bashed in its head if it was still alive. In a wink, it seemed, he'd have it skinned and be off to the next one.

They camped that night and continued upstream as daylight broke. At noon Russell stopped, stood up and turned west. "Camp's that way two, three hours," he said. "Might as well head on over."

Russell talked about the summer's deer hunting, the other hunters, even folks he'd left back in Massachusetts. Time went fast for Matt, and by late afternoon they stood outside Knox's camp.

"Don't look like much," Russell said. "But it ain't supposed to. They's forty or so hunters about, off in twos and threes all over the place. Hunting and running traps. Don't want to bunch up, or the Indians'll get scared we're taking too much o'their game. Easier to hunt with fewer people anyhow."

Four tents ranged around a campfire, a half dozen horses grazed off to the side. As many dogs ran up to Matt and the Hollingers, sniffing and yapping. Three men sitting by the fire stared at them, two more stuck their heads out of tents. One stepped out and walked toward them, pulling a knit hat down over long, tousled hair.

"Russell, dang it, don't do that no more. We thought you'd wandered off and got kilt."

The man's black beard wiggled as he chewed on a small stick, his jaw going sideways like a cow's. He eyed Matt and the Hollingers. "Good to see you, Meager. These your boys?"

"This one here is," Meager said, pointing. "Wouldn't stay home where he belonged. Knox, that there's Matt.

Joined up with us over by the Gap."

"Well, plenty of beasts waitin' to get skinned," Knox said. "Just in time to help out. Come warm up and meet Tony Bledsoe and the others. I'll fill you in."

Matt studied the man. He looked maybe forty years old, was short and slight of build. He didn't have much muscle, but Matt had seen his kind before. His own daddy was built about the same way, but he was as strong as anybody else, could hold his own on any job.

Eight more hunters came in with new pelts that evening. They scraped their catches and piled them in the skin house, a large scaffold covered with buffalo skins. Matt watched one hunter clean his gun and throw the tow over a nearby branch. Noah used to do the same thing, knowing the burnt powder smell would keep the wolves and wild cats away.

At dusk the men ate roasted deer haunch by the fire while they got more meat ready for jerking. Knox cut a piece and squatted next to Matt. He bit into the slab and wiped dripping grease from his mouth with a sleeve. The fire flickered in his eyes as he turned toward Matt.

"You like hunting?"

"Sure. But I guess I'd rather be farming."

The man nodded. "Most of us're in that boat. But this here hunting helps us farm."

"How so?" Matt shifted toward the man, taking renewed interest in him.

"Why, think about it. Three or four men and their dogs can kill ten, maybe twenty buffalo a day. An ordinary hunter can get four, five deer a day. And in one day in the fall he can kill enough bears to get a ton of meat to keep him over the winter."

He tore another piece of meat off with his teeth and chewed it.

"A deerskin'll go for a dollar, and one horse can carry a hundred of them," Knox continued. "Beavers is even better. You can get two, three times as much more'n a deerskin'll bring. And otters'll bring from three to five times as much. So a horse load of beaver furs'd bring five times what deer will. Throw in a few little otters, and you got a real piece of change."

Matt's eyes widened. Why, in a year or two he could load his two horses with enough pelts to buy the best farm there was! His own father and Noah Dandridge never had any real cash to speak of. They just traded for things, maybe sold enough corn to get what they couldn't trade for. But with two loads of pelts turned into cash, Matt could do all right. He'd get that farm in no time, and have a place for him and Mandy to live.

Knox stuffed the last meat into his mouth and licked his fingers. Matt looked at the others around the fire, saw the man they called Bledsoe sitting off by himself, looking up into the black sky. He'd seemed standoffish earlier, only grunted when Knox introduced him. Knox saw Matt's glance.

"Bledsoe'll take one last load to the Cumberland tomorrow, for Mansker and his crew to float to New Orleans," Knox said. "Then he'll start trapping the river. I was hoping you and the Hollinger boy would go along and bring the horses back."

"Why . . . why, sure," Matt said.

"You can keep camp when you get back," Knox said. "Keep the fire going, that kind of thing."

Matt looked away, into the fire. "I guess so. But I was hoping to hunt some."

"Oh, plenty of time for that. Hunters come and go; you'll hook up with someone soon enough. But they're all paired off for now, got their plans made. 'Sides, you can hunt close to camp on your own."

Matt shifted his gaze away from the fire and saw Bledsoe staring at him. Or at least in his direction. He sure didn't look friendly.

❈

Jacob laughed and slapped his leg, startling his horse. "Dang, things sure get done fast here, don't they now! Seems like yesterday I was cutting fodder, and here I am hauling pelts. Ain't that something!"

Matt glanced back at his own load of pelts. Bledsoe was ahead, leading struggling packhorses down a path that wove among the grass-covered hills. Jacob was right. It seemed like just yesterday when he and Noah whittled their little birds by the fireplace. Then that thing with Struthers happened, and —

"There's the river," Matt said. He peered at the horizon beyond Bledsoe. "See those trees?"

"I'll sure be ready to light," Jacob said. "That there Bledsoe don't believe in wasting no time, do he?"

The tree line got closer. Bledsoe nudged his horse off the trail toward a spiral of smoke on the right. Matt and Jacob followed and they soon reached the Cumberland River. Matt dismounted and bent back to stretch his muscles. The Cumberland was a lot wider here than at the Gap. A lot swifter, too.

Chopping sounds came from downriver. "Git those pelts unloaded," Bledsoe said. He pointed to a stockpile of pelts on a makeshift pallet of crossed branches, and disappeared toward the chopping. Matt threw off one of the overlapped buffalo hides that covered the pelts.

"Whooee! Must be a thousand skins here," Jacob said. "Ever seen so many in one place?"

"There's three, four times as many up in Knox's camp," Matt said. "Well, let's get goin'."

They unloaded and stacked pelts for the next hour. When they stopped they were sweating in spite of the cold air. Jacob threw the last pelt on top and they led their horses downstream where Bledsoe had gone.

Two shirtless men stood on two twenty-foot long poplar logs laid side by side on the river bank. Bledsoe and three others stood watching their muscular bodies work in unison; swing their foot adzes pendulum-like down between their legs, swing them back up, grunt and let them fall again, make one chopping sound between them, slice yet another pair of slivers from the logs' insides. They paused, adzes held ready, and the men with Bledsoe cleaned the long chips out. Then the choppers continued, occasionally shifting a half step on the gunwales, striking again. They turned at the logs' ends and started back, cutting more slivers.

Bledsoe approached one dugout, reached into it, and pulled out a handful of shavings. He held it above him.

"They's artists, ain't they?" he said, to no one in particular. He twisted around and looked up the hill. A lone man sat up there on a log, head hung down, staring at his bandaged foot. Bledsoe turned back to Matt and pointed to one of the men swinging an adze.

"You should see that one there square up a log for a cabin raising," he said. "Back in Virginia I seen him swing that damned thing toward his own feet, on purpose. Sliced a sliver off his shoe sole so thin you could almost see through it."

He turned toward the hill again, and the man with the bandaged foot. He cupped his hands to his mouth. "And he done it on purpose, just to show off!" he yelled.

"Gawd dang!" Jacob said.

Bledsoe lived in Virginia! Matt glanced at the older man, trying to ignore the shiver he felt.

"Where in Virginia you from?" he said. He hoped he sounded casual.

Bledsoe turned back to Matt. "Near Fincastle, up in the Valley."

Fincastle. Matt nodded, stared at the men hollowing out the dugouts. Bledsoe probably knew Struthers, maybe was even a personal friend. If he heard about his killing, about a young boy disappearing at the same time, he might put two and two together.

Matt rubbed his jaw, trying to sort his thoughts. Bledsoe

was headed downriver, away from Virginia. There was little chance he'd run into someone who could tell him. Almost none at all.

But knowing that didn't make the nervousness go away.

Matt peeked inside one of the dugouts. "Another six hours," he said, hoping to change the conversation.

"That's 'bout right," Bledsoe said. "You're name's Matt, ain't it?" He nodded toward the man standing beside him. "This here's Casper Mansker. Tomorrow he's taking these dugouts downriver to New Orleans."

"New Orleans. That's a long ways away."

"You got that right," Mansker said. He was tall, clean shaven, looked to be Bledsoe's age. He didn't look strong enough to make the trip down to New Orleans. But then again, it was all downstream. Once there he'd sell the dugouts for firewood, and board a ship headed back to Virginia around Florida.

Bledsoe spat, glanced to his side. Matt followed his gaze to two fresh-made log canoes pulled onto shore. Judging from the cut marks, the trees had been felled and trimmed with a double-bit axe. He couldn't see their insides because of the tarps that covered them, but was sure they'd been hollowed out by the same adzes now at work on the larger dugouts.

"We was going to trap down the Cumberland after Mansker leaves tomorrow," Bledsoe said loudly. He stared up the bank, like he wanted to be sure the man sitting up there heard him. "Sam Warren there thought he could handle an adze as good as this here man," Bledsoe said. "Yesterday he damned near cut his toe off, showing off. He sure can't handle a canoe crippled."

He turned back to Matt. "When you get back, tell Knox to send somebody else. Ross Stoph, if he's still there. Or maybe Schoate."

Matt thought about Bledsoe's situation. He needed someone to help him trap. This was his chance!

"How about me? I'll go with you."

"You? Too young. Too puny. Got to be strong to row a canoe and such all day. No, you do what I said."

"But I am strong! I've been felling trees all year. I've never canoed much, but I can do it as good as somebody else. I just bet you!"

"You heard me."

Bledsoe turned to say something to Mansker, and Matt knew he was dismissed. He walked to one of the canoes and lifted its tarp. It was already loaded with supplies. Shot pouches were lashed to dry wood chunks so they'd float, powder was stored in watertight oiled bags, a buffalo hide bag was filled with something, he guessed parched corn. Other supplies were neatly tied, sealed, ready for the trip. In the center were two tow sacks, blunt edges of animal traps poking out their ends.

Knox wanted him to tend the camp. Well, Sam Warren could do that. The man sure wasn't going hunting, not for a while.

Matt didn't think about it, really. He just pushed the nearest canoe into the river, and jumped in it. He spread his legs wide for balance and wondered what had gotten into him.

"What the hell you doing!" Bledsoe screamed. He dashed over to the water's edge, plunged in, reached out for the canoe. Matt grabbed the paddle and thrust it into the river, pushed away, splashing water on Bledsoe.

"I can paddle, you look!" he yelled. "You just watch!"

Bledsoe lunged again at the canoe. Matt, squatting down to sit, was jerked back. His heels caught on something, and he windmilled his arms to stay upright. His paddle slapped the canoe side and he knew he was headed for the water. As he fell, he glimpsed Bledsoe standing in knee deep water, staring, mouth sagged open.

Matt shoved his feet against the canoe bottom with all his force and arched backward. He back-flipped into the water, feeling his heels brush the canoe's gunwale. Almost instantly he thrust his head up and stared at the canoe. It bucked wildly, slapped against Bledsoe's knees, and stayed there, upright.

Matt stood, up to his knees in the water. Laughter rolled down from the men on the bank, as if it was something solid. He steeled himself for the tongue lashing he knew was coming from Bledsoe.

Bledsoe pulled the canoe up on the shore and glared at the other men, who quieted and went back to work. Matt waded slowly to shore, wishing Bledsoe would get it over with. *Just throw your tantrum and get it over with.*

"Well, at least you didn't turn it over," Bledsoe said.

"No, sir. I tried not to."

Bledsoe looked over its contents and seemed to deter-mine it was all there.

"I'm not going back," Matt said. "If you won't take me, I'll hunt by myself. I got bullets and powder, everything I need."

Bledsoe looked up at the crippled man on the bank, then back at Matt.

"I ain't got much choice. I don't expect no one wants to come down here from the camp. It's you or that bleedy-toed Sam Warren up there on that bank, and he's sure not up to it."

"I'd try real hard to do good," Matt said. "I got to get some pelts so I can get a good home for Mandy."

"Well . . . well, maybe. But I tell you what. I ain't goin' to hold your hand. You don't pull your load, you just hike on down the trail. Now you get out of those wet clothes 'fore you catch your death."

CHAPTER 11

BLEDSOE'S TWO CANOES SET OUT DOWNRIVER THE NEXT day, shortly after Mansker and his crews left for New Orleans with their loaded down dugouts. Oscar Chandler and John Prewitt manned the second canoe, working together with an ease that told of long experience together.

Not so with Matt and Bledsoe. The first time Matt paddled in the back the canoe veered right, bringing sharp comments from Bledsoe. Matt noted that when the older man sat in back he pulled his paddle hard through the water and then pushed it out away from him at the end of the stroke, making a backward "J" shape in the swirling water and keeping the boat straight and true. When they switched places Matt struggled to learn the maneuver. At first his arms ached as he put new muscles to work. But then they hardened. The pain eased, and the outward thrust became second nature. He learned he could paddle almost as well as Bledsoe, and in fact could probably keep it up longer.

They trapped from the canoes until cold weather set in and ice formed along the banks. Each team put into shore to check traps, muscling their canoes around trees and brush and through the cane, checking for animal runs and other signs. Then they pulled into the current and leapfrogged around the other team doing the same thing. At dusk they all went ashore and camped.

After chores Bledsoe often leaned against a tree and looked around like it was the first time he'd seen such a sight. He didn't talk much, particularly to Matt. A gruff "get this" or "do that" was his usual conversation. But once in a great while he said or did something that surprised Matt.

"Nature sure worked on a different scale this side of the mountains," he said once. "Everything's bigger and better over here. Why, look at those red cedars on that hilltop. Four feet thick and forty feet up before you get to the first limb. You won't find nothing like that back to home."

And then he'd turn gruff again, like Matt was his slave or something, somebody put there to fetch and carry for him.

There was still some clover, wild rye, buffalo grass, and pea vine on their trap line route, like in the Barrens upriver. But as they worked farther west, the clearings were smaller and fewer. Mostly the river was lined with thick forests of popular, hickory, black walnut, buckeye and horse chestnut, along with some sycamore, locust, and sugar maples. Noah Dandridge had identified several trees for Matt the summer before he was killed, and later questioned Matt to make sure what he'd said had stuck. "That there's a buckeye," he'd say. "See that shiny black nut? Gets its name from the seed."

Some of the trees on the Cumberland were different,

though, and Matt didn't want to bother Bledsoe with the identifying. The wildlife was also different. The white-tail deer were like the ones Matt had hunted back in the Virginia valley and he'd also seen bears back there, even killed two. But the buffalo still amazed him, as did the huge elk that bounded along the river, and the big turkey flocks. Pheasants, partridges, and quail scattered before them when they went ashore, and pigeons of the like he'd never seen before. Wild geese and ducks flew up when they returned to the river the next morning.

Eventually they pulled the canoes in and set up a permanent outpost camp. Bledsoe picked dense woods with abundant spruce next to a large swamp. As he explained, where there was no spruce there was no sable. Where there was no swamp there was no lynx, or bear.

Swamps held rabbits, the natural prey of the lynx, and wild turnips, the natural food of the bear.

In late winter, Bledsoe started using baits. Parsnips, turnips, sweet apples for muskrats, rabbit flesh, birds, fish, muskrat flesh for mink, scorched and burned meats, birds, and rabbits for fox. "Never make a bait set in a trail, make it at one side," he told Matt. "Hide it under a rotten log, in an opening in the rocks, or under a brush heap. And damn it, don't make it too near a den, like that one there. Wouldn't you be suspicious if you walked out of your cabin and found a nice juicy steak sizzling on your doorstep?"

Matt learned to scatter a few feathers or fur wisps around to disarm suspicion. He learned where the animals lived, and set his traps accordingly. The muskrats built houses out of cattail flags in level flat country, close to the water. Mink were usually in the area, since muskrats were one of their favorite foods. Matt found them mostly at headwaters of creeks and rivers, and where there were plenty of sloughs and ponds. He soon could spot their paths between ponds, identify their droppings by the fish scales and pieces of crawfish shells they contained.

He learned to read fur signs. Overturned leaves, track outlines in the frost, a few stray hairs at a den entrance, a bunch of fur pulled off where an animal squeezed through a tight place — all this he started taking in at a glance. Before long he knew what the animal was doing, where it went and how long ago, and sometimes, by the size of its tracks, whether it was a male or female. He learned firsthand the haunts of deer, elk, bear, wolf, and other animals that roamed the region. He paid particular attention to the winds and rains, and the snows and frosts when they came, since almost every change seemed to mean a change in where the game was.

Snow settled in, and sometimes a blizzard kept them in camp for two or three days. They used the time to repair equipment and take care of the pelts. At night they sat in their lean-to shelter listening to the howling timber wolf and the American lion's piercing scream, wondering when they could get back to work.

Bledsoe gave Matt all the camp work to do. "You was supposed to do it at Knox's place," he reminded Matt several times. But Matt didn't mind, even welcomed the activity. Besides, he was learning valuable things, things he'd later use to keep himself and Mandy fed on the farm he planned to get with those pelts.

Like casing a pelt. He got down on one knee and put his opposite foot on the animal's tail to hold it. Then he picked up each hind leg in turn and cut from heel to heel and around the tail, and pulled the hide over the body. His foot held the animal so that he had both hands free to work with. Skinning the head was the only part of the work he needed to take pains in doing.

Before long he could skin six pelts in five minutes and not cut one hide, all the while listening to the conversation of the others. Split open the hind legs, pull the skin from the carcass, stretch it over a bent stick, fur side in; his knife zipped through its job, his hands and fingers flew, and the furs stacked up.

When they had enough pelts to make the trip worthwhile, they put them in a canoe and one team took them to the camp where Mansker had launched his New Orleans-bound dugouts. They stacked their new pelts on the same crossed limbs that had held Mansker's huge fur pile. At first their own little pile looked feeble in comparison. But, load by load, the cache began to fill up.

Matt lost track of the days. They'd shortened, gotten colder. Snow came, and stayed, piled up to make walking impossible without their makeshift snowshoes. The days got shorter still, and they'd go to bed at dusk and awaken while the wind swirled the snow in pre-dawn moonlight. They'd just sit there huddled, waiting for daylight so they could get back to moving around and warming up.

Then the days got longer. One morning Bledsoe dropped a trap he was repairing and looked at the sun, inching up in the east. "Almost spring," he said. "Time to get home and get some crops out."

They pulled their traps and stacked them in the canoes and started back. Matt's hardened muscles strained, bulged in a deerskin shirt now too tight, too short, as he rowed against the extra load and the spring current made swifter by melting snow upstream. He'd grown almost three inches over the winter, gotten heavier, stronger. He could feel his beard filling out when he rubbed his face with his hand. Once when he saw his reflection in a pool where a creek came into the river, he'd frowned and almost wondered if it was really him. What had been a child's pink cheeks were now rough and wind burned.

On every trip back to the home camp, it seemed, Bledsoe had sat back and stared up at a particular bluff on the river's south side. This afternoon he paused and pointed it out to Matt.

"That there's the bluff Mansker told me about," he said. "Said there's a salt lick up there, and he'd never seen so much game. Let's go see what he was so proud of."

They paddled to shore and tied up where Chandler and Prewitt would see the canoe. Their moccasined feet crunched thin ice as they climbed the rocky animal trail up the cliff. Something roared in the distance, like a far off wind. Bledsoe must have heard it too, because he turned and shrugged, pointed upriver. A storm approaching? They'd have to pitch camp fast.

They reached the top and pushed through a tree and brush fringe until they came out on a level, grassless plain. Matt and Bledsoe saw two deer in its center, nibbling perhaps fifty yards beyond them. They swung their rifles up and fired, and the deer dropped.

"Well, there's dinner," Bledsoe said.

Something wasn't right. Matt strode toward the dead game and realized what had been bothering him. The rough, salty white ground underfoot wasn't covered with rocks, like he'd thought at first. It was covered with thousands of deep hoof prints. And that roar — he turned toward it and stopped in his tracks — that roar! It was the rumble of buffalo hooves!

"Bledsoe!"

The man was looking down at the dead deer. Matt sprang forward, ran toward him.

"Bledsoe!"

Bledsoe turned to the roar and froze in place. A brown, wavy line bore down on them. Huge bushy heads appeared through the dust.

"Run!" Matt screamed. Horror spread across Bledsoe's face. Matt reached him and pushed him ahead. Bledsoe stumbled, caught himself.

"Bledsoe! Get outa here!"

That clump of trees! Matt swung left and ran for it, Bledsoe following. The buffalo mass closed the gap behind them and Matt dived for a thin hickory tree, fell on its roots and wrapped his arms around it. Bledsoe made it to the next tree as the first buffaloes passed, panting, throwing dirt clods, reeking with strong odor, thumping against scarred trees that offered slight hope of protection.

"Damn!" Bledsoe screamed.

Matt couldn't see him for the raging animals and flying dirt. He pulled his own arms from around the hickory, fearful of their being broken and scrunched into a ball with his head against the trunk. It bounced against the tree each time a buffalo hit it. Twice a rampaging animal knocked him aside, and he barely recovered before another beast trampled him there.

God help me! Noah! Noah, help me!

The roar seemed to continue for hours, but Matt knew it was only minutes. The noise, the smells, the herd lessened, moved west. He stayed rolled in his ball until birds called again in the trees bordering the plain. He opened his eyes. Sweat and mud caked his arms, his face. Bledsoe lay prone ahead of him. Matt stood and ran over.

"You all right?" He bent down and saw Bledsoe's wide, staring eyes.

The man grabbed his right leg, grimacing. "I'm alive, but that's all. Damned thing stepped on me."

Matt eased Bledsoe's trouser leg up and stared. A buffalo had mashed his leg, literally pinched a five-inch strip of meat off the calf. Bledsoe eyed it, shook his head.

Matt looked up in the tree. "I'll chop off that limb. Should make a pretty good crutch." He hacked at it with his knife and soon handed the makeshift crutch to Bledsoe.

"Help me get down to the river and get this washed out," Bledsoe said. He pulled himself up and leaned on

Matt's shoulder with one hand, on his crutch with the other. They hobbled across the bare ground, paused where the two deer had fallen. Matt shook his head, studied the mangled animals.

"Looks like stew meat," he said.

"Could'a been us," Bledsoe said. "Well, let's get going."

They made it down the bluff and saw the other canoe coming into shore. They all camped at water's edge that night instead of on the plateau, in case the buffalo decided to come back.

In the morning they thought about shifting loads to lighten Bledsoe's canoe, but both canoes were filled. Bledsoe sat in front, facing the rear, his bandaged, injured leg stuck out before him on a stack of pelts. Matt sat in the back and paddled as best he could. He strained to push the heavy canoe upriver, tried to make it appear easy to his partner. "It's not bad," he said. "How far you figure we got to go?"

"Another day, normally," Bledsoe said. "But with me crippled up here, figure two."

Matt and the other two men took turns in Bledsoe's canoe. As Bledsoe had predicted, it was two days before they saw their home camp. Matt ran the canoe aground, pulled it high onto the bank, and helped Bledsoe out.

"Guess you'll have to hike on up to Knox's camp and get the horses," Bledsoe said. "I sure cain't walk. I . . . " He glanced around the camp. "Something's wrong. Don't know what, but . . . " he twisted around and looked upriver, toward the pelt cache.

"I'll go look," Matt said. He ran into the woods and

moments later came to where they'd stockpiled the pelts. Fresh moccasin prints were all around. He felt a chill.

Gone. The pelts were all gone. Even the buffalo robes that had covered them were gone. The skin-house platform logs lay bare in neat, unnatural rows.

He stared for several moments. All gone! The pelts he was going to buy a home and supplies with, a full winter of hard work, had just disappeared as if in a puff of bitter wind. He turned and trod back down the path to Bledsoe.

"They're gone, ain't they." A statement from Bledsoe, not a question.

"Couldn'ta been long ago," Matt said.

"By God, a whole winter's work!" Bledsoe flung his crutch into the woods. "Those damned Indians! Git me my crutch!"

He stared at Matt. It seemed like Bledsoe shrunk in size while he stood there. The man Matt had feared, tread lightly around, now looked like any other human, not larger than life like he'd seemed before. He was just another man trying to squeeze a living out of the wilderness, and — like Matt himself — got hit with a big dose of reality.

Matt retrieved Bledsoe's crutch and took it to him, waited for him to speak. The man limped to a fallen tree and sat down. After a while he pulled his knife from its scabbard.

He stared up into the branches of the maple tree in front of him as if composing his thoughts. Then he carved something into its trunk. When he was finished, he stood and limped down to the canoe.

Matt walked around the tree and made out the words: "2300 SKINS LOST. RUINATION, BY GOD."

And Matt knew he was right.

CHAPTER 12

MATT HAD NEVER IMAGINED KNOX'S MAIN CAMP SO BUSY. Of course he'd been there only one day before going down the Cumberland with Bledsoe the previous fall, and had been back from a winter's trapping for only two weeks. But now other hunters returned in twos and threes, and the camp was filling up.

The hunters were loaded with pelts and stories about the wondrous things they'd seen. It seemed each one tried to outdo the others in story telling. But the most interesting of all was not even one of Knox's long hunters. He was a man named Daniel Boone, who'd come into camp with his brother Squire just that afternoon. Knox, Meager, and Jacob had met him at the Ohio River falls earlier that year and invited him down. Matt watched him, sitting across the large campfire, laughing and talking with James Knox.

Jacob sat eating next to Matt. He poked Matt's arm. "That Boone feller is somethin' else," he whispered. "Said he come in sixty-nine. You should hear his stories! Let's go listen."

Jacob stood and tugged at Matt's shirt, and he rose. Others had already gathered around Boone. Matt squatted near him.

The man appeared about forty years old. He was broad chested and flat bellied, and his white-flecked black hair was plaited and clubbed up behind. His nose was bent, and his thin, wide mouth pursed when he was deep in thought.

"They was five of us come," Boone said, answering someone's question. "John Finley, 'course he was here the year before, and told me about it. And there was Joseph Holden, John Stewart, James Monay, and William Cool. God, it was beautiful!"

He leaned back and the crackling fire lit up his face. "Everything went good until December last year," he said, frowning. "Stewart and me was out rambling and Indians jumped out'n a thick canebrake and took us. Kept us for a week. We acted like we didn't want to leave them. Then one night after they trusted us, we snuck back to our own camp. But everybody'd all gone home."

Matt leaned forward to hear better over the fire's popping. Boone paused, spat, looked at his hands. After a while he looked up and gestured at his brother.

"Then he showed up," he said. "Him and another guy who got scart and run home a few days later. It wasn't long afore the Injuns killed Stewart."

Squire Boone, his brother, laughed. "Maybe that other guy wasn't so dumb after all, for running."

The hunters laughed nervously, shifted, quieted. Matt watched Boone's eyes squint a smile and Boone returned his gaze. "How old are you, boy?" he asked.

"Sixteen."

"About the age of James, my oldest. Surprised your mama let you come."

"I ain't got one," Matt mumbled, feeling the other hunters' eyes on him. "Did you — you and your brother — did you stay out there all that time?"

"Well, Squire there went home last spring for supplies, and I roamed by myself. He come back last summer and we hunted all over the place. Built a cabin, even. Spent a little time down on the Cumberland, too."

"We just come back from there," Matt said.

"Guess we missed you, but that's easy to do in this country," Boone said.

The subject changed to other things, and before long the other hunters turned in. But Matt stayed behind. Boone got up to leave the fire.

"Mr. Boone . . ."

Boone paused. Matt had said his name, then couldn't think of what else to say. There was so much he wanted to learn from this man. About where he'd been, what he'd seen, the Indians up north. Boone stood a minute, sat down again. The fire had died down considerably, but Matt could still see his face.

"Mr. Boone, the Indians killed my ma, took my sister Mandy. You . . . you didn't see her, did you?"

Boone leaned back, stared at him. "Don't believe so, son. 'Course, I didn't get to all five Shawnee towns. They took me to Chilicothe, on the Little Miami. I didn't see any whites there."

"Well, when they . . . when they kidnap people, what do they do with them?"

Boone thought a minute. He ran his hand over his face, rested it on his knee.

"Well, depends. Now, if they take someone in a battle, sometimes they bring 'em back to camp and run them through what's called a gauntlet. They line up on two sides and beat the man with clubs as he runs through. Sometimes he makes it, sometimes he don't. Guess sometimes he makes it and wishes he didn't, he's so banged up. But I hear that if he makes it they sometimes even take him into the tribe."

" 'Course that don't fit Mandy's case."

"No, guess it don't. We don't know much about the Indians, truth be known. But the traders, they say they ain't all bad. They kidnap an enemy's children . . . sometimes they kill 'em, if they been at war. But sometimes they treat 'em like their own."

"Maybe . . . maybe that's what happened with Mandy. We wasn't at war. Maybe she's up there in one of those towns and has got her a new family and all, and . . . and forgot all about her real home."

"S'pose that's possible, Matt. Take Logan, now, that's what happened to his daddy. He's the chief of the Mingo tribe, up on the Sciota River, right near the Little and Great Miami rivers where the Shawnee are. His daddy was a little French boy, got kidnapped. When he growed up he married a Mingo woman, and they had Logan. His real name's

Tah-Gah-Jute, but he took the name Logan from the secretary of the Pennsylvania Province. They figure it's an honor to answer to a white man's name. They say Logan sticks up for the white man, too."

Matt thought a moment. "I don't know why they're mad at us. We ain't done nothing to them."

"Maybe. I guess they're mostly mad at the Six Nations tribes, not us. They signed a treaty in sixty-eight that took away the Indian rights to the land south of the Can-tuc-kee River, and the Shawnee don't agree with it at all. We're sitting in what used to be their hunting ground right now."

Matt thought about this, about what Boone had said about their adopting people. "Then maybe Mandy's all right," he said, slowly. "We ain't really at war with them. Maybe the Shawnee adopted her."

"Maybe so," Boone said. "Maybe so."

"But . . . but what if they didn't? I got to find her. But I don't know how!"

Boone didn't say anything for a minute. He frowned with thought.

"You say you're sixteen, Matt?"

"Yes, sir."

"Well, that's pretty young. I been around longer, and I don't know if I could find her."

"I got to, though. She's my sister. I got to find her!"

"Well, you be careful. You go up there, they'll kill you right off. What good would that do?"

Boone shifted against his tree trunk. He broke a small stick into little pieces, threw them idly into the dying fire.

He looked at Matt a long time, then spoke.

"Matt, maybe she don't want to come. Ever think of that?"

"Why wouldn't she? She's my sister."

"But she was so little when they got her. Maybe she don't even remember you, or even the language. Maybe you'd not be doing her a favor, bringing her back. Besides, you got no place to bring her."

"Well, I thought I'd get me a farm. A home, you know, someplace to bring her."

"That'd be good. Matt, you get that farm. That's what you got to do. Then maybe you could find her later. That's what I'd do."

Matt and Boone sat there a long time, talking about the wilderness and the Indians. A half moon crept across the sky, and the fire died down. Finally Boone stood.

"Well, I'd best get to bed. I'm leaving at dawn, going back to North Carolina. It's been a long time since I was home."

Matt stood, too. A breeze fanned up the fire's flames. He felt a warm glow as Boone turned and went to his blanket. Yes, Mandy was probably adopted. Up there in one of those Indian towns, with a family and all. Daniel Boone said he was going to come back to the Can-tuc-kee land someday soon. Bring his own family and maybe some others and start a new life. Well, maybe Mandy had started her own new life, up there to the north, and forgot all about him. Like Boone said.

He looked up at the black sky, saw the bright north star.

'Course, maybe Boone was wrong about her wanting to stay with the Indians. Maybe she was looking up, too, right now, staring at that same star and thinking about him, wanting to come home.

Yes, he'd build that farm, that home. Then he'd find her. That's what he had to do. They needed a home to go to.

He stood there a long time, listening to the wolves outside the campfire's glow, off to the north.

Matt awoke early the next morning, but Daniel and Squire Boone had already left. More hunters were readying to leave and Matt volunteered to help them pack. He and Jacob soon loaded almost two dozen horses with pelts. The skin-house stack shrunk a third its former height throughout the day. Some hunters vowed they'd be back next fall. Others said little, just looked back over their shoulders with somber faces. Matt knew he'd seen the last of them.

Tony Bledsoe was one of those leaving. They'd bandaged his leg as good as they could and helped him up on his horse. He gritted his teeth as his horse jostled him and Matt figured the man was thinking about the long trip home.

"Maybe you'd better stay a few days, Tony," Matt said, hitching up his packhorse. "Looks like a lot of pain."

"Got to get back," the older man said.

"Are you . . . you going to buy a new farm somewheres?"

"No, guess I'll stay on at Fincastle, least 'til my leg heals. I can't start a new place in this condition. What about you?"

"Guess I'll stay awhile," Matt said. "I worked all winter and still don't have nothing to show for it."

"I know that feeling. At least I had them pelts I got before we went down to the Cumberland. Well, you take care."

Meager walked over to the skin-house in the early afternoon, watched Jacob and Matt load pelts. He stood around making small talk. Matt knew he wanted to say something. Finally he yawned and stretched and allowed he was going back to start packing.

"Guess we'll head out tomorrow," he told Jacob. "Matt, you're welcome to come with us. You could stay at our place a while, if you wanted."

"Appreciate the offer," Matt said. He finished tying a load and stepped back, wiped his forehead. "But I'll stay on here. Thank you just the same, though."

"Suit yourself. You get in our part of the country, you stop in."

"Pa . . . " Jacob fiddled with the leather strap in his hand.

"Yes, son?"

"Pa, I . . . I think I'll stay on with Matt here, if you don't mind. That be all right?

Meager stared at his son who turned away to tie off his load. It was quiet, except for the birds chattering in the trees, the squeak of the leather being pulled tight.

"I was thinking we'd open up some more land," Meager said. "Off north of the house. Sure could use your help."

"Well, I . . . I sure would like to stay here. They's going to be a half dozen or so staying, and they's plenty of deer.

Figured I could get us some more pelts and you could bring an extra horse or two next fall to carry them back on."

Meager studied him. "Your ma would miss you. She didn't want me to take you away, nohow. She'll blame me if you stayed."

Jacob looked like he was going to object, but thought better of it. "I'll come, Pa. I was just thinking I could get me some land, too, and . . . well, never mind."

Meager, who had turned to leave, stopped. He turned back around.

"Well, now. What you're saying might be a good plan at that. Got any idea where you'd get it? The land?"

"I thought maybe that piece just up the road from you. Where it curves around by the big rocks."

"That's good land," Meager said. "Good spot for a cabin, on that hill."

"It's only two, three miles from your place. I could visit you and Ma all the time, if . . . if I was to stay here and get that land."

Meager smiled. "You thinking on asking that Anna-belle girl to marry you? You are, ain't you?"

"Well, I . . . yes, I guess. But I ain't asked her yet. Don't know if she'd have me."

Meager thought a minute. "Tell you what. You leave your ma to me. It's about time she know'd it's us men what run things."

The long hunters left in four groups over a week's time. It wasn't until the last ones rode over the horizon that Matt knew for sure who was staying. They waved good-byes and looked around at each other, judging their strength.

Six men were left in the camp with Matt and Jacob. The three Skaggs brothers, Henry, Charles, and Richard, had said they'd hunt to the northwest, along the Ohio River. They were already packed, and would be gone by daylight the next day. "We'll come back 'fore summer's out," Charles said. "Got to bring all them deerskins in."

Joe Drake and Obadiah Terrill had talked about staying, too. But it wasn't until this morning that they finally decided for sure. Old Wade Russell had already started packing to leave with the rest, the day before, stopped only when he learned Drake and Terrill were staying. He looked up and blinked, trying to see where the others were standing.

"I ain't got no place to go, noways," he told Terrill. "You don't mind some help, I'll just stay put."

Matt watched the little group break up and settle to their tasks. The packing finished, he sat on a log and gazed toward the northeast where he imagined his sister to be. Boone had said that's where the Shawnee towns were, on the Miami rivers. He tried to imagine Mingo Chief Logan, the half breed whose daddy was kidnapped like Mandy was. But he couldn't. He hadn't seen even one Indian so far, except for those he'd killed in the ambush. Did they all look alike?

Matt looked down at his hands, cracked from dipping into the icy river all winter pulling traps. He rubbed them together and went over to help Jacob. Russell would go off hunting with Drake and Terrill, and Matt and Jacob would pair off. With a little luck they could get a lot of deerskins before fall.

Boone had agreed about getting that farm. The more Matt thought about the situation, the more he liked it. He could get maybe two loads of skins, and that fall trade them for a good piece of land.

But it would have to be someplace far away from Fincastle. Bledsoe would surely find out about Struthers. If he told the sheriff he'd seen him in the Can-tuc-kee land, why, they might even try to come and get him.

Matt looked north once more, then forced himself to turn away, toward Virginia. There was danger in both places. There might even be danger where he was standing.

CHAPTER 13

MATT ENJOYED HUNTING DEER MUCH MORE THAN PADDLING a canoe on the Cumberland. He and Jacob often stayed out two or three days, exploring new regions and returning with several deer skins between them. As time passed and the days got warmer, their kills became surer, more frequent.

Wade Russell went with them on one of their outings. "That Drake and Terrill is just too danged fast," he said. "Don't give a man a chance to aim. I'm still a better hunter'n they are, they just give me a chance."

Drake and Terrill also took two- and three-day trips, usually not returning the same day Matt and Jacob did. But Matt saw smoke as they approached the camp one May evening and knew they were there. They'd already tended their horses and were preparing their skins when Matt arrived.

Terrill glanced up. "Matt. Where's Russell?" he said. He was short and plump, slightly bald.

"Didn't he go with you?"

"Hell, no. We thought he was with you."

Joe Drake came over from the fire, frowning as if

trying to remember something. He was taller than Terrill, more muscular.

"He ain't with you? That son of a gun..."

Jacob nudged Matt. "He done that before, remember? He was by hisself when we come in from Virginia last year."

Matt nodded. "He's probably all right. Let's give him a day or two."

They all stayed in camp the next day, finishing up the skins and worrying about Russell. At dusk Terrill stood and stared out across the Barrens. He sighed. "We'll have to find him. He could be any place."

"He's hunted this whole area," Drake agreed.

"Well, let's go in different directions each time we leave camp," Matt said. "You know, do a circle and come back and check with each other."

Terrill nodded. "As good a plan as any. I like that old man, but he's blind as a bat. Cain't hardly see at all."

They followed Matt's plan for a week without luck. One morning Matt stood by the skin-house gazing out over the rolling grass plain, Benjie's reins in hand, Jacob standing next to him. It occurred to him they were making a daisy blossom pattern on the ground, with counterclockwise loops for the petals. They'd go out a day, camp, come back the next night, compare notes, and repeat the pattern. Their last loop was south of camp.

Matt pointed east. "We come in that way, you and your pa and me. Remember?"

"Sure do. Boy, it was a sight, seeing this camp the first time."

"But remember? That's where we found Russell. Checking traps on the Little Barren. Let's look for him there."

They told the others what they were doing, and rode toward the rising sun. When they reached the Barren River they turned south. Matt didn't recognize much of the land. They'd come in late fall before, when everything was bare. Now the trees all had leaves, the grass was lush and green. He swiveled in his saddle, glanced back. It was a trick Noah had taught him. When you look back, you see things the way you saw them before, when you came from the other direction.

Most of what he saw still seemed unfamiliar, but Matt did recognize where they'd forded the river. It was a wide trail where game crossed the shallow water. They waded over and had traveled north for two hours when Matt saw something off to the side. At first it looked like a dead deer, picked over by the vermin. They rode over to it and dismounted.

"Well, look at that, now," Jacob said.

"Russell's horse." Matt walked over to the animal, and stared down. He shook his head. "Still got his saddle on." He inspected the saddle, saw the bullet hole in the cinch strap, dried blood around it.

"He shot his own horse," he said slowly. "Took it for a deer, I expect, and just shot him down."

"Well, if that don't beat all." Jacob studied the bullet hole. Beneath the saddle and the blanket was mostly bones, well picked over.

"Happened two, three days ago," Matt guessed. "Let's look around for footprints."

They found them, going north. Matt followed them on foot, leading his horses, and Jacob came behind. They reached a low spot where Russell's moccasined feet had dug deep into mud, now dried. The earth was already dusty in the higher parts, and new tracks would be hard to see.

They followed the trail north through the grass the rest of the day, watching it weave like a drunk snake. Matt tried not to think of the most logical string of events, but they popped into his mind just the same. The old man might be just ahead, fussing about the pokey people back at the camp. Then again, he might be dead.

"My God!"

Matt turned at Jacob's yell. Indians jumped out from behind a log.

"Run!" Matt shouted. He lurched forward, but was yanked back by an arm swung around his neck from behind. Something twisted his right arm behind him and he screamed. A shiver shot up his spine.

Movement flashed on his left. "You son of a bitch!" Jacob sobbed. He stared skyward as another Indian squeezed an arm around his throat. He gurgled, grabbed the air.

The pressure lessened around Matt's neck. Something hit his knees from behind and his legs collapsed. Jacob squirmed from the Indian's grip and dived sideways. The Indian kicked at him and he screamed, felt his jaw, and lay still.

Matt saw the folly of resisting and relaxed. His captors took his knife and tomahawk belt. One felt his clothing, found Struthers' pistol, shouted something. Matt slumped, heard sobs, and turned to see Jacob crying. Their gazes locked a second, and Jacob turned away.

The two Indians seemed about Jacob's age. Two more, old enough to be their fathers, stood back watching. Shawnee. They looked like the Shawnee he and the Hollingers killed last year.

One of the older men, about six feet tall and wearing a black beard, jabbered something. He searched their packhorses, and came back with two leather straps. The younger Indians tied them tightly around Matt's and Jacob's necks.

"God, Matt, what're we goin' to do?"

Matt frowned Jacob to silence. The Indians talked among themselves. Black Beard waved toward the woods, and the younger Indians disappeared, returning with leafy branches. They used them to sweep away the scuffle signs.

All four Indians had been on foot. Now they each selected one of Matt's and Jacob's horses, tied the thongs to the two saddles and mounted. They moved north and narrowed into a single file column, the two young Indians leading Matt and Jacob with their halters, the older men following. High grass and bushes closed over the trail.

That bush ahead. Matt reached out and broke a small limb, gritted his teeth at its loud snap, let the broken end dangle. Another ahead, now one on the right . . .

"Hyah!"

Black Beard barked something from behind. He jumped down from Benjie, tore the broken limbs off, waved his tomahawk in Matt's face and remounted.

The trail widened at a low spot where seepage moistened

the soil. Matt edged over and scraped his feet on the trail's side, away from the trample of hooves.

"Hyah!" Black Beard again ranted. He jumped down and smeared Matt's marks with his own moccasined feet. He walked in exaggerated fashion, showing Matt how to set his feet flat so they wouldn't leave marks. It would be futile, even dangerous, to try again to leave a trail. Besides, who would follow it?

They traveled until the red sun slipped past the western horizon, shooting rays upward through darkening clouds. The Indians dismounted and unsaddled the horses. Black Beard turned toward the north, leaned back and put his hands to his mouth. He let out two long, shrill whoops.

"Yeieee! Yeieee!"

"My God, what's that for?" Jacob said.

"I don't know. Maybe he's telling more Indians they got two captives. Or that they're Indians, too, not whites coming to bother them."

The Indians squatted, circled around Matt and Jacob like four points of a compass, and talked among themselves. The sun disappeared and the black sky flashed and rumbled. Large raindrops splashed around them, each making its own small drumbeat on a leaf or grass blade. Soon the rain came in a drizzle. Black Beard tied Matt's neck thong around his own wrist and jerked him to the ground. In the dim light from the weak halfmoon flickering through the clouds, Matt watched the other older Indian treat Jacob the same way.

"What're they doing?" Jacob whispered in the near

darkness.

"Looks like we belong to the older ones" Matt said. "Better do what they say."

Matt lay back on the wet grass and hunched up against the cold rain. No fire, no food, no shelter — how long would they travel this way? He decided to take whatever the Indians handed out without complaining. Do like Boone did, and stay friendly. But even as he thought this, he wondered what lay ahead. He stared into the wet blackness and thought about that for a long time.

CHAPTER 14

Matt and Jacob trudged for three days, sunup to sundown, without food. But the Indians ate nothing, either. Twice the Indians gave them water steeped with poplar bark, which seemed somehow to curb their hunger.

On the third morning, Black Beard yelled and pointed to a tree clump off the trail. The two younger Indians dismounted and pawed through broken dead limbs and uncovered an iron Dutch oven. Black Beard said something and they dragged it over to Jacob. They pointed at him, and one pantomined carrying it on his back.

"Hell, I can't lift that thing!" Jacob said. They motioned again, more angrily. One waved his tomahawk and shouted. Jacob lifted it by its two handles. He staggered, then dropped it. "I really can't," he said. "They'll kill me if I don't, but I can't!"

"I'll help," Matt said. "Grab that handle."

They lifted it between them. Matt stared back at Black Beard. If they both carried, and the Indian wanted to keep holding the rope, he'd have to ride up with them. Black

Beard sat still a moment, then spurred his horse forward. They stumbled back to the trail and continued north.

Matt's left arm soon throbbed with pain. He and Jacob switched sides, forcing the Indians to trade places. They changed several more times before nearing the tree line in mid-afternoon. Soon they'd have to carry the oven single file through the forest.

A movement! A grazing buffalo, strayed from its herd. Black Beard eased off his horse, holding Matt's loaded rifle in his hands. He checked the wind and crept slowly until he was in range. The rifle belched fire and smoke and the animal crumpled into the grass.

"We get to eat!" Jacob said. "An' not a minute too soon."

One of the younger Indians ran to the buffalo, its hind legs still twitching, and sank his knife into its belly. He sawed back toward the legs, at arm's length to avoid spurting blood. He cut a strip of flesh off and reached inside and cut some more, then pulled out the paunch and threw it and the meat strip into the Dutch oven for Matt and Jacob to carry.

The Indians mounted again, and they traveled for another hour until they reached a stream. Two Indians gathered firewood while a third cut the paunch open, rinsed it in the stream and put it into the oven with chunks of flesh and some water. Soon the mixture was boiling.

The Indians dipped their gourd cups into the oven and gathered up broth, leaving the meat behind. They laughed and drank, dipped again, drank more, and talked among themselves. Satisfied, they dipped more broth and handed the gourds to Matt and Jacob. Matt gulped his down and scooped into the oven to get some meat. Black Beard slapped his hand and took the cup, dipped broth, and handed it back.

"That don't make no sense," Jacob muttered.

It didn't to Matt, either. He was weak, and somehow knew Jacob was even weaker. Why couldn't they have some of that buffalo meat? Yet the Indians themselves had nothing but broth, and they would certainly know how to live out here in the wilderness. Matt decided to play their game, whatever it was. Not, he thought, that he had much choice.

The group traveled two more days before killing another buffalo. This time they ate its meat and dried some to eat later. Game was again plentiful, and they killed a deer almost every night.

Matt lost track of time. When they reached a wide river he assumed to be the Ohio, he estimated they'd been traveling almost two weeks. They'd gone in a northeastern direction, according to the moss growing on the north side of the trees and the sun's rising and setting. At the river the Indians conferred, then went east along the bank.

The next day they reached a log raft tied with grapevines. The two older Indians crossed the river on it with Matt and Jacob, and the younger ones swam the horses to the north bank.

Matt tried to picture the land. Daniel Boone said the Indian towns were across the Ohio and beyond the Scioto River, where Chief Logan lived with the Mingos, and where the Yellow River came in. They reached the next river, which Matt took to be the Scioto, and camped an extra day there. He sat on the bank and peered up and down it.

"What you looking for?" Jacob asked.

"Just seeing what I can see. Wonder why we're staying here?"

"I ain't complainin'. I got a stone bruise on each foot."

Matt glanced upriver again. Were the Mingos there? Boone said Chief Logan could talk English better than most white men. Black Beard was on the bank, scratching the mud with a stick. He dragged it toward himself, then moved and pulled it in another direction. When he was finally done Matt wandered over slowly so the Indians wouldn't think he was trying to escape, Jacob following.

There were six stick figures in the mud. Four were grouped together, larger than the other two, and Matt assumed they were supposed to be the Indians. The others would be him and Jacob. Was he saying they were bringing home prisoners?

Each morning and night, Black Beard still yelled to the winds, which Matt took to be an announcement they had two prisoners. The drawing, he concluded, was another way of saying it. Of course, it might just be to show they weren't whites killing the game and causing mischief.

The next morning they swam the river and continued north, and camped that night with no water in sight. Presently, Black Beard came to them carrying a small wooden bucket. He dangled it out to them, pointed east. Another Indian untied their neck thongs.

"They want us to get water," Matt said. He took the bucket and they walked into the woods. Glancing back, he saw only three Indians.

Jacob grabbed his arm. "Matt, this is our chance! Let's run!"

"Quit that!" Matt whispered. "Just walk natural. Act like we done this every day."

"God, Matt, this is our chance!"

"I said to quit it!" Matt whispered through his own fake smile. "They're testing us. I know it!"

They found a small stream and Matt dipped the bucket in. Jacob had tears in his eyes. "I cain't take no more, Matt. I got to get home to Annabelle. They might kill us!"

"Jacob, they're watching!"

"No, they ain't, this is our chance!"

He looked like he was ready to run. Matt grabbed Jacob's neck, hoping it would look like a friendly pat. But he squeezed hard. Jacob's bulging eyes stared at him, and he stood still. When Matt released him he slumped to his knees.

"God help us. Oh, Lord, lead us from this hell. Save us, Lord Jesus. Let me go back home to Annabelle."

Matt touched Jacob's neck, gently this time. "We got to get back to the Indians now," he said. "That's the only way you'll see your girlfriend." He smiled, his eyes darting from side to side. No sign of the Indian who sneaked away earlier and was undoubtedly watching right now. *Come on, Jacob, buck up. We got to act like we like being with them, that's what Daniel Boone done. Come on, Jacob.*

Jacob seemed to read his thoughts. He quit praying, dabbed at his eyes and stood. He wiped his dripping nose with the back of his arm and followed Matt to the clearing.

Matt set the bucket of water down by their captors and sat near them. He forced a smile as his gaze searched the area. Still three of them. No, four now; the other Indian was coming up from the woods on the right. He went to the others and said something. Jacob's owner swiveled around to gaze at Jacob, now staring at his own feet. He stormed over to Jacob, waved his tomahawk and shouted something, then went back to the others. Matt let out his breath slowly. For now, at least, they were safe. And the Indians had left them untied.

But Jacob couldn't be trusted. He was liable to do something foolish, get them both killed. Would it be now? Tomorrow? Matt decided to keep Jacob on a very close rein.

CHAPTER 15

MATT HAD SUSPECTED FOR THREE DAYS THEY WERE NEAR-ing the Shawnee towns. The Indians were more talkative, laughed more, seemed happier. This morning they awoke cheerfully and broke camp. They got black paint from their kits and painted each other.

"What they doin' now?" Jacob asked.

"Maybe we're going to one of their towns."

"Oh, God. I hear they beat whites up, maybe worse."

"Just act like you enjoy their company. That's what Daniel Boone done."

They headed north again. The thin trail opened into a wide path. Soon they met other Indians who shouted greet-ings and stared at Matt and Jacob. Black Beard shouted back, seeming irritated. He said something to the other three Indians in his party, and they all veered off the path to the right onto a narrower one.

Matt stood straight, kept his eyes focused on smoke patches rising from beyond the trees. In moments they were almost overhead and the forest gave away to a large clearing, an Indian village in its center.

The town was shaped like a rectangle. Women and children milled among its bark- and clay-covered log huts. Smoke came from their tops. Black Beard's party squeezed between two huts and entered the village. Matt realized they had avoided the main road. But why?

Then he knew. They probably did that to avoid having to put him and Jacob through a gauntlet. His mind's eye saw the scene Daniel Boone had described; a line of Indians trailing off into the distance, both male and female, beating white men with clubs and whips as they ran past.

But again, why did Black Beard want to avoid that?

The town Indians stared at Matt and Jacob, no different than if whites paraded Indians down Fincastle's main street. The buildings even resembled Fincastle's log buildings. Matt eyed a long structure extending the town's length on one side.

Their captors dismounted and split up, and the other older Indian took Jacob with him. Jacob's eyes showed white as he looked back at Matt, until he and the Indian disappeared behind several huts. Black Beard motioned for Matt to follow him and in a minute they paused before a large hut. Black Beard yelled.

An old woman came out and stood with her hands on her fat hips. Her double chin wobbled as she talked with Black Beard, staring critically at Matt. She shook her head, listened, came over and felt his arm, frowned into his face. Black Beard talked some more, and she nodded. A deal had been struck, Matt knew, and it concerned him.

That was it. Black Beard had avoided the gauntlet because it would damage the "merchandise" he had to sell to this woman. The Indian led Benjie away and left Matt alone with his new owner. She pointed at the small hut next to hers and he went inside.

The days dragged by. For the first week or so, Na-Jeta — she had said the word several times, pointing to herself — watched him closely. She followed him to the forest fringe when he gathered firewood, ready to give warning if he ran. She grunted directions, pointed and gestured, and he did whatever she wanted. But the chores were few. Mostly he just sat around, wondering what she'd want next.

Without warning, one day she went away. She left a kettle of hominy in his hut and he ate it sparingly, not knowing how long it was to last. The first day he went into her hut and looked through her personal items. He found a knife and left it where it was, for the time he might try to escape.

Each time nature called, he walked slowly into the woods. He nodded and smiled to the Indians he met, felt the gaze of hidden eyes. He wouldn't be able to escape easily. It was just like his captors had done on the trail, when they'd sent someone to watch him and Jacob get the water. He had to escape somehow. But he'd watch, pick the right time.

Two, three, four days passed after Na-Jeta left. On the

fifth day he awoke and felt a stiffness in his body. The thought hit him that his muscles were deteriorating, that before long he wouldn't even be able to run if he had the chance. He thought about how he'd lain on the hut floor for hours at a time, and knew he had to build his strength.

The next time he went to the woods he returned with a four-foot long limb. He got Na-Jeta's knife and whittled grooves two inches in from both ends and tied on two large firewood bundles with leather straps he'd found. He grasped the stick's center and lifted the weights chest high, paused, pushed it high overhead. He almost lost his balance and dropped the weights to the dirt floor. He hefted them again.

Soon he'd need heavier ones. Well, he'd look for roots or log sections or something around the town.

For the next week he exercised with the weights in his little hut. He made more and more lifts as time went on, and laid on his back and lifted with his legs. At first his muscles hurt, but over time the pain went away.

His trips to the woods became longer, more frequent. On the first day he did five chin-ups on a tree branch, almost collapsing from the effort. But before long he was doing more than twenty. He took a different route each trip out, looking for just the right thing to exercise with. He finally found it — a foot-thick log fallen across another so its root end sat up at an angle, four feet off the ground. He walked around to that end and grabbed two roots and tried to push the log up. He strained, felt it lift slightly, let it drop. A few more days of exercise in the hut and he should be able to lift it. He'd have to bring the knife out, though, and cut off the roots that gouged his chest. Then he could get rid of the makeshift weight in the hut, hopefully before Na-Jeta saw it.

Na-Jeta finally returned, acting as if she had not even left. She smiled at the large firewood stack, the neat hut. The next day she left for an hour and returned with Matt's rifle, knife belt, and two armed men Matt had seen before in the village. She pantomimed shooting, gave him his weapon, and pointed to the men. He nodded.

He followed them to a hut on the village's other side. They shouted something and another man emerged, followed by Jacob who carried his gun, too. He looked thin and drawn. They wove among the huts until they hit a northbound trail.

Jacob sidled up to him. "God, it's good to see you," he said. "I thought I'd go out of my mind. They treat me like I was a slave."

The Indians jogged north for several minutes, balancing their rifles and bows at their sides. Jacob shortly breathed heavily, huffing at every other step. At midday they squatted and ate dried meat. Jacob slumped down next to Matt and finally caught his breath.

"I'm goin' to escape," he whispered. "Want to come with me?"

"You're crazy. They'd catch you for sure."

"I got to. I cain't keep on living like this. Might as well be dead."

"But you're in no condition. Look at you. You can

barely keep up as it is."

"But I can ride!" Jacob glanced toward the Indians and lowered his voice even more. "I got it all figured out. I seen who they sold my horse to. I'll get up some morning and just take off. I can ride good as any Indian can. You seen me ride."

"But they'll catch you, Jacob! You'd never get away."

"Well, if they catch me, I'll try again. I'll just keep trying 'til I get free and get home to my Annabelle."

CHAPTER 16

A NOISE, OUTSIDE.

Matt jumped up from his pallet and stared into the hut's blackness. What was it that awoke him? He peeked outside, into the pre-dawn gray.

Excited, angry yells came from the south. Na-Jeta was snoring next door and he knew he should stay put. The yelling got closer, somehow more urgent.

Matt tip-toed outside and ran silently toward the sounds, staying low behind a row of dwellings so the noisemakers couldn't see him. He peered from behind a building.

A dozen Indians appeared from the south. They dragged someone by a rope tied around his neck. One clubbed the captive behind the ear, knocking him to the ground. He struggled up amid louder yells, blood streaming onto his shoulders. He turned Matt's way.

Jacob!

Matt ducked down until they passed then followed, staying behind the huts until they reached the council house. They clubbed Jacob again. This time he didn't get up.

Matt squatted in his hiding place. He felt clammy, colder than the slight morning breeze itself would account for. Had Jacob tried to escape, like he said he'd do not two weeks before? Had he . . .

A stabbing pain exploded in Matt's skull.

The bright glare of daylight flooded over Matt. He squinted and pushed onto his elbows and saw the bare and moccasined feet of several Indians surrounding him. He struggled to his knees, and was pulled back onto his haunches.

A weight hung from his neck. He turned to see the rope that tied him to a hut. Jacob, tied next to him, leaned back against the structure. His eyes were closed; dry tear streaks formed muddy paths down his face. Matt's head throbbed. Dried blood covered his leather shirt, darkened the dirt beneath him.

Something moved at the corner of his eye. Pain shot through his back, knocked him down. Again and again it hit, amidst high-pitched voices of women who swung their clubs and switches at him and Jacob. Jacob screamed and begged for mercy. Matt gritted his teeth, fought the all-consuming pain, saw light flashes in his mind with each blow. The pain slipped away, came back, teased him as he hovered between consciousness and total blackness. Were those his screams? Or Jacob's? He couldn't tell.

A stream of liquid hit his face. He opened his eyes. Two, three more streams. Indian boys stood around him, grinning, urinating onto his head. When he tried to move, pain from his back shot spasms through his body. Blackness consumed him.

The sun was high overhead when he came to. Matt turned on his side, fought against the searing pain, finally got to his knees. He heard the sound of wood against wood, and glanced toward its source near the council house. There, women were piling kindling around an eight foot tall post.

"God, Matt! Look at that!"

Jacob was almost unrecognizable. Long open cuts covered his back, arms, and legs, dirt clung in dried blood. He was naked. Matt looked down at himself. He was also naked. Bloody and naked.

"Matt, look what they're doing! Damn, Matt, they . . . they're going to burn us at the stake!"

Indians crowded around them, laughed, piled more kindling on. Some laid long, thin poles on the stacked wood, pointed ends almost touching the post, other ends fanning out from it. A horrible chill went through Matt, momentarily blocking out even the pain from his wounds. Jacob was right!

A commotion came from inside the council house. Na-Jeta's voice. It harangued, pleaded, yelled, pleaded again. Male voices answered. Matt watched the door, listened to the voices, hoped she'd succeed in whatever she was telling them.

They came out. Four, five, six men followed Na-Jeta, all dressed in silver and beads.

A seventh appeared. He was half a head taller than the rest. He wore doeskin leggings and high moccasins laced to mid-calf. Four white-tipped brown eagle feathers stuck up from the back of his head. On each wrist were wide beaten-silver bands. Around his neck was a necklace of colorful beads and silver. He had jet-black hair and matching eyes, a fair complexion, a firm-set mouth. In spite of his Indian trappings, he looked like a white man. He stared at Matt.

Matt knew who it was.

"Logan!" he called out. The man stopped abruptly and stared at him.

"Chief Logan! Daniel Boone told me about you. I'm Matt McLaren, and this here's Jacob Hollinger."

The half-breed walked over and stood with his hands on his hips.

"Daniel Boone said you spoke English. I . . . I want to ask you about my sister. Some Indians took her a couple years ago, on the other side of the mountains."

Logan stood spread-legged. Jacob saw him now. He sat up on his knees, stared up at the half-breed's face. Matt's pain surged, but somehow he pushed it aside enough to talk.

"I asked the others, but they can't understand me," Matt said. "You seen her? She's got blond hair. She'd be seven years old by now. You seen her?"

The man ignored his question. He stood silently for several seconds, then spoke.

"What happened here?"

His voice was gruff. He sounded just like a white man, no accent at all. Matt considered his question, and suddenly it occurred to him that he was so intent on finding his sister that he had forgotten about the trouble he and Jacob were in. Icy fingers again ran through his body.

"What happened? I don't know. I heard something and come out to see what was going on, and got hit on the head."

Logan pointed to Jacob. "He killed a man last night. Tried to steal his horse."

"He *killed* somebody?" Matt turned to Jacob.

"I didn't mean to," Jacob cried. He clutched Matt's shoulder. "He ran out at me, and I hit him with the limb I had. God, I didn't mean to kill him!"

"Damn, Jacob. You *killed* him? I told you not to try to escape!"

"I was just trying to get home, Matt! He . . . he wasn't supposed to come out!"

Logan stood there, watching the two. The other chiefs stood behind him, as if waiting for him to do something. Matt tried to think of something to say. Something that would save him and Jacob from the fire. The crowd's mumbling got louder.

"It was an accident," Matt said, finally. "He sure didn't mean to do it."

Matt frantically searched for something else to say. It was like when he and Noah were burning the limbs, and that church warden tried to take him away, and he couldn't think of words that would change his mind. Jacob peered up at Matt through tear-filled, pleading eyes.

"Maybe . . . maybe we could work it off," Matt said. "You know, tend your crops, hunt your food. We'd sure be glad to do it. I bet we could —"

Logan raised a hand, and Matt knew he had failed. He thought again of his daddy and mama, who were killed by Indians. Now it was his turn.

"You weren't with him," Logan said. It was a statement, not a question. He turned and said something in Shawnee language to the other chiefs, and they talked among themselves. Na-Jeta smiled.

Then Matt knew. *He knew!* Whatever they did to Jacob, they weren't going to do to him. The chiefs nodded, and Logan turned to leave.

"No!" Matt yelled at Logan's retreating figure. He lurched forward, felt the cruel rope strangle him. "That's not right. He didn't mean to kill!"

The enormity of what was happening hit Matt, and he slumped. Logan didn't answer, didn't even look back. He mounted his horse, dug his heels into its flanks. In a moment he was lost beyond the huts.

Matt stood and strained against the rope. "You come back, Logan! You can't kill him. He didn't mean to hurt anybody!"

More Indians gathered, began chanting. They formed a semi-circle around him and Jacob and the pile of wood. One of the chiefs went to the center post and shook it. He nodded.

Matt felt sick, wanted to vomit. He swallowed hard. Jacob stared numbly at the post.

"Jacob . . . Jacob, turn around this way so we can talk."

Jacob began crying. He stared at Matt, catching his breath in ragged gasps.

"C'mon, Jacob, I . . . I want you to tell me about Annabelle."

Jacob quieted. He grinned, turned toward Matt. Away from the council building and the post. It was like he forgot about the post, like it was a dream he'd had.

"She's the sweetest thing you ever knowed, Matt. She's the preacher's daughter, did I tell you that?"

"No, don't think you did. Tell me about her."

Squaws behind Jacob threw more wood onto the stack, spread it around and left. Jacob shifted to see what the commotion was about.

"Jacob! Look at me!"

Jacob turned back to Matt, eyebrows high at the urgency in Matt's voice.

"Jacob, tell . . . tell me something else about her. I bet she's real pretty. How'd you meet her?"

Jacob grinned again, showing his crooked teeth. "I met her when her daddy come to preach. They come in a carriage, and her mama too, and I seen her get out. I never seen such a pretty girl in my whole life!"

The Indian women brought dry leaves, smoothed the pile out, put kindling on it. The crowd was louder now. Jacob started to turn again.

"No!" Matt cried out.

Jacob stared back at him, startled.

"Jacob, tell me about the land! The land, Jacob! I bet it's pretty land."

Matt's head hurt, his stomach was queasy. Jacob looked up at the noisy crowd on each side.

"Look at all of 'em, Matt. Like they was at a party or something. I guess we're a sight, huh?"

"The land, Jacob! Is . . . is any of it cleared? How much is there?"

"Oh, it's such a nice piece, Matt. It runs along a ridge, and they's a stream what comes off it and goes right through, right below where I'll put the cabin. Ain't none of it cleared yet, but I'll get right on it when I get home. It's just like you, Matt, and your sister Mandy. I'm going back and make a home for my Annabelle."

One Indian finished preparing the fire bed and stood. He and the other two turned and walked toward Matt and Jacob.

"I bet it is nice, Jacob, real nice. Remember the land, Jacob. Just think about the land and how nice it is! Heaven's like that, I guess, like having your own place, and tending it, and having cows, and some corn ready to pick."

An Indian on each side grabbed Jacob's arms and dragged him back.

"What the . . . what's going on?"

"Be brave, Jacob! I'll tell your daddy how brave you was!"

"Let go of me!"

They dragged Jacob toward the post, and his heels hit the firewood pile. They heaved him up over it and jerked his arms around the pole and tied them. They tied another rope around his chest. He stood dazed, eyes wide. He looked down, saw the firewood, saw an Indian carrying a fire stick close to his body, protecting it from the breeze. Jacob's knees buckled.

"God! They're goin' to . . . oh, God in Heaven!"

"Be brave, Jacob! Think about the land! Think about Annabelle! I'll tell her you loved her. I'll find her and tell her!"

The fire touched the leaves, sprang to life. Blue smoke curled from between Jacob's feet, hung onto his clothing, hit his face. He jerked his feet away from the fire, lost his footing and slipped down the pole. Flames touched his knees, and he shot up straight.

"They're burnin' me, Matt! They're burnin' me!"

Matt turned and squeezed his eyes closed. A shouted order, and a hand behind him grabbed Matt's scalp and twisted his head back around so he faced the fire again. He heard Jacob's screams, saw his feet hammer the flaming firewood, saw his body straining against the rope.

"You'll go to heaven, Jacob! Mama and Daddy's already there. And Noah . . . he's there, too! They're preparing a place for you, right with Jesus!"

Men picked up the sticks, jabbed their glowing points into Jacob's side. He screamed louder, lost his voice. Hoarse, raspy sounds came out. He stiffened and hung forward against the smoldering rope. More flesh caught fire, and the flames crackled as Jacob's life juices hit them. Matt felt the fire's heat on his own face, for a moment thought himself in the fire, and screamed.

The Indians released Matt. He twisted away from the

flames and slumped to the ground. His forehead touched the earth's coolness. Jacob was burning up, and here he was, thinking about how cool the earth was! Jacob hadn't done anything more than he'd've done, if he'd gotten half a chance. What would they have done if they knew about the three Shawnee he'd already killed, back near the Cumberland Gap? Those Indians might have been from this very village.

Someone untied Matt's bonds, and he stood on shaky legs. Na-Jeta motioned him to follow her. She smiled as if nothing had happened. As if this was just another day. Matt took a step, then another. He felt a pressure on his shoulder, and thought he saw Noah there, guiding him. The image went away.

CHAPTER 17

SPRING TURNED INTO THE DARK GREEN OF SUMMER, THEN the leaves browned and fell to the forest floor. Occasionally, Matt went to sleep and bolted up in the middle of a black night, seeing Jacob's seared body, hearing his screams. He lay there sweating, thinking of others he'd lost to the Indians. His mother and father. Mandy. And Wade Russell? Had they killed him, too?

After Jacob's burning he spent much of his time hunting with the other men. They marveled at his gun's accuracy, didn't suspect he sometimes held back so as not to show them up. But he usually came home with as much meat as they did, for himself and Na-Jeta.

He learned enough of their language to get by. Some considered him their friend, but still he longed for the white man's companionship. His every smile, every gesture was made to ease their minds about his running away. He had to leave, sometime. But Jacob's hard-earned lesson kept coming back. A botched escape attempt meant death.

Matt returned from hunting earlier one cold spring day,

dropped his kill at Na-Jeta's hut and jogged into the woods. He'd long ago lost track of time, couldn't even guess the date within a month. But he'd picked up clues on judging time from Noah and Bledsoe, even from the Indians.

That oak tree just ahead. Noah had said corn should be planted when an oak's leaves were the size of squirrel ears. He guessed it would be another week or two before they were that big. Of course this tree he was looking at was farther north than Noah's, and would leaf a little later.

He trotted through the forest, placing his feet firmly among treacherous rocks and limbs without consciously knowing they were there. It was a daily trip he'd made when not out hunting. Soon he was at his lifting tree. He brushed his hands on his leather trousers and grabbed the tree's rough roots and pushed its end high overhead. He pressed it skyward a hundred times in quick succession and paused, feeling the sweat run down his chest inside his shirt. He'd soon need a heavier tree.

He felt the tightness of his clothes, and knew his exercise was working. Part of it was just from growing, of course. Soon he'd have to make more clothes from the deerskin he'd stored at the hut. He'd grown a good two inches taller since the Indians got him the year before and now stood almost six feet tall. His beard had filled out and blackened, almost covering his cheeks and chin.

He was also bulky. Not fat — he doubted if he had an ounce of fat on him anywhere — but muscular. When he flexed his muscles it seemed his arms might just pop right out of the tight sleeves. The Indians swam in the icy water every morning on their hunts and insisted he do so too, and he'd seen his body reflected in the pools. He was probably stronger than any of them, could run faster, climb higher. But he made sure they didn't realize it.

They'd know, soon enough.

Matt finished his exercises. He stood a moment, breathed deeply. The sharp, cold air cut his lungs like icicles. He gulped air and let it out slowly, and turned toward the village. The trail was to his left, but he'd long ago stopped using it. He bounded across the brush-covered terrain instead, bee-lined toward the village, leaping over logs almost like the deer he killed. Soon the trees thinned and opened into the village clearing. He slowed to a walk and reached the main path into town.

Something was happening ahead, in front of the council building. Curious, he went up that way and stopped at the fringe of a crowd, gathered around a man seated on one horse and leading two packhorses. The man climbed down and spoke in the Shawnee language with those nearest him.

A white man! A trader. The man unloaded bundles from one of the horses and, struggling, carried them toward the council building door. He spotted Matt.

"Well, I'll be damned. You a white man?"

He set his load down and reared back to examine Matt. He was middle-aged, heavy-set and spectacled, and he wore a long blue greatcoat. He cocked his head and frowned through his glasses, as if trying to focus his eyes on Matt.

"Yes, sir," Matt said. "You're the first white man I seen in months."

"I'll be damned," the man said again. "You look just like my boy Anton, bless his soul. Died a couple years back. Look . . . let me take care of business, then let's talk. A white man, out here!"

The man and several Indians went into the council house. Matt breathed cold fog into the air, rubbed his hands together. The trader's saddle horse, a young chestnut gelding, stamped for warmth. Matt ran his hands through its mane, felt its muscles. The packhorses were older than Benjie, but still had strength he admired.

Indians went into and came out of the council building until the sun hung low in the western sky. The crowd finally left and the trader stuck his head out and saw Matt, who had stood stone-still all afternoon, waiting. He motioned with his hand.

"Come in here, warm up," he said. "You must be froze."

Matt went inside, rubbing his eyes to focus in the dark room. "You're the first white man I seen in a long time," he said. "I'm Matt McLaren."

"Batest Ariome. I trade out of Fort Pitt."

"Batest. That's French."

"How'd you get here, Matt? They catch you?"

"Yes, sir. That they did."

Matt told Batest his story, leaving out some of the parts he didn't want to remember himself. The trader nodded, sat on a crude stool, motioned for Matt to do the same. Matt finished with a bare-bones account of Jacob's death.

"I seen the charred post," the Frenchman said. "Must'a been tough, seeing it and all. Make you think twice about escaping, though."

"But I got to," Matt said. "Got to get a farm going. They think I like it here, that I'm going to stay 'til the cows come home. But I can't."

"Well, it ain't right to keep you here. You know, you really do look like Anton. How old're you?"

"Seventeen. Say, maybe I could go with you." Matt tried to say it casually, as if the thought had just occurred to him. He stared into the man's face.

"That's how old he'd be if he was still alive," Batest said slowly, looking down. "Died of the pox, like a lot of others that year. Almost killed his mother."

Matt inched forward on his own stool, peered into the Frenchman's eyes.

"What do you think? I could work for you. I'd do whatever you wanted me to do. Anything at all."

The man glanced up, then looked down again, at the bags and packages that surrounded him. He didn't say anything for a long time, just sat there. Finally, he spoke.

"Well . . . I don't think so. Don't need no help, really. " 'Sides, them Indians don't take to interfering. They put up with me 'cause I bring them things they want. Like them things right there."

Batest glanced at a bag that leaned against his stool leg. He ground his teeth together, spat, and reached down and opened it. He fingered some of the things inside, withdrew his fisted hand and opened it slowly. Jewel-like objects sparkled when a shaft of light from the doorway hit them, crosses and broaches shined like silver.

Matt turned his attention back to the man's face, leaned even closer. He smelled the reek of the man's clothing, but ignored it.

"I'm going to escape," he said, softly. "If you won't take me with you, I'll just get up tomorrow and walk away. Just head on down the trail."

"You wouldn't get a mile," Batest said. "Them Indians'll chase you down and kill you, for sure."

Matt stood. He towered over the man, who now looked small and confused. "Maybe so," he said. "But I got to do it for Mandy."

Batest frowned. He peered up at Matt, then back down at the bag of trinkets. He stared a long moment, like he was adding something up in his mind, then looked back at Matt.

"Maybe I could buy you," he said, quietly. "If they'll sell you."

"Buy me?"

The words sounded strange, applied to a person, not a horse or something else. People didn't buy people, except for Negros, and Matt wasn't even sure he approved of that. It didn't seem right for one man to buy another. Yet Na-Jeta had bought him. Someone had bought Jacob. He guessed it was at least all right to buy somebody back.

"What do you think?" Batest said. "Tell you what. If I can get 'em to sell you, you work for me for a while, say through the summer, so I can get my money back. That be agreeable?"

"Sure . . . sure is! But she won't sell me. I do all her hunting and the other work."

Batest grinned. "Hell, she's a woman, ain't she?" He stuck his hand back into the bag, pulled out a fistful of the shiny things. "Sometimes vanity takes over where it shouldn't. I seen it work time and again."

Matt returned to Na-Jeta's hut. He took in some firewood, tidied up, sat down to wait. She sat hunched over with her back to him, working with some leather. They'd often sat like this for hours when he was in her place, as if they were in separate worlds. An hour passed, then two.

A sharp voice came from outside. She peeped out the door, mumbled something, glanced back at Matt and left.

He waited for another hour. Approaching footsteps sounded outside, and she opened the door and came in. She wore three necklaces, and several rings, none of which he'd seen before. Matt recognized a pendant he'd seen in Batest's bag.

"*Wehpetheh*," she said. Go. She pointed at the door and he jumped up and went out. She gathered his gun and the belt with his ammunition, knife, and tomahawk, and followed.

"*Wehpetheh!*" She pointed toward the council house. He put the belt on, shouldered the gun. He walked ahead, felt pressure on his arm, and turned. She stood there, her hand on his sleeve, staring into his face. She turned and went back inside.

Batest had already packed and sat on his horse, waiting.

His two packhorses stood behind him, with another saddled horse.

"Benjie!" Matt grinned and stepped up to his old friend, patted his nose.

"I'll just put it on the bill," Batest said. He spat and stared ahead, and kicked his horse. Matt mounted and followed.

They rode east out of town, single file. Matt said nothing. Batest would talk when he was good and ready. Matt knew the slave's role, he'd played it so long. He followed Batest as the path wove through the forest. After an hour they reached a fork, and the trader reined in his horse and turned in the saddle.

"Well, this is where we part company."

Matt wasn't sure he understood the man's meaning. "We part company?"

"Unless you got an urge to go to Pennsylvania or someplace. In that case you can go with me."

"But I thought I *was* going with you. Work off my debt."

"Changed my mind."

Batest eyed the back of his hand, scratched it briefly with his other hand. He glanced up. "I can't keep you, Matt. Wouldn't be right."

"But I owe you for that jewelry and whatever else it was you had to give."

"It wasn't much, truth be known. You just do someone else a favor and think of me when you do it. Then we'll be even."

"I . . . well, I sure appreciate it. You sure?"

"How you doing for ammunition?"

Matt thought a moment. "Maybe two more loads. They don't give me much at a time."

"I figured."

Batest reached behind him and retrieved a small leather bag, swung it toward Matt.

"That'll last you. Powder and balls. Some jerky, too, enough maybe for a week. Then you're on your own."

Matt took the things, and looked down the path going south. "Know where that goes?"

"Hooks up with what they call the Warrior's Path," Batest said. "Goes to the Cumberland Gap, they tell me. And Matt?"

"Yes?"

"Get the hell out of here, and fast. First time that Indian woman needs some food killed, she'll send them others after you."

Matt nodded. He gathered his reins. "Thanks again."

Batest touched his horse with his heels and headed east, away from Matt.

"I'll sure do that favor, you can count on it," Matt called after him.

The Frenchman waved over his shoulder, then stopped and twisted around. "I can't get over how much you favor my Anton," he said. He disappeared around a stand of trees.

Matt flicked his reins against Benjie's neck, starting him into a slow lope. He felt his old horse's familiar movements under him, hefted the rifle, and looked south toward the Warrior's Path. Was he really free? Yes, it was true enough. After a couple years hunting animals and killing

Indians, then being their prisoner, he was finally going home. Home!

He added it up in his mind. It must be four hundred miles back to the Gap. He'd soon be back in Virginia, and . . .

And what?

He reined Benjie in and sat there. It was quiet, except for a gentle stirring of leaves. A crow cawed off in the distance.

He couldn't go back to Virginia. Certainly not up into the Virginia Valley. The sheriff was looking for him there. What if Bledsoe saw him and reported him?

Matt opened the ammunition bag and looked in it. It would last him hunting for several months, if he were careful. He knew how to call game, stalk it, bring it down without wasting a shot. How to skin it.

Mandy needed a home, but it didn't have to be in the Virginia Valley. Why, he'd get a farm someplace else. Maybe on the Yadkin River in North Carolina, where Boone was from, or on the Virginia frontier where there wasn't much law yet.

He needed pelts. Knox said that was how others built up their farms. Why, with enough pelts, he could get a fine home, a place his sister would be proud of.

.Matt touched Benjie's rump and started down the trail. It felt strange, out on a horse by himself. No sound at all, except that made by Benjie's hooves.

He couldn't go back east. There was nothing there for him. No, he'd hunt deer this spring and summer. He'd get him a stockpile of skins, then trade it someplace on some good land. He'd clear it, put in some corn, get some cattle.

He stroked Benjie's mane. "Well, old friend, ready for some more hunting? Just you and me and them varmints?"

He smiled and prodded Benjie into a fast walk. He looked ahead to the right, into the wilderness, toward the setting sun. Out there was freedom. Freedom to hunt, to lie under the stars, to dream about what might be. Like Boone must have done when his brother Squire went back home and he'd stayed out there by himself.

But would he really be free? Matt looked back toward the Indian towns. He then looked east to the mountains, imagined Struthers' frozen body, the sheriff, Bledsoe pointing his finger at Matt. He prodded his horse to go faster.

Maybe, no matter how far he ran, he'd never be free.

CHAPTER 18

A RIFLE SHOT ECHOED DOWN POWELL'S VALLEY ON A CHILLY October morning in 1773, bouncing off tall oaks and hickories and the Cumberland Mountains behind Matt. The slug plowed into the log in front of him, and he hugged the earth closer.

Matt scratched his bearded face, chewed his lower lip. His beaver cap lay a few feet to his right, where it had fallen when he dived for cover after hearing the first shot. The hat cast a long shadow from the sun peeping up over the forest ahead.

The Shawnees had thundered past him not a half hour back almost like ghosts out of the night. They'd shot him in the arm, snared Benjie's reins and took the horse off with them. Matt had rolled down the hill into thick cover and they'd just kept on going with his deerskins, headed back toward the Cumberland Gap he'd just come through, for the Can-tuc-kee wilderness beyond.

A summer's work wasted. The furs he'd gotten since leaving Batest and the Indian village the spring before would warm the bottoms of Indian squaws, or more likely the shoulders of English society, thanks to the white traders.

And now this. Matt reached for his rifle. Gone! He panicked, breathed out slowly. No, it was just out of reach, its stock near his right foot. He inched a moccasined toe toward it and pushed the stock away. The gun pivoted slowly on its hammer and he grasped its barrel, felt pain, saw blood oozing from his forearm. He gritted his teeth and refilled the pan with powder.

Another shot. A bullet chipped bark from his log and spat into a tree behind him. He hunkered down and buried his face deeper into the dew-moist leaves.

The gunman was obviously alone. Matt struggled the rifle barrel up until it rested across the log. A plan played around his mind, seemed to make sense. He waited one, two minutes, then abruptly poked the rifle barrel into the air.

"Yeiah!" he cried out.

Another shot. As it echoed, Matt pulled himself up on his good arm and looked over the log. Telltale blue smoke stood out against a spiny locust tree trunk. He aimed just below it, squeezed the trigger lightly. One, two, three — at the count of seven, a head appeared. He squeezed . . . but wait! He jammed the stock down as the powder flashed in the pan and the bullet burst from the barrel. It splintered the locust tree. The head disappeared.

He watched where it had been. Was he wrong? Several seconds passed.

"Hello!" he shouted.

No answer. Had he hit the shooter?

"Hello!" he tried again. "You a white man or an Indian?"

Several more seconds crept by. His shot still seemed to echo up the valley.

"White! What're you?"

"If you're white, stand and show yourself."

"You think I'm crazy? Some Injuns can talk white!"

Matt smiled and relaxed. "They're gone. They stole my things and run off. Unless you're one of them."

"They just kilt 'most everybody here," the man said. "Look . . . don't shoot. I'm gettin' up. But don't shoot!"

A white man stood up. He appeared to be about fifty years old. He brushed his stringy gray hair back and stood still, his gun hanging, barrel down, in his right hand. Satisfied, Matt also rose.

"I thought you was the Shawnees come back to finish the job," the man said.

Matt eyed him. He'd heard far-off shots earlier and thought it was hunters until the Indians shot him and stole his pelts. His right arm ached, but he decided to ignore it.

"I'm Jonas Jernigan. Got a cabin up on the Clinch. Who are you?"

"Matt. Matt McLaren. You say the rest of your party's killed?"

"All but me and Adam, a slave what belongs to my neighbor, Russell. He just hightailed it out of here, and I don't blame him!"

Jernigan turned and walked several paces back east. Matt followed. Within a minute he saw Powell River, then-smelled the camp: the burned-out fire, wisps of cooked food, an unknown odor he couldn't put his finger on. They passed a copse of sycamore trees; he saw the bodies, and stopped.

"My God. They're all dead!"

"I'd have been dead, too, if I hadn't been off on a nature call. They kilt seven, all but me and Adam. Don't know how he escaped."

The bodies lay in puddles of drying blood. Matt's knees buckled and he grabbed a limb for steadiness, forcing himself to view the death scene. Every one of them was scalped. The odor he couldn't place before was blood. Or maybe it was death itself. Blood was all over the place, splattered on the trees, the ground.

"They shouldn't of had the fire," Matt said. "When the Shawnee saw the fire, they knowed they had them some sittin' ducks."

Jernigan glanced quickly at him, then down. He nodded. He sat next to a young man's face-down body and stroked it softly with a gnarled hand. Flies rose from the bloody scalped head and relit.

"Shouldn't a made that fire, that's for sure," Jernigan said. "I shouldn't a let them. Hell, I knowed better. Guess that makes it my fault. Oh, God, God . . . " He sat there crying for a minute, then dabbed his eyes and looked across the fire at the body of another young man, who appeared to be about Matt's age.

"That there's James Boone," he said. "His daddy's getting ready to take some people through the Gap and settle over there. Look at that. Not even a man yet, and he's dead."

"Daniel Boone? Daniel Boone's boy?"

It sure looked like Boone's boy would know not to make a fire. Yet Boone had left his family on his North Carolina farm while he'd roamed the wilderness. Maybe the boy just never had a chance to learn from him. Of course, they could have had a fire, and not be seen, if they made it with white oak bark like the Shawnee did. Then it would burn almost without smoke and still put out a lot of heat. Matt considered telling the old man, but thought better of it.

Jernigan looked surprised. "You know Boone? Boy, he sure paints a purty picture of that Can-tuc-kee land, don't he? Look . . . somebody's going to have to tell him."

Matt looked down at James Boone. There was a resemblance. The boy wasn't any older than Matt himself, and already dead.

"They should have knowed better," Matt said. "But maybe they thought they wasn't any Indians around, or maybe they was tired and didn't think about it at all. God, all of them scalped."

"Somebody's got to tell Daniel and them others," the old man said. "I cain't go. If we was to both leave, the wolves or something'll come and . . . well, I got to stay with them."

"I guess I don't understand. Some of these are your people and some are Boone's?"

The old man stroked the corpse again. He turned away, and his upper body shook. He waved a hand near the scalped head. Flies rose, came back.

"Only three's Boone's," he said. "They come to Russell's place for flour and things, and we was helping carry it back. We stopped here when it got dark."

Jernigan pointed across the dead fire. "That there's Russell's boy, Henry. The others was just helping him out some, from upriver."

"I'll tell Boone," Matt said. "Where is he?"

"They ain't but three, four miles west of here. We got off the trail somehow when it got dark and decided to camp. I . . ."

His eyes teared again, and he turned back to the body. "Boy, it's sure goin' to hurt him and Rebecca! They're strong people, but it's goin' to hurt bad."

Everything was quiet for a while, as if the birds and varmints knew something bad had happened. Matt watched the old man, hunched over the body. Presently the man looked around at him, saw his stare.

"This here's my own boy, Zach," he said.

"Oh." Matt didn't know what to say. The man looked back at his son, stroked him again. The silence became almost unbearable.

"He's the only thing I got since his mama died," the man said, finally. "He was going to get married next week." His shoulders shook. He turned away and covered his face with his arms and cried softly. Matt looked away, then down at his own wound.

It wasn't much. No broken bones, nothing like that. It didn't even hurt as bad, now. He'd find Boone, then get that bullet hole wrapped up. He picked up his gun and left the man crying over his son's body.

CHAPTER 19

THE SUN INCHED DOWNWARD BEHIND MATT AS HE STARED at the seven new graves lined up before him. The river whispered quietly beyond.

There must have been fifty to sixty people there all told, heads bowed and uncovered, including both Boone's party and the Clinch Valley settlers who'd come down from the north. Captain Bill Russell stood before them on the other side of the graves. The slanting sun shined off a stark white bald spot, obviously kept covered when he was out and about. He was short and heavy set, looked nothing like Wade Russell, who he'd said the day before he didn't know.

"We give you back to God," Russell was saying. "May the Lord love you, as we do, and take you into his arms."

The river whispered a benediction while the mourners stood quietly in their grief. Someone blew his nose, another coughed, and one by one they left the grave site. Matt walked over to where the Russell and Boone families gathered, along with some others.

"Well, what're your plans, Daniel?" Captain Russell asked.

Boone didn't answer at first. He glanced back at the graves, then at Rebecca. She returned his gaze with large dark eyes and a question on her tear-streaked face, then stared off to the side. Matt had seen that look before, when a deer looked up and saw his gun trained on it. She pushed her black hair back over her shoulders and hugged their middle girl Lavinia tightly to her side. The other six Boone children were gathered behind her.

Daniel Boone shrugged. "Well, we can't go back to North Carolina. We sold out there and come with everything we owned."

"I expect you're right," Russell said. "You got nothing to go back to." He looked off to the northwest. "You still going up into Can-tuc-kee?"

Amos Norton, one of the men who'd come with Boone, kicked at a small rock and watched it bounce a few inches. He stared around at the others, who were mostly looking down at their feet. "Well, we're going back," he said. "We sold out, too, but we got folks back there. I ain't goin' to get my family kilt."

The others turned toward Boone, whose own gaze followed that of Russell, toward the northwest and the Cumberlands. "The Shawnee do seem riled," he said.

"Guess we've been lucky until now," Russell said. "The Shawnee've been boiling mad ever since the Six Nations Indians gave up rights to everything below the Ohio. They're getting real touchy."

"We sure got their attention," Boone agreed.

"Our valley's a skinny little thing," Russell said. "Guess

they never noticed us before. Why, when we came three years ago there wasn't a sign of an Indian ever living here."

As they talked, Matt glanced around at the women. They were the first white females he'd seen since he'd left the Fincastle courthouse three years back. He'd noticed Boone's oldest girl Susanna watching him a minute before. He looked down, walked away, inspecting the bandage Rebecca Boone had wrapped around his arm. The wound still throbbed.

"Watch out!"

Matt stopped abruptly. The woman was only inches away, standing by Zach Jernigan's grave.

"Oh, I'm sorry! You all right?"

She mumbled something and stared at the fresh earth piles. Her long brown hair was stuffed under her bonnet, like it was put up in a hurry. She was tall and slender, almost as tall as he was. Her red eyes had no tears, and he realized she must have already cried herself out.

"Was you his fiance?" he said. He wished he hadn't said anything, had just turned and snuck away.

"We was going to get married next week," she said. "You're the one that just come from Can-tuc-kee, aren't you?"

He nodded. She appeared about twenty years old. Her well-formed breasts pushed out, and he fought off ogling them. He looked away, toward the Boone party.

"I'm Clare Ryborn," she said. "Isam and I moved here last year, but he died from some disease in the fall. What's your name?"

"Matt McLaren."

"Where you going now? I mean, you're coming back from Can-tuc-kee, where everybody else is headed."

"I don't know."

"Isam and I come from Staunton. You ever been there?"

He shook his head, looked toward the others. Boone was saying something to his traveling party. Some of the Clinch River people were walking back north, shovels over their shoulders, heads down.

"They'll camp upriver and get home tomorrow some-time," Clare said. "But some of us'll camp with the Boones tonight. Captain Russell says the Indians won't be back."

"I 'spect that's right," Matt said. "Well, I'd best find out what's going on, see if I can help."

"Here, I'll go with you." She stared at her fiancé's grave once more and shuddered. Then she turned her back to it and fell into step with Matt.

Captain Russell's wife had her arm through her husband's. She dabbed her eyes with a wadded piece of cloth.

"Dan'l, you'd best sleep on this," Captain Russell said. "Wait 'til morning to make your decision."

"I guess I already made it. We got a few cattle and some supplies, I got my rifle. Maybe we'll just stay on the Clinch for a while."

"Well, you're sure welcome," Russell said. "I didn't mention it, didn't want to color your thinking. But David Gass's farm is a couple hours south of our place, and he's been gone a good while. The cabin's not much, but it's better'n nothing."

"Why, thank you for thinking of it. We'd get by real

well there."

Boone looked over at Matt. "You'll stay the night, won't you? You're sure welcome."

Matt mumbled his thanks. Pretty soon they all went back to the graves and prayed again, then headed toward Boone's camp. Matt stayed at the rear to watch for Indians. But Russell was right. There were too many whites for a stray Indian band to attack.

They reached the camp as darkness covered the valley. Matt found a smooth spot for the blanket Rebecca had loaned him, off to the side from the rest. The others talked in murmurs, passed around jerky and cold cornbread, made their own beds. One by one they lay down and turned over to sleep.

For an hour or more Matt just lay there, listening and thinking. Occasionally he heard a muffled sob. He turned over and tried to push the pain away with his thoughts. Sleep crept around his mind, and he dozed off.

"Matt . . ."

It was only a whisper, softer even than the river. Something touched his shoulder.

"Matt, it's Clare. You awake?"

"Yes," he finally said.

"I can't sleep. Can we talk?"

Her lips were only inches from his ear. He turned onto his back and saw her silhouette above him, kneeling.

"I miss Zach something terrible. I thought maybe if we just . . . you know, just talked, maybe it'd help."

"Well, sure, I . . ." He lowered his voice even more.

"What you want to talk about?"

"Oh, you know. Things. Maybe you could tell me about yourself. That'd take my mind off him."

His mind raced, trying to think of something to say, something interesting. Nothing much had really happened to him, he figured, at least that someone else would want to know about.

"Well, my . . . my mama was killed by the Indians, just like Zach was," he said, thinking that might somehow help. "An' my sister Mandy, she was took by the Indians back on our farm in Virginia. I . . . I . . ."

"Now, don't talk about it if it bothers you," she said quickly. She rubbed his shoulder softly, slowly, and lay on her side next to him. "There, there. We can talk about something else."

He lay still a minute, listened to the small voices of the settling starlings overhead, then of the animals in the forest around them, the ones he knew were there, could hear, but couldn't really pin down. Snores came from the main camp. A breeze shook the leaves above him, and Clare's body touched his. He wasn't sure which caused the tingling sensation, her or the wind.

"I ain't never found her," he said. "I asked about her and all. But I guess . . . I guess I don't really know how to find her."

"Oh, you poor thing." Clare hugged his chest, and he felt her breasts against his arm. "You poor darling thing! That's the saddest thing I've ever heard."

She stroked his chest now, and he smelled her body's

musk. She rubbed in an ever-widening circle, and soon her hand was on his stomach, then lower. Sweat popped out on his forehead and feeling surged in his loins.

"You poor thing," she said again, softly. Her lips brushed his ear, and her hand touched his face. She turned his head toward her with a gentle pressure and he felt her lips on his, felt her hand on his stomach again, moving down. His body cried for her. A cloud hid the moon. His hand touched her bare hip, and she rolled over onto him.

CHAPTER 20

RAIN PATTERING ON HIS BLANKET AWOKE MATT. COLOR streaks showed in the east, but the sky above was black. He made out several gray blotches, tent cloths and bed-coverings stretched between upright poles and trees, or just lying on the ground. He glanced again at the sky. It wouldn't rain long.

He scooted back against a protective sugar maple tree, pulled his cover up under his chin, and sat thinking about what he and Clare Ryborn had done the night before. What had happened? Clare had just lost her fiancé, just buried him, in fact. But she had come to him and began touching him, and strange powers took over his body. Before he knew it, he was on top of her, doing things he'd only dreamed of. And doing it while her fiancé lay dead, less than a mile away, his body hardly cold!

A spoon clattered against an iron pot, mumblings came from the tents, campers swished through wet underbrush and tree limbs to relieve themselves. Men clustered in the center, squatting around a fire's cold remains. Matt shook his troubling thoughts from his mind and ambled over to them, trying not to call attention to himself.

"Well, we're goin' back," one was saying. It was Norton, the man who spoke up the night before. "We was lucky it wasn't our own kin killed yesterday. Beggin' your pardon, Daniel, I didn't mean . . ."

"We'll go with you," another said. He was a tall, skinny man. "We can be ready in an hour."

Boone stared at the cold ashes, saying nothing as others announced intentions to return home. Finally they'd all had their say and just squatted there, like they were waiting for his permission to leave. He looked them all in their faces, as if he were trying to memorize how they looked.

"Well, I wish you all luck," he said, finally. "You got your own lives to live."

"You ain't goin'?" Norton said. "We cain't talk you into it?"

"No, we'll stay on here. Someday I'll settle over there in Can-tuc-kee, I'll promise you that. But I guess we've got to own that land first."

"I sure don't see how that's going to happen," Norton said. He rubbed his chin and looked around at the others, most of whom were still staring down at the ground. "Well, guess I'll finish packing."

He left the circle, and all but Boone followed. Matt waited for a while out of his line of sight, then stepped up and sat across from him.

Boone looked up. "Well, Matt. You going, too? What're your plans?"

"I don't have none," Matt said. "I got to get more pelts so I can get that home for Mandy, though, but I don't have any ammunition. No supplies."

"You can go with them others."

"Guess so," Matt said. "'Course, I don't know where they're going."

"Well, some's from North Carolina, some's from Virginia. Ain't that where you come from? Virginia?"

"Yes, sir."

Boone sat back and frowned. "Things've changed since you left. They've moved the Virginia boundaries out to here, made this Fincastle County. Split it off of Botentort County, and named it after Botentort's county seat."

"I didn't know that," Matt said.

"People are moving in. Like those Clinch River folks. Some have settled on the Holston, some even south of the Virginia border, in Cherokee country. I've spent some time down there myself."

"Maybe that's where I'll go," Matt said. He figured the sheriff wouldn't reach him there.

Boone eyed him, then picked up a stick and drew with it in the ground.

"Tell you what. You go on up the Clinch with the rest of us, then east through Moccasin Gap. Cross the Holston's north branch with the others, right here. They'll keep going, but you head up Reedy Creek headwaters. Go on to the mountain's edge, and you'll find a place called Sapling Grove."

He drew the two Holston forks coming southwest and meeting, then made a jiggly line for Reedy Creek and stabbed a place at its end.

Matt squinted at the crude map. "Sapling Grove. Don't remember the name."

"Wasn't there when you left. Evan Shelby opened his store there in seventy-one, seventy-two. Other folks're moving into the valleys around him. Tell him I sent you."

"Sapling Grove. I'll do it."

"Fine. And Matt . . ." Boone's eyes sparkled, and he motioned Matt to lean down. He looked around, then back at Matt.

"That Ryborn gal's something else, now ain't she?" he whispered.

They left camp before the sun was fully up. Matt had never seen so many people traveling together in all his life. He'd seen buffalo herds a lot bigger in Can-tuc-kee, going from horizon to horizon even. He'd seen a lot of other animals crowding the salt licks. But this was people, and it was something else.

The cattle went first, herded by the young boys, followed by their families. The men led horses that carried their wives and the supplies gathered for the trip to Can-tuc-kee. At first the youngsters played tag around the horses, but soon tired of that and walked beside their daddies or their older brothers and sisters.

The caravan headed up the Clinch, which meandered between two irregular ridges, then crossed the river at

Neil's Ford. The river stayed centered for two or three hours, then hooked right and hugged the ridge. It looked to Matt like a huge sausage, like Noah made once, laying in a bed of greens.

"What're you thinking?"

It was Clare Ryborn. She had dismounted and was walking her horse by Matt's side.

"Nothing. I was just walking."

"But you was thinking about something. Me, I was thinking about getting home. It'll be good seeing it again."

"I guess so."

They walked together for a while, the silence crushing in on him.

"I guess I was thinking about what's up ahead," he said. "Whatever's up there."

"You don't know where you're going?"

"Not exactly. Leastwise, I never been there before. Someplace called Sapling Grove."

"Well, it's sure nice to have a place to go to. Isam left me that four hundred acres and a good corn crop, right up there on the Clinch. Zach was going to put the corn up for me. Too bad about his dying."

Too bad about his dying? Matt said nothing, but glanced at her, then forward again. She was his fiancé! How could she say "too bad about his dying," like he was an animal or something? Matt's thoughts shifted to the night before. How could he find fault with her, when he bedded her right after Zach had been killed? He now thought of the surging feeling he had had in his belly, the all-consuming passion, and his face seemed to catch fire.

They walked silently together as the sun crept up over-head, absorbed in the rhythm of squeaking leather and occasional voices. At noon the settlers stopped for lunch beneath the oaks next to the Clinch and watered their horses. Matt tore off some meat Rebecca Boone had given him and held the main piece out to Clare. She smiled and shook her head.

"I got food here," she said. She reached into her saddle-bag. "There's one thing about me, I know how to take care of myself. Let's sit over there."

They sat on a decaying log and watched the Clinch flow by. Matt tried to think of a way to excuse himself.

"You like farming?" she said.

"Well, yes. Nothing I'd rather do than open up good land."

"I see." She stared down at her food, then flashed him a smile.

"Like I told you, I got that four hundred acres. Prettiest land you ever seen."

"Awfully good land around here," he said.

"I got the land, but I can't work it myself. Isam worked it, and then Zach helped out. But they're both dead now."

"Yes'm."

"Did you like me last night?"

"What? Oh, you mean . . ." His face stung again with heat.

"I know how to treat a man. The man what marries me gets a good prize. I work hard, too."

Matt scooped some water and slurped it to wash down his food. He splashed more on his face and rubbed his hands on his trousers.

"Boy, that's cold. Well, the rest're leaving. Suppose I ought to see what I can do to help out."

He got up and walked toward the others. She sat there a moment, then jumped up and started after him.

"When we get to Moccasin Gap, you come on with us," she called. "We got nice farms and good folks. You can stay awhile and . . . you know, rest up."

"Well, I really ought to keep going." He walked faster, struck a long stride, pulled away from her.

"Maybe you could stay one night?" she called after him. "And catch up with them later? That'd be all right, wouldn't it?"

He walked faster and didn't stop until he was in the middle of the group. He looked around for something to do. Maybe he could help with the cattle. He'd never tended cattle, but . . . well, what's to know? You just follow the things and keep them in line. If the young boys could do that, he could, too. He looked back, but couldn't see Clare among the milling people and horses. Yes, he'd go help with those cattle. He could learn about them. But women? He started jogging north.

At mid-afternoon, the Clinch River bent westward toward the left ridge, and they stopped the cattle to let the rest catch up. Boone had said Moccasin Gap was just ten miles off to the right from where they stood. The Clinch people and the east-bound settlers stopped at the bend, told each other to "come see us, now," and "don't be a stranger," and the eastern travelers prepared to cross the Clinch and start for Moccasin Gap.

Captain Russell spurred his horse and rode up to Matt. "Son, would you do us a favor?" he said.

Matt stopped. "Sure, be happy to."

"Boone says you're headed to Captain Shelby's place. Give him this message to read and pass on to Colonel Preston at the Lead Mines, will you?" He handed Matt a folded piece of paper.

"Sure." Matt stuffed the paper into his bullet bag. "Well . . . well, I'm sorry about Henry."

"Thank you, Matt. You take care, now."

Captain Russell turned his horse and galloped back to the others. Matt saw one horse standing to the side and recognized its rider. It was Clare Ryborn, sitting quietly, watching him. He turned back and walked quickly to catch up with the others.

CHAPTER 21

CAPTAIN EVAN SHELBY'S PLACE STOOD ATOP A CLEARING that ran uphill to the north. Matt saw the buildings and stopped, memories crowding his mind. It was like Noah's place three years back, when he'd stood on the log and seen Reverend Ashbrooke approaching, and Noah came up from behind to see who it was.

He blinked the memory away and started up the path separating the corn from the forest. There were differences, of course. This clearing was clean of stumps and burn piles and covered with dry, ear-laden corn stalks, their brittle leaves snapping and rattling with each hint of breeze. It was just like he'd pictured his and Noah's field would look.

And the buildings were different. There were actually two main ones in front, lined up along an invisible line and separated by sixteen feet or so. Beyond them, at the far edge of a grassy yard, were a spring house, a stable, a shed, and an almost empty corn crib. The house on the right looked no different than Noah's, or his own parents' place for that matter, before the Indians burned it. The October gusts swirled blue smoke around the chimney and set it dancing with the tree tops.

The store was on the left. It was slightly larger than the house, but was also made of logs chinked and daubed with wood scraps and mud. Matt studied it, noticed the empty hitching rack.

A mongrel dog ran from behind the house, yipped and snarled at him, lunged and retreated. A long-legged, long-bodied hound loped around the store and uttered a deep-throated snarl. Matt stood still, respectful of them and their owner, who obviously used them to help put bear and deer meat on the table.

"Hello! Anybody here?"

The stable door opened, and a middle-aged man with a massive frame and large features stepped out. He held the door ajar, his deep-set eyes staring at Matt from beneath bushy eyebrows. "Yes, sir. Can I help you?"

"Name's Matt McLaren. Daniel Boone told me to stop by."

"Oh, now, did he!" The man grinned broadly, relaxed his big hands down to his sides. "C'mon up. How is old Daniel, anyhow? Satch! Blue! Let this boy by!"

The two dogs slunk away as another man emerged from the stable. He was in his mid-twenties, and judging from his looks, the older man's son. He had the same big frame and features, the same eyebrows, compressed lips, heavy chin. He directed a frown at Matt.

"This here's my oldest boy, Isaac," Evan Shelby said. "Say, did Boone ever move to Can-tuc-kee?"

"He's staying on the Clinch for now," Matt said. "His . . . the Shawnee killed his boy."

Both men's faces clouded, and it seemed their shoulders slumped. Captain Shelby scratched his big whiskered jaw and thought a minute.

"Well, c'mon to the house and tell us about it," he said. "Isaac, go get the others. It's dinner time."

Matt tried to act polite, but ate like he'd never had food before. He fished another meat chunk out of his stew and chewed it three or four times before swallowing and scooping for another. The Negro girl spooned him more from her serving kettle.

"Now, there's plenty where that come from," Letitia Shelby said softly, the corners of her eyes wrinkling. "The Lord has blessed us. Tizzie, you keep his bowl filled."

Tizzie looked to be in her early twenties. She added an extra spoonful and returned to the wide hearth to refill the serving kettle from the larger kettle hanging on the fireplace crane.

Matt glanced at Mrs. Shelby, seated next to her husband. She was thin, had small white ears with red hair knotted above them. His gaze shifted around the cabin's interior. The sliding shutter of the single window, opposite the fireplace, was closed against the chilly evening air. Feather beds ranged around the walls, and extra clothing hung on pegs above them. A wooden cupboard occupied one corner, and a crude ladder rose to the loft in the other. A curve-handled gourd leaned against a water bucket on a shelf just inside the door, and a broken looking-glass hung next to it on a leather thong.

Tizzie returned and ladled more stew for Captain Shelby and his four sons.

"Now, be sure and get some salt, Matt," Mrs. Shelby said, nodding toward the high salt cellar on the plank table. "We got plenty."

"Thank you, ma'am."

Captain Shelby and his boys ate noisily, barely looking up when Tizzie refilled their bowls. Isaac, the oldest, seemed thoughtful. Occasionally he whispered to his father, sitting next to him, and was answered by a nod or a one-word response. The other three, ranging in age from Evan Jr. to James to Moses, barely a teenager, had their mother's red hair and slim build.

"It sure is terrible about Boone's and Russell's boys," Captain Shelby said. He pushed his bowl away and unfolded Captain Russell's note again. He read it slowly to himself. "Terrible. How many Indians were there?"

"Dozen, maybe more. Took 'em by surprise while they was sleeping."

"Well, looks like we can expect company," Shelby said. "I knew the peace wouldn't last. I'll send word up to Colonel Preston about how things stand with the Indians."

"Colonel Preston. I heard Boone and Russell mention him."

"He's in charge of Fincastle County's militia and its

surveying to boot," Shelby said. "Russell and I both report to him. Damn. If it ain't the Cherokees, it's the Shawnee."

"I always thought the Cherokee was peaceable," Matt said. " 'Course, I been away for three years."

"Well, they used to be. But a year ago they gave the Watauga people — James Robertson and that crowd — a ten-year lease on the land they're sitting on. Got a thousand pounds worth of trade goods for it, which ain't bad in my mind. But now some're not happy with the arrangement."

Isaac looked up at his father. "We'll have to build a fort now. No gettin' around it."

"You're right there," Captain Shelby said. "The Reedy Creek fort's too far away, and not big enough at any rate. We'll get started in the morning."

He retrieved his pipe from the mantle, lit it with a stick from the fire. Just like Noah used to do. Smoke wafting throughout the room brought flashes of Noah's image.

"Matt, let's get us some air," Shelby said.

They walked outside and were absorbed by the darkness, broken only by the glow of Shelby's pipe and the sparse moonlight that barely outlined buildings and trees. Matt followed Shelby's form past the woodpile to a log at the clearing's edge, recently cut according to the moist sycamore fragrance. The older man sat down on it.

"Take a load off," he said. "Guess this is one of my favorite things, to be out here when it's dark, watch the stars, and feel the nip of winter."

For several minutes they just sat there, listening to a whippoorwill's call from the corn field down the hill. Each time Captain Shelby drew on his pipe the glow lit his face, and Matt saw he was staring at him, not at the stars. The tobacco smoke teased Matt's nostrils, rode away on a cold northern breeze.

"What's your plans, Matt? Where you go from here?"

"I . . . I don't really know. Guess I'll just get a job some place, so's I can get me some more supplies and go back to Can-tuc-kee."

"Back to the wilderness? By yourself? You must have a pretty strong reason to go."

"Yes, sir. I guess I do." Matt started talking, and before long he'd told about his sister, Noah, Jacob getting killed, all the rest. The whippoorwill called again, and an owl hooted in the distance. The breeze picked up, and Matt hugged himself for warmth. Shelby grunted when he finished.

"This'll have to be a big fort," he said, slowly. "Folks think of the store as their meeting place, so we got to protect them if trouble comes. Going to take a lot of log cutting and dragging. Want to help out?"

"Why, sure. I've done that before, cutting trees. Be glad to help out."

"Good. Tell you what. You help build the fort and get the corn in, help out at the store awhile, and I'll give you a good horse and room and board for your pay. A man needs a good horse in this country. What do you think?"

"I . . . of course. I'd sure be obliged."

"If you were of a mind to, you could stay on at the store. Business is really picking up, what with all the new folks moving in. Of course, if you need to go do some more hunting, why, you could do that instead."

"That would be fine, working here," Matt said. "I'm a good worker. I've got corn in before, too, and I'm a good learner, on the other things you might want me to do."

Shelby stood. "Don't doubt it one bit. Well, let's get to bed. We got a lot of work ahead of us come morning."

At daybreak, Matt stood with Captain Shelby and his boys by the woodpile. The Captain turned in a complete circle, his gaze following an invisible line around the clearing.

"I want all our buildings inside the fort," he said. "That'll take a lot of logs. We'll cut in that oak stand back of the place. Isaac, you go tell the neighbors, then bring the team out."

He pulled the ax from a well-sliced stump. "We got more axes in the store. James, you get 'em and meet us out there."

Matt and the two other boys followed him between the stable and the corn crib. They passed the spot where Matt and Captain Shelby had talked the night before, wove through the hickories and the sycamore until they reached the tall, straight oaks.

"Cut those logs pointy on the top, now. I'll go lay out the walls and keep an eye on the store. Isaac will be in charge. Any questions?"

There were none. Captain Shelby left, and moments later James appeared with two shiny axes and a sharpening stone. Matt hefted one ax, liked its feel. He looked at the trees, spit on his palms and looked for a target. Maybe the Shelbys had some gloves he could use, or leather scrap he could make some from. He'd check later. He swung at the nearest oak, and the ax made a deep, satisfying cut. He swung again, and again, and the chips flew. The valley rang with the thwacks from the three axes, sometimes stuttering in individual voices, other times combining in a single loud chord.

They hacked each fallen tree to length, and trimmed the branches off. Isaac came with his draft horses and wrapped chain around two logs. The team snaked them through the forest, huffing and grunting as their harnesses snapped and jingled. They returned for another load, and another. Matt kept chopping trees, his muscles working, finally hurting, yet feeling good.

The sun was almost overhead when Matt became conscious of other chopping in the woods about him. First it was a single pecking far to his left, then other, closer hacking. A stranger slammed his ax home again and again to the right. There was more movement farther down, and more beyond that. A span of oxen appeared. The teamster hooked them to a log and snapped his whip, and the oxen bellowed and lunged forward. The air shook with thwacks and bellows and whinnies of axes and oxen and horses and the shouts of neighbors who had come to help build the fort.

After a while, the commotion quieted in stages, from the left to the right.

"Eating time," Isaac said as he passed Matt on his way to tell others up the line. "Come down to the yard."

Matt fell into step with the others heading back to the clearing. He looked at his left hand, fingers spread wide.

Skin from open blisters flapped at him. He would be hurting more before the day was over.

The yard was almost filled with perspiring men, aproned womenfolk, playing children.

"My God, where'd they all come from?" he asked James.

"Well, Isaac told some. Some heard the chopping. Others come by the store and found out what we're doing and spread the word or stayed to help."

The men and older boys gathered near the woodpile, and Matt went over there with James. He smelled the reason before he saw it — ham, venison, beef, vegetables, breads, pies — a feast was spread out on rough planks lying across sawhorses. He got in line and unsheathed his knife and began cutting and stabbing at food. The women on the other side of the table put more out when there was room. They had already run out of trenchers and pewter plates, the latter prizes from an earlier life across the mountains. Matt put food between two slices of turkey to make a sandwich.

"Here's one you can use."

It was a soft female voice. A pewter plate magically appeared before him. He glanced up to see a girl, perhaps fifteen years old, holding it. She thrust it at him. Her hair was stuck up under a sunbonnet that shaded her face. She had sparkling eyes and dimples that deepened with her nervous smile. She was thin, but almost as tall as he.

"Thank you, ma'am," he said. "I didn't see any plates there."

She turned away quickly to get more food, and Matt moved down the line. James poked him in the ribs from behind.

"There wasn't no plates there, which is why you didn't see any." He laughed. "She saved that one for you, dummy. She just took that plate out of a sack under the table."

"Oh, she did not!"

"She sure did. I guess she likes you."

"She prob'ly just found it when I got there," Matt said. He stabbed a piece of meat. "Who is she?" He hoped he sounded casual.

"Naomi Grubbs. Her daddy's Archelam Grubbs, farms west of here. He's an odd bird."

Matt leaned against a tree to eat, away from the others. He glanced back at the table. She was looking at him!

Before long the men wiped their mouths and returned to the woods. Matt stood to follow. Captain Shelby came over.

"How's your hands?" he said.

"Doing all right." Matt looked down at them. "Just need to build up some callus."

"They look like hell. Look, you be my string man. We've got to mark where to put the fort walls, and get things ready."

Matt grinned. "I ain't going to argue with that."

He followed Captain Shelby across the clearing toward the back side of the store. As he rounded the corner he glanced back at the food table. Naomi Grubbs. It was such a pretty name!

CHAPTER 22

Ringing axes and cries of "Timber!" shattered the fall air for more than a week. Horse and ox teams grunted and tugged and dragged the logs to the fort perimeter Matt and Captain Shelby had marked off and lined them up side by side just beyond where the trench dirt mound would be. Matt had helped clear and burn brush away from both sides of the line, savoring the smoke that clung to everything around him. That done, with healing hands, he returned to the stand of oaks to help Isaac and the other teamsters hitch their loads for dragging.

Matt couldn't keep Naomi Grubbs from his mind. He looked forward to mealtimes, when he would see her again. Today, as he had done each day, he watched until all the plates had been passed out, then stepped into the food line. She smiled, like she'd done every day, and pulled her pewter plate from its sack beneath the table.

"Here's your plate," she said.

"Thank you . . . Naomi."

He moved down the line, stopped. No one was behind him.

"Look . . . can I talk to you some place? I've wanted to all week."

"I don't know . . ." she glanced behind her.

"Will you be here if I come back?"

Another timber cutter got into line behind him, and he moved forward.

"Well, I . . . Daddy doesn't want me to. . . ."

The heavy older woman behind her frowned and set her platter of ham down. "I need you back here, Naomi," she said. "Now!" The wattles under her arm shook as she tugged Naomi's wrist. Huge, deep wrinkles formed around her eyes and ran from her nose to her chin, and black holes gaped where teeth should have been. As she pulled Naomi away, she shuffled with a limp Matt hadn't noticed before. Only now did he see the crutch tucked under her right arm.

"All right, Mama. Careful now, don't fall." She looked at Matt. "I guess not. I . . . I won't be able to."

Matt gulped his food and stormed into the woods before the rest were done eating. He grabbed an ax and attacked an oak tree with vicious force, exploding large chips that ricocheted off other trees. Why had she flirted with him, then turned him away? He undercut the tree with savage thrusts and watched it crash to the forest floor. He hacked at its middle, cursing with each lunge, each flying chip, until it surrendered and lay in two pieces.

"What in hell's got into you?" It was Isaac, back with others to start the afternoon's work. He coaxed his team of horses backward into place. "Come help me hook up. Something eating on you?"

"Just thought I'd get an early start." Matt snaked a chain around the log, jumped back, and Isaac slapped the reins against the horses' rumps. They jerked forward. Matt flung the chain around the second log and tied it off. He stood back, hands on his hips, breathing heavily.

"Sure nothing's wrong?"

" 'Course." Matt rubbed the horse side, smelled its sweat. He eased up near its head, stroked its neck, and glanced at Isaac. "You know that girl?" he said.

"What girl?"

"The one that serves the food. Naomi, something. Scruggs? Grubbs, I guess it was."

Isaac laughed. "You know her name. What about her?"

"Just wondering about her daddy. James said he was odd."

"Oh, he just keeps to himself," Isaac said. "I'm surprised he let his womenfolk come. Guess he wants to guarantee a spot in the fort, case there's trouble."

"Oh. Well, I was just wondering."

Isaac touched his shoulder. "You like her, don't you?"

"Just curious, that's all." Matt turned away.

Isaac jiggled the reins, and the horses lurched forward. Matt jumped back as the logs plowed past him.

"So, you got a girl, do you?" Isaac called over his shoulder. "Watch out. You know what terrible things that can lead to."

Matt turned his back on Isaac, then thought again about Naomi, and paused. How would it be with her? Clare had introduced him to an earthshaking desire, in a way he was now ashamed of. When he thought of Naomi, those feelings began to return. He listened to the sounds coming from the cabin yard, hoped to hear her voice. But he knew he wouldn't. He picked his ax up again, and attacked another tree.

When Matt awoke the next morning, Naomi was in his mind's eye, smiling and holding out her personal pewter plate. He tried to block the thoughts, but she kept coming back. Her dimples, her smile, her soft voice surrounded him, called to him. He ate breakfast and followed Captain Shelby and his boys outside, still thinking of her.

They hoped to finish the fort today. They finished digging the stockade wall trench the day before, except for part of the north wall, and logs had already been upended and tamped into place in the south wall. Early-arriving settlers were digging the remaining trench, their shovels and picks clinking and thumping as they hit and removed rocks. The foundation logs had already been laid for the corner blockhouses. Crews were preparing to build the east and west fort walls, drawing from logs that lay just beyond the dirt mounds.

The Shelby party stopped in the fort's center where a roast pig turned on a spit, grease droppings spattering in the glowing ashes. Other volunteers ambled over and stood there too, awaiting instructions and taking in the roast pig's warmth and rich aroma.

"That's the best part of a job," James Shelby said to Matt, nodding at the pig. "The celebrating's always more fun than the doing."

"I s'pose so," Matt answered. "Think we'll get done today?"

"Probably. But we'll launch this fort tonight, either way. There'll be dancing, and games . . . it'll take our minds off things."

Captain Shelby spoke up. "We've got to finish the blockhouses," he said. "I'll take one team. Isaac, you take the other."

He divided the assembled men into two crews, and Matt followed him to the corner closest to the store. Matt looked down the outside of the completed stockade wall and realized the Captain had intended the south walls of the store and house to be part of it all along. The new gate leaned against the store, waiting to be hung between them. Shelby was obviously a capable man, someone who thought things through.

As the captain had predicted, the blockhouses went up fast. Half the men adzed notches into the log ends to fit them in the corners, and Matt and the rest rolled, carried, and hefted the logs into place. When the logs stood shoulder high they chopped four loopholes into the top ones facing out, so rifles could be fired at attacking Indians. That done, Matt carved his initials into the top of one log. They would be covered by the next log in a few minutes, but he'd know they were there. His signature to a job done well.

More settlers showed up as the day passed. They tied their horses and unloaded baskets and sacks onto the makeshift table until it was covered with food. Letitia Shelby bobbed around the table, helped clean up after the midday meal, directed Tizzie's efforts, talked with the other women. She helped with their loads, complimented them on their donations. Most had worked on the fort or served food the past week.

Then Matt saw Naomi, helping her mother down from her horse. The older woman leaned to the side and crushed down on Naomi, who staggered a moment and found her support. "Careful, Mama. Careful, now!"

Naomi leaned into her mother until the older woman's feet hit the ground. She hugged her tightly. "That's my mama. Here. Here's your crutch. You all right?"

A tall, heavy-set man stood next to them. Archelam Grubbs was the biggest man he'd ever seen. He watched his wife and daughter with bloodshot eyes, half hidden behind puffy lids. A scar ran down his left cheek, ending in a black, bushy beard.

Grubbs plucked a sack from behind his saddle and carried it, dangling, to the table. He plopped it down in front of Mrs. Shelby and turned back to his wife and Naomi. "Get over and take care of this!"

Naomi helped her mother to the table. She opened the sack, took things out and placed them among the food already brought. Matt stepped closer and was hit with the aroma of bear and venison, roasts, wild turkey, pheasant, and other dishes. Johnny cake and corn pone lay covered with towels next to covered milk pitchers.

His gaze turned to Naomi. She must have seen him watching her, because she glanced quickly around at her parents, then back at him, smiled and slipped the sack under the table. The shape of a pewter plate pulled down inside it.

Well, he wouldn't play the part of a fool again.

Archelam Grubbs spotted Captain Shelby at the block-house. He sauntered over and watched Matt and the others add another course of logs to the top. "Where you want me?" he asked. He twisted a finger in his nose and wiped it on his trousers.

"Wherever you want to fit in," Shelby said. "Maybe over on the wall."

Grubbs clasped his hands behind him and leaned back, observing the crew working on the west wall. He turned and watched the east wall workers. Both had advanced about ten feet from the corner.

"Hell, it'll take these woodpeckers all week, slow as they are," he said. "They need lessons handling those logs."

He walked to the western trench and jumped over it.

"You pansies're slower'n molasses in January. Here, get out of the way. You tamp, I'll throw them logs."

He lifted a log like it was a toothpick, walked it to the trench, and dropped one end in. He grinned. "Hey, you on the other wall! You're a bunch of pansies."

They paused, then continued working.

"We challenge you to a race! The side what gets to the other end last has to . . . " he thought a moment, then grinned wider ". . . has to climb on top of Shelby's house there and holler, 'I'm a pansy' ten times. We got a deal?"

They stopped again, looked at him, at each other. "You're on," one said.

It was Darass Hutchins, a man Matt knew had probably felled more trees than any other worker over the previous days. He had big muscles, but was not as enormous as Grubbs.

"But you got six people, and we only got five," Darass called. "That ain't fair."

Captain Shelby turned to Matt. "Go help them."

Matt went over while the rest of the settlers gathered along the two lines, laughing and joking. He scanned the crowd, saw Naomi by the table. Their gazes locked and he thought he saw an uncertainty, like she was trying to decide something. When the other workers dropped their tools and moved toward either wall to get a good view, she came to his wall.

Darass looked at Matt. "You help me pitch them logs," he said. "The rest of you throw the dirt in and tamp. "We can beat that big-mouthed bastard."

"You think so, do you?" It was Grubbs. "Tell you what. I'll make a side bet. Your team wins, I'll carry you around this here fort on my shoulders. We win, you do the same for me. Deal?"

"You got it. What's the rules?"

"Rules! Hell, there ain't none. 'Ceptin' we got to fence all the way to the corner, and it's got to be tamped in proper. The captain'll be the judge. Right, Shelby?"

"I will," Shelby said. He walked out to the center by the roast pig where he could be seen. The crowd had by now divided into two groups and stood back so Shelby could see both teams. "When you're ready, I'll signal you to start."

"Hell, I been ready all m'life," Grubbs said.

"And you, Darass? All right, here we go. One, two three . . . go!"

` Matt and Darass jumped to work. Each grabbed and carried his own log, dropped its end into the trench. Two men held it vertical and shoveled dirt at the logs from either side, and the other two tamped the dirt in place, with saplings cut flat on one end. Occasionally Matt and Darass stumbled over each other, as did Grubbs and his other log handler.

"God damn it, stay outa my way!" Grubbs shouted. "You can't do it right, don't do it atall!"

Matt strained every muscle to grab, carry, and drop each log, then run back to get another. Before long he paused, panting, and glanced at Grubbs' wall. It was growing faster than theirs. Grubbs tossed his logs as if they were weightless. It looked like there was no struggle at all — just reach down, pluck it off the ground, carry it, toss it in, and do it all again. Grubbs' strength made the difference.

Matt turned back to get another log.

"Watch it!"

Darass shouted too late. Matt knocked him off balance, and his log twisted around and slipped. He grabbed for it, but it fell and smashed his foot.

"Oh, God, that hurts!"

"Jeez, you all right?"

Darass gritted his teeth and tried to stand. He fell back. "Damn, that hurts. It ain't broke, but I ain't goin' to run no races for awhile."

Matt turned to Grubbs.

"We got a hurt man here," he called. "The contest's off."

"The hell you say! I don't recall no rule about that." Grubbs saw his teammates standing and watching. "Get back to work! We got a contest to win!"

Grubbs hefted another log, and in moments his crew was back at work. Darass stood gingerly, tried to walk. He hobbled in a circle. "Boy, that smarts. Don't think I can carry a log like this."

Matt thought a moment. "Well, how about we two-man them? Maybe that'd work."

"Hell, I'll try anything. What does that mean, 'two-man them'?"

"You stay at that end, I'll stay here near the trench. We'll swing a log toward the hole, then get under it and push it up."

Darass hobbled to the first log and lifted his end in the cradle of his clasped hands. Matt did the same nearer the trench, and together they swung it underhanded for a distance of about three feet. It dropped with its end propped up on the dirt mound that paralleled the trench.

"Get under it now!" Matt said. He ran back to Darass and they both lifted the log's other end to their shoulders. They strained and pushed up higher, to the extent of Darass' reach, and Matt walked his hands down the log as he moved toward the hole. The log arced upright and slipped on the mound, its bottom end thunking into the trench. He kept walking and pushing until the log was vertical.

"It's going to work!" Darass hobbled to the next log. "Damned if it ain't going to work!"

"Let's count it off," Matt said. "Ready? One!" They grasped the log, and lifted it from the ground.

"Two!" They swung it back and then forward toward the trench. Matt ran back to in front of Darass.

"Three!" They grunted the log up to their shoulders and put their palms under it, ready to push. A picture flashed in Matt's mind, of him exercising with the log near the Shawnee camp. Up, down, up, down — he hoped he still had some of the strength he'd built then.

"Four!" Some of the crowd joined in the count. The two log handlers strained their load upward until it left Darass' hands, then Matt walked down its length until it dropped into the ditch, and the two dirt shovelers took over.

Matt and Darass grinned at each other. "It's going to work," Darass said again. "Let's keep going."

Soon they set a fast pace that was timed by the crowd's chanted numbers.

"One! . . . Two!"

They threw each log toward the trench and lifted its end to their shoulders.

"Three! . . . Four!"

They upended each one, and Matt dropped it in. Darass Hutchins limped one step down the line between throws, ready for the next log.

Sweat rolled down Matt's body. He paused to remove his shirt and saw Naomi Grubbs on the front line of spectators. He reached over to lift the next log.

"One!" she shouted with the others.

"Two!" she cried, when they swung it at the trench. He lost

sight of her in the tension of pushing the log up, but her slight voice fought its way through the chorus. "Three! Four!"

Matt lost contact with the people around him. The numbers they shouted became peaks of physical exertion, spears of pain. He groaned with each swing, each push. The agony expanded, almost consumed him. Occasionally he glimpsed Grubbs on the opposite end of the fort, a bright target in a forest of haze. Now the man was ahead of them, laughing, calling them pansies, other names. One! Two! Three! Four! Now he was even, directly across the pig spit, yet somehow standing out through the smoke, silent except for grunts of effort. One! Two! Three! Four! Now Grubbs was behind! He slowed, was obviously hurting, but still picked up logs, carried them, threw their ends into the trench. One . . . Two . . .

Matt stopped. Something was wrong. He stood there, the log end pulling down on his tortured muscles, ready to throw it toward the trench. But there was no trench. He stood for a moment, then realized what they had done. He and Darass dropped the log.

"We're at the end!" he gasped. The dirt throwers had kept up, but the tampers were a good ten feet up the line behind him, their blunt poles thumping the thrown dirt. A tamper. They needed another tamper! He gazed about, saw nothing he could use. Then he spotted the roasting pig. He ran over and grabbed one end of the spit, cradled in the "V" of a forked limb.

"What the hell you doing?" the pig's attendant cried out as he jumped out of Matt's way. Matt didn't answer.

He lifted the spit from the fork and swung it around, and dropped the pig on the ground. He ran to the other end and did the same there, and the smoking pig lay smoldering in the grass. He pulled and jerked until the pole slid out of the animal, and ran back to the stockade wall. The crowd was silent, wondering what he was up to. Then they laughed and clapped as he tamped the dirt with his new tool. He worked feverishly for ten, fifteen minutes as they cheered him on.

Finally, it happened. He ran out of dirt to tamp.

Captain Shelby looked down the new stockade wall and grinned at Matt.

"I declare this wall the winner," he said. "Let's quit work now and celebrate!"

Matt bent over, hands on his knees, breathing heavily. His arms and chest ached, his throat was tight. He turned and saw the other tampers and shovelers doing the same. They grinned at each other, then laughed. He looked back at the unfinished wall at the other end.

At first he didn't believe what he saw. Grubbs, standing by the roast pig, swung his arm around and knocked Naomi to the ground. The smack sounded just like he would imagine a similar hit on the pig's side.

"You was cheerin' 'em on, I seen you!" he screamed. He kicked her. "Get up and take what's comin'!"

"Don't hit her, Arche!" His wife limped over and grabbed his arm. "Not here, where people can see it! Oh, please, don't! It ain't right, out here in public."

"Get out of the goddamned way!" He turned toward his daughter. "You little whore. You was eggin' that boy on agin' your old man!"

He kicked her in the side. She crawfished away, looking up at him in horror.

"Hey, stop that!" Matt shouted. He started for Grubbs, but Captain Shelby got to him first. Shelby grasped the man's shoulder, held out his other arm to keep Matt away.

"You got no right to hit her!" Matt tried to fight his way around Captain Shelby. His strength was almost gone, but he managed to break the older man's hold, and lunged at Grubbs. Shelby grabbed him before he reached his target.

"Stay back, Matt! Grubbs, there's no need to hit and kick. Take it easy, and we'll celebrate the fort building."

"Yeah, and we'll watch you dance on Shelby's house, telling us what a pansy you are," Darass called. "An' we'll watch you carry me around the fort!"

A nervous chuckle traveled through the crowd. Grubbs glowered at Darass. "In a pig's ass, you will. You two double-teamed me, and that ain't fair."

He turned to his wife and daughter, who had gotten up and was rubbing her side where he'd kicked her. "Get on those horses. You're goin' home where you belong. And you're goin' to stay there!"

He twisted around and eyed Matt for a long moment. "You steer clear of me. I got your number."

They mounted and went out through the gate. Naomi looked back at Matt from her perch on her horse. She lifted a hand to wave, then dodged as her daddy slapped at her. It was quiet for a while, then someone — Matt thought it was Isaac — cried out, "Let's celebrate!"

The spell was broken. They gathered around the table and pulled whiskey jugs from saddles and other hiding spots. Matt looked toward the gate opening, stood there for a minute, thinking. Then he stalked into the woods.

CHAPTER 23

OCTOBER FLEW INTO NOVEMBER, AND SUDDENLY CHRIST-
mas was there and past. The snows came and went and
thoughts turned to a new corn crop. Matt helped plow the
fertile land and drop the seeds into the furrows, and in
early May felt aglow as he watched green corn spikes peep
through the black earth.

Matt had set up housekeeping in the blockhouse where
he'd earlier carved his initials. He'd have to share it if Indians caused trouble and settlers moved into the fort, but that
wouldn't be a problem. He had only two blankets and basic
cooking utensils the Shelbys gave him. No, moving over
would be no problem at all.

He liked working at the store. Each morning after hoeing the corn he went inside and enjoyed the comfortable
smells. Sacks of seed, wooden handles, oiled metal imple-
ments, barrels of salt, leather — they all added to a flavor he
loved to sample each day. He liked to visit with the neighbors who came to buy them, listen to the gossip that tied the
far-flung community together.

Occasionally word came from the outside world about things that could affect them all. Like the news they'd heard from Boston. Fifty men dressed like Mohawk Indians threw chests of tea off a ship in the Boston harbor. They didn't like having to buy from England and pay a heavy duty to boot. The man telling the story had laughed and said they called it a "Boston Tea Party".

The job Matt liked most was delivering goods to customers. Captain Shelby gave him a horse the week after they finished the fort, a young white-speckled chestnut. He named it Benjie, after Noah's horse, the one the Shawnees had stolen with his pelts. Every chance he got he rode it out on the wilderness paths. By Christmas he often led a packhorse, carrying goods to customers farther and farther away, learning the trails to isolated farms dug in wherever a family's instincts took them. Mostly the people came to the store, seeing the trip as a social event, a chance to catch up on the news. But if they wanted something that wasn't in stock, they sometimes ordered it and made delivery arrangements.

Twice, Matt's runs took him near Archelam Grubbs' farm. He rode to within shouting distance and sat there, protected from sight by the trees, and watched the house. The first time smoke came from the small cabin, but there was no movement, and he left. The second time Naomi was working in the cluttered yard. He sat there for an hour, wanting to talk to her, but was afraid if he did her daddy would hit her again. The whole trip home he cursed his cowardice.

One May afternoon, Matt returned from delivering goods on an eastward loop. He stabled Benjie and patted

Shelby's dog Satch, a ritual they'd formed long before, and went into the store. He swept the floor, sorted the harnesses on their pegs, put away stock that came in that morning. Captain Shelby walked in, glanced his way, and went behind the counter.

"Friend of yours came in yesterday," Shelby said.

"Oh? Who's that?"

"Name was Tony Bledsoe. He just bought seven hundred forty acres on the Meeting House branch."

Matt stared at Shelby, then at the wall. "Did . . . did he say anything?"

"Just ordered supplies. I said you'd deliver them. He recognized the name, said the Matt McLaren he knew was involved in a killing north of Fincastle. Course, that was another McLaren altogether."

Shelby pulled out his account book and slowly thumbed through it. Matt stood still, feeling the silence crush in on him.

"Here it is. Flour, salt, other provisions, and some tools. Why don't you take them to him?"

Shelby laid the book open on the counter. He arranged some things on the shelves, glanced at Matt, and walked toward his cabin.

Matt stood in the middle of the floor for several minutes, until he heard Shelby's cabin door slam shut. It had finally happened. Bledsoe found out who he was. It would be only a matter of time before the sheriff came.

Matt looked around at the shelves, frowning. In moments he took a hesitant step to the counter and read the order, reached up and fingered a small sack of gunpowder. His mind's eye saw snatches of his past: Noah and Struthers dying, Bledsoe limping down the hill after the buffalo stepped on him, the empty cache of pelts, Bledsoe staring back as he left the hunting camp, headed back to where Matt had shot Struthers.

Yes, he had to do it. There was no other way out.

Matt grabbed the sack and set it on the counter, then gathered other items from the shelves and bins and stacked them next to it. He went out to the shed and saddled Benjie and brought him to the store and tied Bledsoe's order across the horse's back behind the saddle.

He returned to the shelves. Bullets, powder, jerky — he selected these and other things, wrapping them in a second blanket. Shelby could deduct their cost from what he owed Matt for the clerking.

Matt led the horse back to blockhouse where he lived and went inside. Not much to pack, not much at all. He picked up things, stuffed them into his load. In five minutes he was done. He mounted Benjie, stood in the stirrups, gazed around the fort. He'd miss it, that was for sure. He'd miss the people, his friends. He kicked his horse into motion and rode out the gates onto the trail west.

Bledsoe's new place was two hours out. Matt had admired it several times. Someone had previously home-steaded part of it, built a cabin and an outbuilding, then moved on. Bledsoe had obviously used his pelt money to good advantage.

Somehow, he'd drop off Bledsoe's order without the

man seeing him. His first thought had been to head out to the Can-tuc-kee land without making the delivery, but that wouldn't be fair to Shelby. No, he'd tie Benjie away from Bledsoe's cabin and carry the load in on foot, and put it where Bledsoe would find it. Then he'd go west and get more pelts.

Matt clicked his tongue and prodded the horse. Can-tuc-kee. It seemed ages since he'd been there. Trapping pelts, then hunting deer. Twice he'd tried to get money for a home for him and Mandy. Twice he got the pelts, then the Indians stole them and he had nothing for his troubles. Well, this time he'd bring some back.

Wait a minute. Back to where?

Matt thought about that, let the horse slow down.

Back to where?

He couldn't go back to Shelby's. Word about his killing the innkeeper would probably spread like wildfire. And he couldn't go back to Virginia, to his folks' place, or Noah's.

Back to where?

He saw Bledsoe's cabin ahead, peeping through the oak trees. He halted the horse and jumped down, grasped the supply bag, ready to take it off.

He paused.

If he went to Can-Tuc-Kee, where would he come back to?

He stood a long time, leaning against the horse, watching smoke rise from the cabin chimney. Bledsoe was in there. If he didn't resolve the innkeeper problem, he could never come back. Back to anywhere.

Matt let out a long sigh and climbed back on Benjie. He snapped the reins, and the horse bolted toward the cabin. He entered the cabin yard and stopped, and put his hands to his mouth.

"Bledsoe!" he yelled. "Bledsoe, you come out here!"

The door opened, and Bledsoe limped out. He looked just like he did the day he left Knox's camp, except maybe he was bent over a little more. He squinted at Matt, shielding his eyes in the bright sunlight. Then he smiled.

"Matt! That you?"

"Bledsoe, I got to talk to you."

"Well, light, and let's talk. That my supplies?"

Matt climbed down and untied the load, took it to the cabin and set it down. Bledsoe opened the top and peered in.

"You heard about what happened north of Fincastle," Matt said. "To the innkeeper." He watched Bledsoe's face, tried to read his thoughts.

"Yeah, you killed a man. I heard."

"Well, I'm sorry it happened. I didn't mean to. It was an accident."

The older man stared at him. He stood to full height, planted his fists into his sides. He shook his head slowly, side to side.

"You mean you didn't sneak up behind him and blow a hole in him with that rifle of yours?"

"No! It was an accident. He shot Noah, and my gun went off. He killed Noah. He . . ."

The corners of Bledsoe's lips quivered. "You didn't hide behind a tree and shoot him when he come out of church?"

Matt paused. Bledsoe frowned, worked his mouth. "You didn't poison his grub, and club him on the back of his noggin, and . . . and . . . " Bledsoe burst out laughing. Matt stood stunned as the man doubled over, holding his stomach, and cackling like a chicken.

"You mean you didn't shoot him with a bunch of arrows, then hack his head off with your tomahawk? You didn't . . . Gawd, Matt! Everybody knows you didn't kill him on purpose!"

Matt just stood there. What was Bledsoe saying?

"Hell's fire, Matt. Even if you did, they'd thank you for it. You got to give people credit. They seen where you drug the old man to his grave. They seen how nice you buried him, they was real touched by it all. You think they're after you? Boy, you got nothing to worry about on that score."

Matt felt a weight lift from him. Bledsoe kept laughing and Matt grinned, then laughed with him. It was quite a picture in his mind, him shooting arrows into Struthers, clubbing him, and the other things.

"You had me going there," he said. "You really had me going."

"Now, you come in and take a load off," Bledsoe said. He turned and pulled the cabin door open. "Just leave that stuff right there where it sits. You and me, we got a lot of talking to do."

Matt visited with Bledsoe a good part of the afternoon. He learned Wade Russell had returned to camp after being lost for eighteen days. The old man had showed up in Fincastle with Terrill, who was headed back to his farm up near the Pennsylvania line. According to Wade, he'd hired on as Terrill's farmhand. But Bledsoe said Terrill's smile and secret wink told a different story.

Back when they were on the Cumberland, Bledsoe had been gruff, abrupt. Downright ornery sometimes. But now he smiled and joked like he was a long lost buddy. Matt thought about that and figured it was probably close to the truth.

Matt left Bledsoe's place mid-afternoon. He went out to the fort trail and paused. That trail also led the other direction, toward the Can-tuc-kee land where all those pelts were. It led to the only way he knew to get that home for him and Mandy. It also led to the Shawnee, who'd kidnapped him and killed Jacob and twice stole his pelts. After the French trader had bought him from the Indians he'd wandered all over it. He'd killed deer, camped alone at night, listened to the animals' screeches and roars, saw no humans at all. There'd been an emptiness that getting pelts couldn't quite fill.

Matt chewed on his lower lip, looking toward the west. Then he clicked his tongue at Benjie and headed east, toward Shelby's fort. Maybe he'd wait. If someone else wanted to go to the Can-tuc-kee land later, maybe he'd go along. Besides, it wouldn't be fair to leave Shelby without store help. What with people working their fields and needing supplies and all, it just wouldn't be right.

Matt arrived at the store that evening and went inside. He was putting the bullets and powder back onto the shelves when Shelby walked in.

"See you got Bledsoe's order delivered," the older man

said. "Everything all right?"

"Sure is," Matt said. Shelby didn't ask why he had the ammunition out, and he didn't volunteer the information. "I trapped with Bledsoe over on the Cumberland."

"He said you did. Well, glad you're back."

Shelby puttered around a few minutes, then left. Matt watched him go back to his cabin. Shelby knew about his Virginia Valley problem, but he didn't say anything. And he knew Matt had confronted Bledsoe about it. He was probably dying to know the details, but didn't come out and ask. Of course, Bledsoe might have told him the whole story. In that case the storekeeper was letting him handle his own problems. The more Matt thought about that, the more he realized what a good friend the man was.

One morning two weeks later, wagoner Burton Boyd brought another wagonload of supplies in from Staunton. Matt set the small gunpowder casks on a high shelf, away from any chance of fire, and placed lead bars under the counter. He methodically put the rest away, and by mid-morning he'd done everything he could think of. He leaned back against the counter.

Captain Shelby came in and grunted a greeting. " 'Pears you got everything under control."

"Guess so. Wish there was something else to do. This standing around's the hardest work of all."

"Well, I saw dust up the road. We'll get a customer

pretty soon. I see you already got that stock up."

"Yes, sir, everything's already done that I know of."

Shelby looked over the shelved items and grinned. "Well, you were a little too fast. James Robertson's supposed to pick most of that up for his people down on the Watauga River. We could'a just left it all stacked in the corner."

The dogs barked outside and both men went out to see what the commotion was about. Captain Russell appeared at the opened stockade gate and swung down from his horse. He tied up at the hitching rack and looked back at the gate.

"You got to keep that thing closed from now on," he said. "The Indians are real touchy, at least on the Clinch."

"I've heard," Shelby said. "Come in and sit."

"I've been on this horse ever since Preston's place at the Lead Mines, before that all the way from Williamsburg. My sitter's 'bout wore out."

"Williamsburg. Must be something important up."

Russell rubbed his bottom and cocked his head at Shelby. "Might be life or death," he said. "You heard about the soldiers killing those Indians up on the Ohio?"

"No. You thirsty? Come get some water and tell us about it."

They went to the spring by the west fort wall and Matt filled a gourd dipper with icy water. He handed it to Russell, who took long sips, then sighed.

"Well, a Captain Michael Cresap killed three friendly Indians." Russell wiped his lips. "Then men named Baker and Greathouse invited some others to drink some liquor, and murdered them. When more Indians came to check on their friends, those two bastards killed two of them, and wounded the rest."

"Damn," Shelby said. "What were they thinking? You know, we had an Indian murdered not long ago, an hour north of here. Shot in the back, and left naked. He was a friendly Indian, too, hung around the fort. We figured it had to be a white man that did it."

"That's too bad," Russell said. "But these two I'm talking about turned out to be Chief Logan's brother and sister. He vowed to take ten white scalps for each one that got torn off the heads of his kin. He goaded the Shawnees and the Delawares to war against the whites. They scalped thirteen whites in Pennsylvania. Six were children."

Logan! Matt's mind conjured up troubling images. He saw Jacob burning, smelled his flesh, recalled how Logan had spared his own life. "Logan was the white man's best Indian friend," he said. "He talked the Shawnee out of warring against us once before."

Russell eyed him. "Isn't he the one that saved your skin?"

Matt nodded.

"The Shawnee want the Cherokee to join them and fight us, and Logan won't talk them out of it anymore," Captain Russell said. "Governor Dunmore says we've got to protect ourselves."

Shelby stood and brushed his trousers. He looked northwest for a long minute, as if he could see right through the fort wall and the mountains beyond, clear to the Ohio River.

"They'll come up the Big Sandy and its tributaries," Shelby said. "The Tug, or the dry Tug fork, maybe the Louisa.

There's nothing to stop them until they get to the Clinch." He turned to Russell. "You'd be right on the firing line."

"That's how Preston and I see it," Russell said. "He's also worried about John Floyd and the others, out surveying Can-tuc-kee tracts for Patrick Henry. He's afraid the Shawnee'll kill them on the way."

Shelby stared toward the south. Matt knew he was thinking about James Robertson and his settlers below the Virginia border where the Cherokee were. Could the Shawnee talk the Cherokee into fighting for the common cause?

"The Cherokee might go along with them this time," Shelby said, echoing Matt's thoughts. "Robertson says the Indian agent ordered them back to Virginia, and North Carolina won't protect them if they don't move. That whole keg of gunpowder's ready to explode."

Russell got another dipper of water. He sipped, paused, frowned at the gourd. Then he grinned and looked over at Matt. "I almost forgot. Clare Ryborn says to stop by and see her next time you visit the Clinch."

Both the older men laughed, and Matt's cheeks burned. It looked like the whole world knew about him and Clare.

Russell mounted and prodded his horse into the west. Matt watched him until he was out of sight. He thought about Clare, then Naomi Grubbs. Maybe the next time he went by Naomi's place he'd find a way to talk to her without her daddy knowing it.

CHAPTER 24

WOULD CHIEF LOGAN REALLY TRY TO GET EVEN?

Every day, it seemed, more whites moved in around Shelby's fort and along the Clinch River. The Shawnees could just swoop down and kill them all in their beds, if they wanted to. Yet Chief Logan was a good man. He had, after all, saved Matt's life. But you could sure see why he was put out about the whites killing his kinfolk.

Why, the white man had done other things to the Indians that Logan could get mad about if he wanted to. It seemed like a month didn't go by without Matt hearing about a white mistreating an Indian, maybe killing one for no reason at all. Of course the one that did the killing seemed to always have a reason that satisfied him, at least.

But killing your kinfolk was something else. Matt's parents were killed by Indians, so Matt knew first-hand how it felt. Maybe Logan himself killed them. Would Matt kill Logan if he had the chance? He pondered that question over the next few weeks.

One mid-July morning, wagoner Burton Boyd pulled

his freight wagon to the store's front door. He usually went to the back and unloaded, then socialized. But this time he jumped down from the wagon and stalked in through the front.

"It's them damned Indians," he said. He handed Captain Shelby an envelope. "This here's from Colonel Preston."

Shelby tore the envelope open and read the message. He laid it on the counter.

"They going to attack?" Boyd asked. "That's what they say up in Royal Oak."

Shelby drummed his fingers on the counter. "We'll help you unload," he said, finally. "Just bring it in through the front door."

For the next few minutes they unloaded the wagon. Shelby frowned at the letter every time he passed the counter. Finally they were done. He paused, turned to Boyd.

"Tell Tizzie to give you something to eat," he said. "We'll finish here."

"Sure looks like trouble, don't it?" Boyd said. He started to leave, but paused and looked at Matt. "Say, boy, you ever seen Indian things up close? You know, bows an' arrows, knives, that type of thing?"

"Sure have." The man was short and pudgy, wore the same clothing every trip. Matt stepped back from Boyd's smell as the man hovered over him.

"Well, I got some out in the wagon, thought you might want to see it. Bought it off a guy a couple days back. Figgered I'd take it back east sometime, and make me a little money fer my retirement."

He stood there a few seconds longer, as if he thought Matt might decide to come out to see it. Finally he shrugged, and walked for the door. "You boys take care, now," he said. "I'll see you next trip."

As he left, Shelby pinched his nose between his thumb and forefinger. "He's sure no rosebud," he said, grinning. He picked up the letter, read it again. "Well, the Shawnee are about to raid the Clinch settlements. Dunmore wants me and Russell to take some men up to meet him and Colonel Lewis and some others where the Kanawha River hits the Ohio. Wants to solve the Indian problem once and for all."

Matt leaned against the counter, thinking. Those rivers formed a land triangle some called Point Pleasant. It was just north of where the Big Sandy hit the Ohio, maybe a hundred fifty or so miles north of where Matt stood. The Shawnee towns weren't more than two day's ride northwest of there. Jacob Hollinger's burning body flashed in his mind.

"When you leaving?"

"A month. That gives Preston time to get the word out and let people tidy up at home."

It didn't take long for the news to travel. Just like when they'd built the fort, people came out of the woodwork to help. And it wasn't just local people. Twenty or more came up with James Robertson from the Watauga River settlements, down in the Cherokee territory, where they had settled illegally. They camped on the fort grounds, wrestled and joked and just waited to leave for the battle. Within three weeks at least forty men were signed up.

Shelby came in at mid-morning that day. He glanced back out into the fort yard. "Thick as flies," he said. "Well, time to get to work. Here comes Boyd with a load."

Matt joined Shelby outside the store, and Boyd pulled his freight wagon up and stopped.

"It's started," he said. "They killed six children up on Sinking Creek. Mangled them something terrible. Three was John Lybrook's, one just a sucking infant."

"Damn," Shelby said.

"Looks like they come up the Tug, down Wolf Creek to the Kanawha, then up Sinking Creek. They shot Lybrook at his mill, shot him in the arm."

"Didn't Preston have scouts out?" Matt asked.

"Damned Indians just went around 'em. There's fifty miles of hills where they can dance a jig around you and you wouldn't know it."

Boyd reached into his greasy shirt and pulled out a folded piece of paper. He handed it to Shelby. "Major Campbell just sent this here message to Russell. Said you should see it, too."

The Captain unfolded the paper and glanced over at Matt. He read it aloud:

"Dear Sir – I have this moment received intelligence of several people being killed last Monday by the Indians on Sinking Creek about ten miles from Colonel Preston's. This makes it necessary that we should be strictly on our guard lest some straggling party should visit us. Therefore endeavor without loss of time to get the inhabitants in your Company collected together in two or three convenient places for forts, and let them keep up strict and regular Duty until more men can be sent to assist them, which I will endeavor to have done with all possible speed. This alarm will retard the expedition at least a week, therefore all young men that choose to do regular duty may be taken into pay. I expect an Express tomorrow from Colonel Preston, after which you shall have further instructions. Pray do everything in your power for the safety of the inhabitants."

"I am, dear sir, very sincerely yours,
Arthur Campbell."

Shelby refolded the paper. "Thank you, Burton. Well, let's get this stuff into the store."

Matt and Shelby helped Burton unload, and the wagoner stabled his horses for the night. Shelby busied himself with the stock. Finally he turned squarely to Matt.

"I need you to help Russell get his forts ready," he said. "Then to stay and help protect the Clinch women. Hutchins will be in charge here, you'll take over there. Both places'll be short-handed when Russell and I leave."

Matt fidgeted with a bag of flour he was holding. He didn't have to decide whether he should kill Logan or not. At least, not yet.

"If that's what you want."

"I know you want to go with us, but we need you here.

You're tall and strong, got a good head. I . . ."

Shelby leaned back against the counter and busted out laughing. He peered at Matt through thin slits under his bushy eyebrows, then slapped his leg and roared so loud the Indians might have heard him up in their villages. It had been a long time since Matt had seen him even smile. The man threw his head back and laughed even harder, like he'd just heard the world's funniest joke. Finally, he caught his breath.

"I just thought about you besting Arche Grubbs building this fort," he said. "Throwing that pig on the ground and all. That was the funniest thing I'd seen in ages. In a month of Sundays, like they say."

Grubbs. Matt frowned. He should check on Naomi, stuck out there so close to the Cherokee boundary, over toward the Reedy Creek fort.

"When you want me to go?" he asked.

"Today." Shelby wiped his eyes and caught his breath. "Those Indians go through scouts like water through a sieve. Russell's people could be in desperate trouble."

Shelby got a can of gunpowder from the shelves. He measured some into a small leather pouch and handed it to Matt. "Take this to Arche Grubbs when you go," he said. "He didn't order it, but might as well be on the safe side."

He got his journal from under the counter and wrote something in it, like Matt was the farthest thing from his mind. Matt watched him a minute, wondered if Shelby was somehow making fun of him with Naomi, like he'd done with Clare Ryborn. No, probably not. But it beat all, the way Shelby knew what Matt was thinking and then did the right thing. Matt stepped outside to saddle his horse.

Matt heard noises from the Grubbs place while still three miles away. First a series of thunks, then their echoes from over the ridge. Grubbs' ax? It didn't sound like an ax.

The path opened into the clearing. Naomi's mother was hoeing in the corn, her crutch lying next to her. Arche Grubbs worked his team farther down, dragging logs from the woods. The thunking continued, from the other side of the cabin. Then, far off, its echo.

Grubbs stopped his team and wiped sweat from his face with a dirty arm. He stared at Matt. "Well, what the hell you want?"

"Shelby sent this gunpowder. Said the Shawnee might be planning something."

"Hell, there ain't no Shawnees around. All we got is them tame Cherokee. Three or four come trooping down that there path 'bout every day, like little bitty ants."

"Peaceable now, maybe. But Shelby says the Shawnee're trying to rile them against us. I can take this powder back."

"No, leave it — you done brung it. Tell Shelby I'll settle up later. Take it over to the cabin."

"I'll set it inside out of the sun," Matt said. "All right to get some water?"

"I s'pose. Then get on out of here. I don't need you gettin' in my way." Grubbs slapped the near horse's rump, and the team jerked against its load.

Matt walked his horse around the cabin. Naomi was working at a sweep and mortar mill. The wooden pestle in her hands was tied to a bent-over sapling. When she pulled it down it thunked into the hollowed stump, mashed the corn, and sprang back up. He set the gunpowder inside the door.

She looked up. "Oh! God, you scared me!" She held her hand to her throat, looked to the sky. "I didn't know who you were!"

He nodded. "You . . . you doing all right?"

"Goodness, give me a minute here . . . you startled me! Does Daddy know you're here?"

"He said I could get some water." Matt went to the well and dropped the bucket in, pulled it up. "I wanted to see you, Naomi. I come by a couple times, wanted to stop, but . . ." He filled the gourd dipper and held it out to her. She sipped from it, and he gulped the rest down.

"Well, I'm glad you came. Real glad. I . . . I've been thinking about you, almost every night."

The thunk, thunk, thunk echoed from across the ridge. Matt looked toward the noise. "That don't make sense. How can that echo come when you're not even working?"

She laughed, her low voice sending a chill down his spine. Just like water over a waterfall, he thought. That beautiful, beautiful sound. When the thumping echoes stopped she grabbed the pestle and pulled it down hard into the corn. She did that a dozen times, and the thunks got louder as the grain pulverized into powder. She let the pestle dangle from its rope and held up a hand to him for silence.

"Now, listen!" She pointed toward the ridge. In a moment he heard the far-off thunks.

"I don't know who that is," she said. "But we talk back and forth like this just about every day. I may be hoeing, or spinning yarn, or whatever, and I'll hear her and run over and make my samp, too. Or sometimes I get lonely, and I start first, just to hear from somebody else."

"Don't know who that'd be," he said. "I never delivered over there."

"I've never met her, but we're good friends. We've been knowing each other almost since we moved here. They's nobody to actually talk to, and Daddy wouldn't let me if there was. Oh! I almost forgot!"

She ran into the cabin, and Matt looked around while he waited. The thumping stopped. Sounds of clanking chains, mixed with yelled curses from Naomi's pa came from around the cabin. In a few moments Naomi returned with a bundle. She shook it out and he saw it was a fringed hunting shirt.

"This is for you. It . . . it should fit real good. I didn't know for sure, just took a chance."

He held it to himself. "Nobody's ever made me anything before, 'cept Ma and Noah. I been making do with what I could find."

She smoothed it out on his chest with busy fingers. "Don't tell Daddy I give this to you! He thought I was making a dress. I wish I had some flax to make it with, but he didn't plant any yet. I made it out of some nettle growing back of the clearing. Mixed some buffalo hair in and just wove it into a cloth. You like it?"

"I've never seen anything so pretty," he said. "Really, I haven't."

He held the shirt out before him and knew that was true. He looked at her upturned face and dropped one side of the shirt, wrapped both arms around her and squeezed tight. She seemed to melt into his arms, just like she was supposed to be there, and he felt her lips on his, her arms around his neck. They stood that way a long time, until he heard the thunking from across the ridge again. He turned her loose and glanced around to get his bearings. The team's harnesses jingled on the other side of the cabin.

"I brought some gunpowder," he said, remembering. "The Shawnee killed some people north of here. Shelby wants me to help build up the Clinch forts."

"Oh." She stared at her hands. "How long'll you be gone?"

"Hard to tell. Maybe a month."

"I'll miss you. I know you haven't been by to see me, but I'll miss you something terrible."

"I wanted to come, but . . ."

"Daddy," she said. "You're right for being careful. He can be mean."

"Listen, if the Indians cause trouble, you go to the fort, hear?"

"If Daddy'll let us. He doesn't like Mama and me to be away. Says we'll take our chances out here."

"God, I hope not! You go to the fort! I seen with my own eyes how the Indians can treat people."

Something flashed on his left, and Arche Grubbs came into view. He stopped and stared at Matt.

"You 'bout got that water drunk?"

"Yes, sir. Just fixing to leave."

Matt mounted his horse, nodded to Naomi, and headed back toward the Clinch River. The thunk-thunk-thunk started again, and stopped. Then it echoed from across the ridge. Naomi was talking with her closest friend.

CHAPTER 25

CAPTAIN RUSSELL TAPPED THE PAPER RHYTHMICALLY with the quill pen and peered at the cabin ceiling like he was looking for answers. He leaned forward and wrote something else, blew on the ink, and squinted at the paper sideways to make sure it was dry.

"That should do it," he said. He folded the paper and handed it to the waiting messenger, who tucked it into his pouch and left. Russell leaned back and turned to Matt. The afternoon sunlight streaming through the window lit his face and the cluttered table. Chopping noises sounded outside, on the Clinch River bank.

"So, how's things at Sapling Grove? Busy as we are here, I suppose."

"I guess so," Matt said. "But things'll settle down when they leave in a day or two."

"Well, I sure appreciate your coming. Wish we had a hundred more like you. Wish my boy was still alive, so he . . ." He let the thought trail off, and nodded toward the door.

"That letter I just wrote was to Preston, telling him we're ready to march. I also said we need more guards on the Sandy River branches, that those Indians'll be on us like vultures on a dead horse. Of course, we're not the only ones with problems."

"You got the biggest ones," Matt said. "The Indians'll hit you first."

"That depends on your view," Russell said. "At least we have some forts, sorry as they are. But there's none at all on Holston's north fork, and only two on the middle fork — Major Campbell's at Royal Oak and Thompson's at Town House. They can't come help us without putting their families in those two forts, and there's just not enough room for everybody."

He looked out the window, at the men chopping down trees. The chopping stopped and a tree fell, vibrating through Matt's moccasin soles. The chopping started again. The captain turned to Matt.

"We're not even closest to the Indians, you think about it. John Floyd and the other Can-tuc-kee surveyors are about ready to get killed. I sent Boone and Michael Stoner out the last of June to warn them. But, hell, they may not even be able to find them. Well, let's get going."

They went outside. Matt squinted at the afternoon sun, reflecting from the Clinch River below. He couldn't see much of the Clinch Valley from there, but he'd seen how pretty the land was while riding along the river earlier that morning. It was every bit as pretty as Clare Ryborn said it was. Certainly pretty enough to clear, and to fight the Indians for.

Russell waved at the four men chopping trees. "What do you think? That a good spot for a fort?"

"Looks good," Matt said. "You're away from the river, on top of a hill."

"The Indians scared the Cowans off this farm a few weeks ago," Russell said. "It'd be poetic justice to put the fort here."

Matt gazed around. The Cowans had cleared enough trees to build their cabin and plant a little corn. A lean-to stable stood off to the side of the cabin. Next to it were three makeshift tents. A woman stirred a kettle over a small fire there, talking with another woman. Four toddlers played nearby.

He studied the area again. It didn't make much sense, them asking his opinion about forts. He was only seventeen years old, what did he know? Hunting in the Can-tuc-kee wilderness didn't make him an expert. Living with the Shawnee for a year, that didn't do it. Of course, he did help build Shelby's fort, and before they were done Shelby had pretty much let him run the show. But even that didn't make him an expert.

"Any ideas on how we should build it?" Russell asked.

"Well . . ." The layout was similar to Shelby's place. The land had the same roll, and Cowan's cabin was in the right place to be part of the wall. And those oak logs were just about the right size. He pictured the oaks all chopped down, and arranged around the perimeter like so many pickets in a fence.

"I'd probably make it like we done at Shelby's. Face it

toward the river, put blockhouses on the corners, the whole thing. Let the house be part of it."

"That's what I had in mind," Russell said.

Matt noticed the tents again. "If you got a lot of people around, we could build a big shelter right in the middle." He walked over to where he pictured it to be. "Right here. They'll be bunched up and uncomfortable, but at least they won't get rained on or catch a bullet or an arrow."

Russell nodded. "Good idea."

"What's your other forts like? You said they weren't much."

"Well, they're little. We got Thomas Witten's station up at the Crab Orchard, and Rees Bowen's at Maiden Spring. And there's Bill Wynne's fort at Locust Hill. There's a couple others, too, like the one at Moore's, downriver six miles, near where Boone's staying. And the Blackmore fort. But they're just little things, wouldn't hold more'n a handful of people, any of them. Mostly just the families that built them, maybe a couple neighbors. And some're so weak you could almost rear back and blow them over. This one's got to be a whole lot bigger and stronger."

"It'll take a lot more people than just me and those four to build it."

Russell nodded. "I'll make some rounds tomorrow, get some neighbors over. I imagine they'll turn out in swarms, what with the Sinking Creek massacre. Come on, let's eyeball a couple of those forts."

He started to leave, but stopped. "You know, I think I'll call this Fort Preston. Maybe Preston'll take to it and give us enough people and supplies to protect it. It wouldn't hurt."

Russell left. Matt watched the men chop the trees a moment, and smiled. Soon he'd be with them, swinging an ax, working up a sweat. Store work was all right, but it was making him sluggish. He thought about his exercises at the Indian town, about just sitting around getting weak. Well, he'd been weak and he'd been strong, and strong was sure better. Exercising with an old tree stump was all right, but it really didn't get anything done. But working on the fort? It was probably the next best thing to putting a new crop into the ground and then harvesting it, when the frost nipped the air and everything felt so good. That kind of work was good for both the body and the soul.

❊

Matt was ready when Captain Russell came at daybreak. They rode along the river path, stopped at cabins snuggled into the forest. Russell introduced Matt to the occupants, told them to come to the Cowan's place the next day, and moved on. The names jumbled together: Henry Dickenson, Charles Bickley, Simon Oscher, James Bush, William Fraley, and more he couldn't remember.

Mid-morning they rode into a particularly neat cabin yard and hallooed the house. The flower border spoke of a woman's hand, as did the stacked firewood pile. Even the wood chips had been gathered.

Matt turned toward Russell and waited for him to say

something about the owner like he'd done at all the other stops. But Russell only stared at his saddle horn, inspected it as if it were a very novel object. Was that a smile he was trying to hide? The plank door opened on its leather hinges and a woman came out. She wiped her hands on her skirt.

"Why, Captain Russell, how are you!" she said. "What can I . . . why, Matt! Matt McLaren!"

Matt bolted upright. He glared at Russell, still inspecting his saddle horn.

"Well, Clare, it's . . . it has been a long time. You doing all right?"

"Good as can be expected. Say, you two light. I just made some cookies. Matt, I'm so happy to see you!"

"You two go ahead and talk," Russell said, sidling his horse away. "I'll be up at the next cabin. Just take your time, Matt, take your time. There's no hurry."

"Captain . . . Captain!" But Russell had already spurred his horse and was out of sight. Matt looked at the trees where the man had disappeared. Damn Russell! He'd deserted him for sure. Hostile Indians he could take. But a pretty woman who had set her cap for him? He vowed to get even with the man, if it were the last thing he did.

He turned back toward the cabin. Clare had disappeared. She returned in a moment with a platter of cookies and a pail of water.

"At least get down a minute," she said. "Here, have some water. You're probably parched."

He jumped down and sipped from the dipper. He nibbled on a cookie, ate the rest of it in one bite. "That cookie was sure good," he said. "Water hit the spot, too. Well, I better get on."

"I've got something to show you, first. It won't take a minute."

"Well, I . . ."

"Don't you want to see my corn?"

"Your corn?"

"I got some of the best looking corn in the valley, you just ask anybody. Come on, I'll show you."

He followed her around the cabin, and stopped at the corner. She was right. It was some of the prettiest corn he'd ever seen. It was tall and green, just starting to brown, and there wasn't a weed in it. He looked left and right to gauge the field's width, estimated its depth to the tree-tops poking up behind it.

"Why, it's a fine crop, sure enough. You do all this by yourself?"

"Oh, no. No, I had help." She set the cookie platter on the ground. "You remember Jonas Jernigan? Zach's father? He helped me plant. Helped hoe, too. Sure looks good, don't it?"

"It sure does. But it needs a fence around it. Don't the varmints bother it?"

"They sure do. Seems like I spend 'most all my time out here with my gun scaring them off. 'Bout used up all my ammunition."

"You sure need a fence."

"Jonas was going to build one. He even split the rails, see over there under the vines? When he didn't come back,

I found out he broke his leg."

"That's too bad," Matt said.

"He gets around with a cane pretty good. Say, what're you doing here?"

"I came to help build Russell's fort."

"Oh, you'll be here a while."

"I guess."

"Well, if you could help me build that fence, I'd sure appreciate it. Shouldn't take long."

Matt gazed out at the field. She'd done well. You could tell if someone liked farming or not, the way they took care of things. Jonas had helped plant and weed the corn, but he hadn't planted the flowers. He hadn't decided the field should be there in the first place, and he probably didn't keep her cabin yard neat and trim like it was. That was the work of someone who loved farming, who made sure the seeds were planted, had faith they would come up, and made sure they'd be cared for, one way or another.

"We start building the fort tomorrow," he said. "That'll take up most of my time."

She laughed. "I heard about your wall-building contest, over in Sapling Grove. That was all we heard for a long time."

"Well, a lot of it was luck."

"No. No, it wasn't." She crossed to him, squeezed the muscle of his left arm. "Here's your luck. When I saw you at Zach's funeral, you looked like you was one of the strongest people I'd ever seen. And that night when we . . . you know . . . why, I thought you could protect me from anything that came along. Were you always this strong?"

He stepped back. "No. I decided I had to be strong when the Shawnee had me, so I set about getting strong. But I've got strong just growing up, too. Just growing up and working."

She ran her hand along his shoulder, rubbed it up his neck. He shivered.

"And here's your luck, too," she said, patting his head. "Your muscles throw things around, but your brain says what and how to throw. Like it did when you beat that Grubbs man."

He stepped back again, felt his face redden. His mind's eye saw Zach's prone scalped body, his father stroking it, the graves by the river. And not twelve hours later, the outline of Clare hovering over him. Had she seduced Jonas Jernigan too, Zack's father, to get her corn planted and weeded? Her hand moved down his body, below his waist.

"Captain Russell's waiting for me up the road. I got to go. Thanks for the cookie and the water."

"You sure you can't stay a few minutes? He said take all the time you wanted." She followed him around to the front of the cabin, watched him mount his horse.

"No, I got to go. We got too much to do. But thanks."

"You take care, now."

He turned his horse toward the path, went a few feet, stopped, and twisted around.

"That fence does need to get built," he said. "I'll try and get out here some evenings and help you get it done."

CHAPTER 26

Matt awoke before dawn. He pulled on his clothes and stepped into the gray morning, joining several men who talked in low voices, waiting for the sun to get high enough to make chopping safe. In a few minutes the woods rang with their axes. They worked until the sun sank at night and made chopping dangerous, if not impossible.

The next day they showed up again, surely some with aching muscles, but none admitted it. Matt's own muscles felt the pain, and it felt good. He slammed his ax into the trunks time and time again, grunting with each swing, felt a joy as the trees crashed through the limbs of others. They would become part of the fort. But when peace came, the fort would be torn down and crops planted where the trees once stood.

Matt gauged his own progress by comparing how many trees he and the others cut. He soon realized others made the same comparison with him. Men content before to watch others drag their felled trees away, now impatiently helped hitch the teams to the logs so they'd get out of the way faster.

Soon Matt had to leave the chopping to others and make decisions on the fort's structure and location. Captain Russell stayed busy getting his company together for the Point Pleasant battle, and left the building details to Matt. Every day, as new battle recruits arrived, Matt assigned them fort-building jobs.

On his first day at the site, Matt had sized up the four tree choppers. He decided to keep an eye on Ansel Davis, who was not much older than he. Ansel volunteered first for the hard work, yet was quiet about his accomplishments. He worked well with the others, offered and took suggestions with equal grace. On the third morning Matt made Ansel his assistant, to serve as Matt had served Shelby. Together they laid out the fort.

On the last day of August, Matt rose before dawn and toured the partially built fort by moonlight. The timber cutting was almost done, the logs were lined up along the perimeter. The trench was dug, and two stockade walls were already up. He smiled as he recalled the contest of the day before, when wall builders challenged each other as Grubbs had challenged Darass Hutchins. They'd made a game of it, even double-teamed and threw the logs like he and Darass had done. They'd even counted out the movements — One! Two! Three! Four! — as they strained and lifted and threw and erected the logs in the trenches. It was as if forts had been built that way since the beginning of time.

They'd built the center shelter first, and several families already lived there. Now he heard low voices from the shelter, saw movement as families started their day. Dark blotches took shape, and soon the sun brought form to the fort. More voices sounded, more people moved about. The aroma of frying venison drifted by on a warm breeze, water splashed from bucket to kettle, a baby cried, a mother's soothing voice answered. The day was off to a good start.

Matt walked back to the newly-finished blockhouse he shared with four others. Captain Russell had slept there the previous night. He stood outside when Matt got to the cabin.

"We leave today, just after noon," he said. "You'll have to finish the fort without us."

Matt nodded. "How many men did you wind up with?"

"Forty, all told." His gaze shifted past Matt. "Well, look who's coming up the path!"

Matt turned toward the newcomer. Daniel Boone appeared, rifle over his shoulder.

Captain Russell waved. "Back already? I didn't expect you until at least . . . well, another month, at least!"

"Sixty-two days," Boone said. "Well, hello there, Matt. You've growed up."

"You must have run every step of the way," Russell said.

"Stoner and me don't let no moss grow under our feet. Hurried so I could go up north with you."

"Well, glad to see you. But I need you here, Daniel. Not up north. There's precious few left to protect the forts."

Boone's face showed disappointment, and Matt knew first-hand how he felt. Boone set his rifle butt on the ground and stared off toward the shelter. "If that's what you want."

"It has to be," Russell said. "Preston's got sixty men guarding the lower Clinch settlements, but we're still alone up here. He wants Captain Smith to draft thirty men from Herbert's and Doack's companies, but there's no telling when we'll see them. If ever."

Russell leaned against the cabin doorframe. "Daniel, you supervise the forts below Elk Garden. Be in charge of the one at Moore's. That's pretty central, and it's the one nearest you."

"Whatever you think. But those forts ain't much."

"They're better'n they were," Matt said. "Still and all, they're bad off. We had to almost rebuild two."

Boone turned to Matt. "Sure surprised to see you, Matt. You taking up Clare Ryborn's offer on her farm?"

Matt smiled, not knowing what else to do. Boone winked at Russell, who grinned and winked back. Matt was still angry at Russell for stranding him in Clare's cabin yard, but he'd gotten back, in a way. When he'd rejoined Russell that day he didn't even mention it, and finally Russell came right out and asked about it. Matt had said, "Oh, we had cookies. We discussed farming and such." He left it at that. It seemed to get Russell's goat Matt hadn't flown off the handle or something.

The fort workers laid their tools down at noon and gathered around the food-laden tables near the shelter. The Point

Pleasant recruits got their food and stood off to the side, talking in low tones with their families.

There were more tables set today than before, more people to feed. Matt got in line, watched the serving women and thought of Naomi Grubbs. If she were there, she'd smile at him right now, reach into that sack, and pull out that pewter plate. She was safer where she was, of course. The Indians would have to get by the Clinch River forts first, then go through Moccasin Gap and pass by the King's Mill fort on Reedy Creek. She was probably pretty safe.

But what about Clare Ryborn, out on that farm all by herself? Matt looked around, confirmed she wasn't there. He got his food and walked over to Ansel Davis, squatting under a tree eating his own meal.

"You seen Clare Ryborn lately?" he said.

"Not for a week or so. There a problem?"

"Just wondering."

Matt took a bite and glanced around again. He'd half expected her to show up before now, if for no other reason than to ask about her fence. He'd been meaning to get out there, but working on the forts from dawn to dusk left no time.

"Let's take the rest of the day off," he said. "Most'll leave 'fore long, and the ones left won't be in any mood to work."

"I agree with that," Ansel said.

"I told Clare I'd help put up her fence. Guess I'll go do it."

"I'll help," Ansel said. "A change of scenery'd do me good."

They walked around the fort, listened for their horse's bells in the clatter and clamor of the rest. They found their horses and saddled them, slipped quietly out of the fort, and headed toward Clare Ryborn's farm. As they entered her clearing, Matt heard a scream from behind the cabin. It sounded almost like a wildcat. It sounded again, then again.

There was no question. It was Clare Ryborn!

CHAPTER 27

"GOD, WHAT'S THAT?" ANSEL SAID.

Matt spurred his horse and rounded the cabin's corner, then jumped down, rifle in hand. He heard rustling in the cornfield and peered down the rows. A flash of movement. A Shawnee! Two more Indians rattled through the dying stalks and turned toward him. One dragged Clare by her hair. She screamed again, grabbed at a passing stalk.

Matt shot at the first Indian and he fell. A shot fired from behind Matt hit the second Indian. He staggered, fell on his back and lay still.

The third Indian froze. He held Clare's hair in one hand, his knife in the other. He jerked her head to the ground, placed one foot on her neck and twisted a hand in her hair. He slashed the knife around the skull's top and tugged until the bloody trophy popped loose, then stuck it under his belt and ran down the corn rows to the woods. In moments his horse's hooves beat a muffled retreat on forest floor. Clare screamed again and again, almost not taking time to breathe.

"Oh, God, Matt . . . they've scalped her alive!" Ansel said. "Look! Oh, my God . . ."

"Damn," Matt whispered. "Clare!" He dropped his rifle and ran to her. She scrambled up and stood screaming. The top of her head spurt hundreds of small streams of blood, pumped it onto her shoulders and the ground.

"Help me! Help me!" She stared wide-eyed at him. She felt her bare skull with a hand, and blood streamed down her arm. She screamed even louder than before.

"Ansel! Get something to wrap her head up!" Matt led her out of the cornfield and, for the first time, saw the half-completed rail fence. Her blood-drenched dress was torn and dirty from handling the split rails. She'd given up waiting for him and was building the fence herself.

Ansel brought out a piece of cloth that might have been a dress. Matt wrapped it around her head.

"God, Clare. I tried to get out here sooner."

She stopped screaming and sobbed uncontrollably. Matt looked back at the Indians and picked up his rifle. "Get her to the fort, Ansel. I'm going after him! Go on, now!" Ansel's horse galloped toward the fort, carrying him and Clare. Was Matt hearing her cries still? Or was it the wind?

Matt ran to the two Indians on the ground. Dead. He jogged back to his horse and rode down the corn rows past their bodies following their footprints into the woods. Two Indian horses watched him with casual interest. Only three Indians before, only one escaping now.

Matt circled the horses until he found single tracks

leading away and followed them. Slanted light flickered through the trees. Six hours until dark. Six hours to find the Indian. He spurred his horse and leaned down to watch the trail.

The trail meandered between the gently flowing Clinch River and the mountains. Matt rode around a bend and halted. Ahead, a naked cliff thrust more than two hundred feet above the mountain's common level, as if squeezed up from the earth's bowels. He followed the trail to the cliff's base, where the Indian's tracks disappeared into an upward slash cut through the rocks. Matt urged his horse into the slash and climbed the steep trail through a series of jagged clefts. More naked rock towered still higher and Matt stopped at the brink of a narrow ledge. Plants covered the valley floor almost a hundred feet below. Beyond stood another, even taller cliff.

Matt dismounted and looked for sign. He found scratches from a horse's hoofs and led his mount into an irregular cleft that sloped downward into the abyss. Huge rocks towered above him. It seemed the slightest wind gust would start them rolling.

Matt shook off the feeling of danger by concentrating on the trail. He followed the tracks downward over huge loose rocks into a shadowy pit. The horse snorted and balked and Matt stopped to listen.

A rattle. A coiled rattlesnake. He extended his rifle

barrel toward the snake and flipped it through the air. His startled horse lunged sideways and hit the stone wall. It lost its footing and slid a ways before scrambling back to its feet.

They continued through the pit, finally reaching the bottom, and he dismounted. The Indian's trail continued, wound up a steep cleft toward the second cliff top. Matt stopped to collect himself, and as a vision of Clare swept his mind, her screams engulfed him. He tugged the horse's reins and started the climb.

Alternately riding and leading his horse, Matt climbed and descended three more peaks over the next two hours, each taller than the one before. He paused atop each to study the wild confusion of rocks thrown together below and around him, as if God had collected the rubbish of his building materials here. He reached the fifth summit and found clear, ice-cold water in a natural rocky basin.

The Indian had stopped there to drink. Did he know Matt was following him? He had to.

Matt took long sips from the pool and forced himself to continue. He scaled the sixth and tallest rock ledge and gazed down at the Clinch, now a thin, watery ribbon which ran through hazy green. A blanket of trees, canebrakes, and pea vines covered the valley. Tiny patchwork shapes showed where settlers had already cleared. Beyond the valley, mountains rose above mountains in endless succession, until far in the smoky distance he could see the faint outline of what he figured were the Cumberland Mountains.

Beyond that, certainly beyond sight, was the Can-tuc-kee

land where he'd hunted and trapped with Knox and the others. His mind wandered briefly, took him to the campfires there, the fellowship of the other hunters, the excitement of the hunt itself.

He turned north. A large flat-topped mountain sat starkly before him; beyond it other mountains gradually faded into indistinctness. Someplace beyond them, far away, was the Ohio River, home of the Shawnee.

Someplace, just ahead of him, was Clare's scalper.

Sun glinted off metal and Matt dived for the ground. A slug ricocheted off a rock next to him. A far-off gunshot sounded. He grabbed his loaded rifle and ran toward the glint. The Indian reloaded, raised his gun to fire. Matt shot his own rifle from the waist, and the Indian lurched around, blood spurting from his shoulder. Matt dived for cover once more and the Indian's gun spit a bullet into the rocks next to him. Matt's rifle slipped from his grasp and clattered down the rocks, wedged twenty feet below among boulders that had rolled down in distant history. There was no chance to retrieve it, with the Indian watching.

Matt hunched down and ran north into the brush, eyeing where the Indian had disappeared. He crawled quietly to the right, through a small gully, hidden from the Indian's sight by boulders and scrub brush. No noise, except a bird off somewhere, far enough away to not be bothered by the life-and-death struggle taking place. Matt turned a fist-sized rock over and over in his hand, held it at arm's length and heaved it sideways over his head. It cracked against a rock beyond where the Indian had seen him earlier.

Matt jumped up and stared out ahead. The Indian shifted around a boulder, stared toward where the rock had landed. Clare Ryborn's scalp hung from his belt, its bright red inside flashing when he moved. The Indian slowly poured powder down his gun's barrel.

Matt grasped his tomahawk, jumped up, and ran screaming at the Indian, who twisted around and reached for his own tomahawk. Too late. Matt smashed his weapon into his skull. The Indian grabbed for Matt's arms and missed, tried again to lurch up. Matt crashed the tomahawk down again and again, exploding blood and tissue onto the tree, the ground, himself. The struggling grew feebler and Matt dropped the tomahawk and pulled out his knife. He plunged it into the Indian's chest.

"For Mama!" he screamed. He plunged it again. "For Mandy!"

The Indian lay still. Matt grasped his scalp lock and pulled it taut. He slipped the knife around it until the scalp was free, then slumped to his knees, looked at the black, hairy form in his hands, and dropped it. "For Clare," he murmured.

Matt stood on the platform behind Fort Preston's front wall and watched for movement on the Clinch River. There was none. There had been none since the full alert caused by Clare Ryborn's scalping, except that made by settlers coming in for the fort's protection.

He gazed around the enclosure. It was like he'd imagined a city to be, with all the people milling around. The blockhouses were filled, as was the center shelter. Every day, it seemed, more people came. Braver ones — or more fool-hardy, he wasn't sure which — left each morning to do farm chores and returned at night.

Clare shared the northeast blockhouse with other women and their children. He'd seen her only rarely since that day of the scalping. Not that she was angry at him or anything, she just didn't want anyone to see her. The women said her wound was healing, leaving a wide white area of skull showing on top. Someone devised a leather cap for her, and twice Matt saw her wear it. Most people glanced at their feet or at the clouds when they passed her.

Matt stared at his own feet. Surely he could have found a little time to help her with that fence. It was his fault she'd been scalped. If that fence were already built she wouldn't have been out there working in the field, an open target for the Indians. Maybe they wouldn't have done anything to her, her being inside the house. Maybe.

Something sounded outside the fort. A small mounted figure approached from the south, riding fast.

"Open the gate," Matt shouted. He jumped from the platform and ran to the entrance. Daniel Boone rode in, dismounted and leaned against his saddle.

He looked like he was hurting.

CHAPTER 28

BOONE'S EYES WERE BAGGY, RED. "THEY KILLED JOHN Duncan," he said. "Matt, they come at dark and shot at him and two others standing right in front of the fort. They scalped him and run off before we could do anything."

"Sure sorry," Matt said. "How can we help?"

"We need to get word to Major Campbell. Logan and his Shawnees are sneaking around Fort Blackmore like they own the place. We got to get help."

It was happening just as Matt had figured it would. Panic hit the Clinch settlements when Clare was scalped, and families moved into the undermanned forts. The men who didn't go with Captain Russell seemed to think Matt was in charge and he'd played that role as best he could. No one else wanted it.

"Those soldiers from Doak's and Herbert's companies haven't come," Matt said. "And most folks've used up their ammunition protecting the crops. We even run out of flour."

"Well, I got to get a message to Campbell, Matt."

"Get it ready; we'll find somebody to take it."

Matt returned to his post and stared toward the river. He'd have to be careful who he sent. If the Indians weren't afraid to attack the forts, what would they do to a lone man? A dozen or so Indians killed John Henry's family near Witten's Fort nine days after Clare's scalping. Five days later, three Indians shot at a soldier hunting only a half mile from the Maiden Spring fort. Another soldier shot an Indian and they trailed him to a nearby cave and finished him off.

The Blackmore incident was the latest. The Shawnee captured two Negroes, some cattle and horses. They were so unafraid of the weak garrison they'd made the Negroes run the gauntlet right in front of the fort, like they dared somebody to do something about it.

And there was no question who was behind the raids. Chief Logan, the half-breed who'd saved Matt from the stake, was getting revenge for his brother's and sister's murders. He'd been seen in the attacking parties. One of the Witten fort soldiers saw a whole Indian camp west of there, complete with a handful of women and children. Logan was making it a family affair.

More galloping hooves. The gate opened and a young man rode in and swung down from his horse. He saw Matt and ran over.

"Another Indian raid," he said.

"Where?"

"King's Mill, on Reedy Creek. They —"

"Reedy Creek! Why, that's just this side of Sapling Grove! Anybody hurt?"

"Not hurt, killed. They killed John Roberts and his children, and cracked another boy's head open so you can see the brains. He was took up to Major Campbell at Royal Oak."

Naomi. She was just beyond Reedy Creek. And her daddy had threatened to keep the family away from Shelby's fort even if there was trouble.

Matt strode to the cabin and threw the door open. Daniel Boone sat there, talking with some others.

"I got you somebody to take that message to Campbell," Matt said. "I'll do it myself."

Matt rode down the valley and crossed over at Moccasin Gap. He stopped at a settler's house for water. No one was home and, curious, he went inside. The furniture was there, and tools, but guns and clothing were gone. A scrap of bread lay on the table. He picked it up and squeezed it. Still fresh. They'd just left.

He stopped at two more cabins, found the same thing. Had they run back east for safety? Or had they been kidnapped — or worse?

He hit Reedy Creek above the King's Mill fort and took it northeast to its source. Soon he recognized landmarks, places he'd passed making his store deliveries. A knob appeared off to the right, and in an hour he reached it. He stared down the valley to the south.

It was Naomi's valley.

He turned his horse into it. Within an hour he saw smoke from the Grubbs' homestead, heard rhythmic knocking. Not the muffled thump of Naomi's samp mill, but the sharp ringing of wood or metal against wood. He rounded the last bend and saw Archelam Grubbs, bare-chested, splitting logs.

Grubbs' back was to Matt. He was bare-chested, and sweat poured off his thick, hair-matted chest and arms. He sank the ax blade lengthwise into a log and drove it home with several blows of a wooden maul until the log end split. He hammered a wedge into the crack. He straddled the log to drive the wedge in farther, spotted Matt, and leaned back.

"Something I can do for you?"

"I come from the Clinch," Matt said, glancing around. Neither Naomi nor her mama was in sight. "Indians attacked the forts there. The Reedy River fort, too."

"That supposed to mean something to me?" Grubbs shifted and squinted up at Matt.

"I figured you'd be at Shelby's fort by now. Those Shawnee could come crashing in here any time."

"Oh, you think so, do you? Well, we ain't all pansy-asses. Now, if you'll excuse me, I got work to do."

Grubbs turned back to the log and swung his ax up, ready to strike the wedge. He looked up the path and stopped.

"Well, lookee here," he said. "Here come those piss ant Indians."

Three Cherokee Indians walked down the path. Matt raised his hand in greeting. "You'd best be careful," he whispered to Grubbs. "The Shawnee're trying to get them to go against us."

"The hell you say. Why, they're as weak as cat pee, wouldn't hurt a fly. You afraid of them?" He chuckled, waved at the Indians. "Hey, come over here! I need your help!"

He laughed and peered at Matt through puffy eyelids. "I'll show you how worried I am 'bout them weaklings. You watch!"

The Indians came over. Matt recognized them from Shelby's fort, and knew them to be friendly. At least they had been back in the summer. But a lot of things had changed since then.

"Now, you watch," Grubbs said. He grinned at the Indians and they smiled in return.

"Need your help," he said, louder. "Need help splitting logs. Splitting logs."

He said it more distinctly the last time, and pointed to the log he'd started. He knelt at the log's split end and motioned the Indians to do the same. Two kneeled on one side, the third on the other.

"Now, put your hands here," Grubbs said. He placed his hands side by side on the log and extended his fingers into the split. "Need you to pull. See? Pull. Pull." Grubbs pulled back and grunted, as if straining. The Indians glanced at each other and shrugged. They placed their fingers into the crack and pulled hard, put real force behind their efforts. Grubbs jumped up and grabbed his ax.

"That's right! That's good! Just keep it up . . . pull harder now . . ."

He swung downward and knocked the wedge out of the

crack. The split sides slammed together, mashing the Indians' fingers. They screamed and tried to pull free.

Matt leaped from his horse. "God, what you doing! You crazy?"

"Ha! You call these Indians dangerous? Why, look at 'em! They ain't nothing but animals. Ha! I never seen anything as funny. Listen to them!"

Matt bounded over to Grubbs. "Give me that!" He grabbed the ax, stuck the wedge into the log, and made one long swing. The wedge drove opened the split, freeing the Indians' fingers.

"You're a crazy man!" Matt screamed at Grubbs. "Damn, you're crazy!"

The Indians held their bloody hands before them and screamed. Something moved behind Grubbs, near the cabin. Naomi ran toward them, hands to her mouth. Her mother leaned on her crutch behind her.

"You scared of these Indians?" Grubbs said. "They won't be botherin' ol' Archelam Grubbs, I'll wager. I just teached them a lesson!"

The Indians wailed and jogged up the path holding their bleeding hands before them. In a minute they were lost in the woods. Even their cries could not be heard.

"What's going on?" Naomi asked.

"Get back inside," Grubbs said. "Nothin's goin' on. Get back in there."

Matt moved next to Naomi. "You got to get to the fort. There's Indian trouble about. And after what your pa just did, there'll be more. Right here!"

"She ain't goin' nowhere," Grubbs said. "But you are. If you ain't gone in one minute, I'll kill you."

Grubbs picked up the ax and stepped up to Matt. He swung it back, as if winding up to fell a tree.

CHAPTER 29

ARCHELAM GRUBBS SWUNG THE AX WITH CRUSHING FORCE and Matt lunged away. He felt a breeze across his chest, tripped backward over the log, but sprang back up onto his feet. Grubbs grunted when the swung ax missed and threw him off balance.

"You damned piece of trash. You get off my property!"

Matt crouched, arms extended. "I'm taking Naomi and her mama with me," he said.

"Matt, he'll kill you!" Naomi ran forward and grabbed Matt's arm. "Leave, Matt! We'll be all right. He'll kill you for sure!"

"You got that right," Grubbs said. He swung the ax back and skipped a step toward Matt. He grunted, and the ax blade hurtled at Matt's head. It barely missed as Matt lurched and fell again. He crawfished backward and scrambled to his feet. The ax thudded into the log and Grubbs see-sawed it out.

"You've give me all the grief you're going to," Grubbs said. "Naomi, get back in that cabin!"

The maul Grubbs used earlier lay next to Matt's hand. It had been cut from a five-inch thick log, its handle whittled down two-thirds of its length. Matt jerked it up and felt its solid strength.

"Stand back, Naomi!" he shouted. "Get back!"

Grubbs grinned. "You made me look like a fool at the fort. You cheated, and they laughed at me! My own flesh and blood was against me. But I got even!"

Grubbs leaped over the log. Matt scrambled sideways, crouched forward, held the maul the same way Grubbs held the ax. They circled each other and Matt studied his opponent. He'd have to disarm the man somehow, and stay away from those viselike fists.

"You beat up on Naomi, don't you? I saw the bruises. You beat your wife, too."

Grubbs swung the ax again. Matt stumbled back, felt the breeze.

"The bible says women is supposed to obey their husband. Sometimes you got to train 'em like a dog so they'll obey. Stand still, goddamn it!"

He swung again. This time Matt jumped forward and brought the maul down hard on Grubbs' arms. Before Grubbs could react, Matt dropped the maul and smashed a fist into his face. The man yelled and dropped the ax, grabbed his face and caught blood gushing from his nose.

"Goddamn you! I give you your chance. You could've just left. Now I got to kill you!"

Grubbs reached for his knife, but Matt's fist splatted his face again and Grubbs' hand stopped. Matt hit him in the stomach, saw no effect and Grubbs swung a ham-like fist into Matt's shoulder. He fell.

"Thought you was smart, didn't you? Tricking me like that in front of all those people! Well, you beat me, but you cheated. Let's see who's strongest now. We both got knives, but let's throw them away. We'll just fight man to man."

Grubbs undid his knife belt and held it out, waiting. Matt undid his. "On the count of three," Matt said. "One, two, three!"

They both swung their belts out. Too late, Matt realized Grubbs kept a hold on his and it swung back down. The man grinned and reached for his knife. "You tricked me, and I tricked you. Makes us even."

When Grubbs grabbed the knife handle, Matt kicked out and hit his hand. Grubbs screamed and the knife flew away, bouncing among the stacked logs. Grubbs cursed and put his hand to his mouth.

"You son of a bitch!"

"Matt, leave! Please go, he'll kill you!" Naomi looked up at him with pleading eyes. "We'll be all right here, Mama and me."

The next thing Matt knew he was on the ground staring up at Archelam Grubbs' hovering body. Grubbs' right fist had just hit Matt's jaw. He swung it back the other direction and smashed Naomi's mouth with the back of his hand.

"Get out of here, girl! Get back to the cabin!"

Pain stabbed at Matt's face. But when Grubbs hit Naomi it dissipated and he shot up from the ground like a striking rattlesnake. His body hit Grubbs full force in the stomach and Grubbs hit the ground on his back, arms slamming down on each side, his lungs letting out a whoosh of air. Matt scrambled on top of him and smashed Grubbs' jaw with his right fist, his left. Grubbs tried to protect himself with his hands, but Matt struck him over and over and Grubbs' arms finally dropped.

The pain returned to Matt's jaw. Both his fists felt broken. He stood and looked down at the blood-spattered man.

"Get up!" he said. "You hit Naomi for the last time. Get up!"

Grubbs leaned up on his elbows, felt his jaw, then shook his head violently. Matt got the ax and held it high over Grubbs' head.

"Grubbs, I'm an inch from killing you. I'd do it, too, 'cept for Naomi."

He looked at her and saw the blood on her face.

"Naomi, you got to come with me. Your mama, too. Come to Shelby's fort. You'll be safe there."

Naomi knelt and rubbed blood from her father's face with her petticoat hem. "Daddy . . . oh, Daddy . . . Daddy . . . I have to go with Matt. You and Mama come, too."

Matt stood back and dropped the ax. Mrs. Grubbs hobbled over and knelt by her husband's head. He looked away from them all, like he saw something interesting out in the woods. Mrs. Grubbs wiped her eyes and glanced up at Naomi.

"He don't mean to do bad. Deep down he's a good man. You go on."

Naomi went inside the cabin and a minute later was

back out, carrying a small bundle. Matt took it from her and she went to her mother. Archelam Grubbs rose, his back to them, still staring into the woods.

"I love you, Mama. You too, Daddy. But I got to go with Matt."

She kissed her mother's cheek and touched her father's arm. They stood like that for several seconds, then Grubbs slipped an arm around her waist and squeezed, still looking off into the woods.

Naomi came over to Matt and he helped her onto the horse.

"You sure you won't come?" he asked her mother.

"I got to stay with Arche. Naomi, you take care. I tried to raise you good, you know that. The Lord knows I did. And don't think too bad of your daddy."

Naomi mounted and Matt led the horse down the path. Soon they were out of sight of the house.

Another two hours. In two hours they'd be at Shelby's fort. It seemed so long ago since he'd planted corn there, tended the store, when the Indians were friendly and all. Would things be the same again? He glanced back at Naomi and knew they could never be.

Matt and Naomi got to the fort just before dark. He called out and the gate opened. Darass Hutchins waved them in.

" 'Bout time you got back," Darass said. He grinned and pulled the gate closed. "Good to see you."

Matt clasped Darass's outstretched hand. "This is Naomi. Archelam Grubbs' girl. She'll be staying on awhile."

"I recognize you from the fort building," Darass said. "Your folks not coming?"

"Not right now," Matt answered for her. He glanced about the enclosure. There must have been more than a hundred people there, cooking and washing and standing around. "You got more people'n they do at Fort Preston," he said. "Folks really getting scared?"

"You got that right. Hear what happened on Reedy Creek?"

Matt nodded. He helped Naomi down from the horse and glanced over at the blockhouse he'd lived in. A half dozen women sat on benches out front, talking and tending to their children.

"Lot more women than men here," Darass said, watching his gaze. "Women and kids. Naomi can stay with them. Wish we had more room."

"Looks pretty good to me," Naomi said. She started to dismount, and Matt took her arm and helped her down. She put a hand on his shoulder to balance herself, left it there a moment. "I'll go on over and get set up," she said.

He watched her walk toward the blockhouse and turned to Darass.

"How bad are things?"

"Real bad. We're damned near out of food and ammunition. See that there store? Might as well be a stable. Burton Boyd won't haul nothing below Royal Oak. We're getting desperate."

"Royal Oak . . . I'm taking a message to Campbell there for Boone. Tell me what to tell them and I'll do it."

"Just tell him where things stand," Darass said. "That's all I can say."

Matt excused himself and walked over to Shelby's cabin. He called and Letitia Shelby came out, briskly drying her hands on her apron.

"Matt! You're just in time for dinner. Get on in here and tell us about what's happened to you."

He stepped inside and was hit with familiar smells. Three of her boys sat in the same chairs they'd been in the day he first came to Shelby's place. Isaac's stool was empty, as was Captain Shelby's.

Mrs. Shelby sat down and waved toward Isaac's stool. "Sit, Matt. Tizzie, get him some food. Hurry, now!"

The black girl went to the large cauldron on the fireplace crane. She scraped the bottom with the ladle, scraped again, then stared into the pot.

"Missus Shelby, they's nothing in here," she said. "Not enough to feed a fly."

"Oh, what was I thinking of! Of course! I just got the last bowl, 'cause I didn't want it to go to waste. Here, Matt, you just help yourself to it. Don't think I could eat any more if my life depended on it."

"No, ma'am, I don't want your last bit of food."

She pushed it at him. "Now, don't let me hear you talk like that! We got plenty, just have to cook it is all, and we'll do that tomorrow. You eat this!"

"Yes, ma'am."

He ate the soup and answered their questions as best he could. He told about what had happened to him since he'd left several weeks before. He helped build a fort, saw a woman get scalped, killed an Indian -- it seemed like he was just destined to kill people.

"An' what's happened around here? Hear anything from Captain Shelby?"

"Not a word. But we should soon, you'd think. You going to be around a while?"

"I got to go see Major Campbell. Thought I'd leave at dawn."

"Well, you'll sleep right here tonight," she said. "Isaac's with his daddy, so you can take his place."

"Yes, ma'am, and I thank you for that. You and Noah Dandridge, I don't know how I . . . well, I guess I'd better get me some sleep."

CHAPTER 30

THE TRIP NORTH TO ROYAL OAK TOOK A DAY AND A HALF. Matt paused at the town's edge and eyed the small cabins on each side. Royal Oak looked something like Fincastle, only smaller. There was no courthouse, of course. There was only one inn and a couple of stores, not nearly as many people walking around, and only three horses in sight, not counting the wagon team in front of the store. The Indian panic had obviously reached Royal Oak.

A man came out of the store, got something off the wagon, and took it inside. Matt dismounted and stood by the wagon until the driver came back.

"Hello, Burton."

"Why . . . why, Matt McLaren! How you doin'?"

"All right. Making deliveries?"

"Sure am. Say, you back from the Clinch River settlements?"

"Well, for now." Matt gazed at the loaded wagon. "You haven't been to Shelby's fort for a while. Headed there now?"

"Well . . ." Burton Boyd busied himself with another

load. "Back in a minute," he called, muscling a bag of flour into the store. He returned shortly, pulled another bag to the back of the wagon.

"On your way to Shelby's fort after this?" Matt said.

"Well . . . no. I got to drop off loads north of here tomorrow, then get back to Staunton." Boyd picked up the bag of flour and took it into the store. Matt was waiting for him when he came out.

"They really need supplies at Shelby's," Matt said.

"Yes . . . yes, I know it. But damn it! They's Indians down there! I ain't goin' to get myself kilt."

Boyd got up on the wagon and uncovered some more of his load. He grabbed an armful of packages. Matt looked over what was left, knew in spite of the wrappings what was there. He'd put enough of it up on the shelves at Shelby's.

"Well, I got to go find Major Campbell," he said. "Where you spending the night?

"North of town. Good seeing you, hear? Major Campbell's down that way at the fort."

Matt led his horse the direction Boyd had pointed. The gate opened and a guard waved him in. A lot of people were inside, standing around and talking. A man in buckskins and a blue-dyed shirt came out of a log structure and mounted one of two horses tied to a hitching rail. Matt tied his own horse and knocked on the door.

"Come in!"

Matt entered. The man sitting at the table was tall and heavy set. He looked up.

"I've got messages for Major Campbell from Shelby's

Fort and the Clinch River people," Matt said.

"That's me." Major Campbell leaned back. "Guess I know what the messages are. Who are you?"

"Matt McLaren."

"Shelby told me about you. Let's go outside and get some air."

Matt followed him out the door and they walked along the fort wall to a large oak tree where a table and two benches stood. Campbell dragged one bench against the wall and sat down. He waved at the other.

The fort was larger than Shelby's, seemed to have more people. Russell had said it was one of only two forts on the Holston River's middle fork, so there was every reason for it to be packed.

"I know what you're going to say," Campbell said. "But tell me anyway."

"Well, we don't have enough men to protect the forts. And we're low on food and ammunition. The Shawnee and the Mingo are raiding the Clinch, and the Cherokees might be helping them."

He told Campbell everything he knew about the Indian situation at all the forts, and about what Grubbs had done to the Cherokees. The Major seemed to get older as he listened. He looked down, eyelids half closed, like he was nodding off to sleep. Suddenly he stood up.

"Here's what we'll do," he said. "I'll get a message to Colonel Preston, ask him to send Russell and Shelby and their people back home as soon as he can. Let those who don't have Indian problems at home fight that battle up there."

He grasped his hands behind him and paced up and down by the wall. "'Course, maybe Logan cooked up these raids just so I'd do that, leave fewer for him to fight. No matter. Right is right."

He paced again. The sounds of people around them faded away, like only Matt and Major Campbell were there.

"Matt, how serious do you think the Cherokee threat is?"

"I don't know. I been away for awhile, but they were friendly before that. Those Indians Grubbs tricked was friendly right before he mashed their fingers. But I'd be mad about that myself."

"Right," Campbell said. "The Shawnee been pushing the Cherokee to fight us for a long time. That might help make up their minds."

He paced again, stopped. "I'll send a letter to Colonel Carter down at the Watauga settlements first thing tomorrow. Have him get it to Oconostota, ask him to help us keep peace."

Oconostota. Matt remembered he was the Cherokee war chief who lived at Chota, the Cherokee nation's capital.

"As far as manning the forts, I can't do much. I could spring maybe eight men loose, that's all. Four for you and four for Bledsoe's little station."

"It'd sure help," Matt said. "Anything'd help."

"When you going back?"

"Tomorrow morning."

"All right. They'll be ready to go with you. Anything else?"

"Well, we could use some food and ammunition."

"Can't help you there," Campbell said. "We don't have enough ourself."

"Oh, I almost forgot. I stopped at three cabins near Medicine Gap, and nobody was there. Looked like they'd just left."

Campbell sat down and stared around the fort yard. "I suppose some of them people are right out there," he said. "A neighbor came in yesterday, said a Medicine Gap family just moved in with him. I've been expecting troops to come in that I could send over there, but they haven't showed. Matt, we don't have enough fighters to go around."

They sat there a minute, neither speaking. Finally Major Campbell stood. "Well, I'd better get back to work. Anything else?"

"No. 'Cept I've been thinking about that boy that got his skull cracked open down on Reedy Creek. How's he doing?"

"He died this morning," Major Campbell said.

Matt stared at the fort wall, not seeing it. Presently he looked at Major Campbell. "I'm staying with a friend just north of here," he said. "I'll be back bright and early."

CHAPTER 31

MATT AWOKE AND EYED THE WET FOLIAGE THAT GLISTENED in the early morning sun. He was glad Burton Boyd parked the wagon on a high spot. The big raindrops had thudded onto the tarpaulin over them most of the night, splashed onto the ground, and run down the hill. He stretched and looked out from under the wagon toward a snapping fire Boyd had started. The wagoner waved at him with his spatula.

"Morning! Sure glad we put that firewood under the tarp. Get a good sleep?"

"Did fine." Matt crawled from under the wagon and rose. He heard bells and looked west where their three horses munched rye grass and pea vines.

"I got some eggs here, always carry them," Boyd said. "That's an advantage of ridin' a wagon 'stead of a horse." How you like yours?"

"Stomped on," Matt said. "I'll hitch your horses."

"That'd be good. You know, I was sure surprised when you showed up last night. Sure surprised." He scratched his belly with the spatula handle and flipped the eggs. Matt slipped halters over each of the horses' heads, untied their hobbles, and walked them back to the wagon.

"Here, let me get them harnesses," Boyd said. He laid the spatula down and jerked back as grease splattered. He threw the tarp back to expose the wagon's interior, and got one harness, threw it on the near horse, then got the other one. Matt started to pull the harnesses around the horses and walk them to the wagon tongue when he spotted something else in the wagon.

"What's that?" he said. He leaned over the wagon's tailgate and pulled a small bundle toward him.

"Just some things I got," Boyd said, quickly. "Here, help me with these horses."

Matt started to, but couldn't pull his attention from the bundle. "This wasn't here when you left Royal Oak yesterday," he said. He unrolled the bundle. It was Indian things: a bow, arrows in a quiver, a breastplate, and other items. He studied the cloth they were wrapped in. It was a breach cloth, covered with a dark red stain. He frowned. "That's blood," he said, mostly to himself. "Dried blood."

"It is?" Boyd looked nervous. He shifted from one foot to the other, all the time holding the second harness in his big hands. He finally threw the harness over the horse. "Bought it that way, off'n a stranger last night. After I left you at the fort. Here, you walk these animals up to the front, an' I'll snap the lines."

No, something was wrong. Things just didn't add up. Matt glanced around and spotted an opening into the thick trees, the start of a path. From the lighter shade of a strip of grass, it looked like something had been drug into the forest. His trapping instincts took over. Now he saw little red spatters on some of the blades.

Boyd held a hand up. "Now, don't you go in there! I tell you, I bought these here things from a stranger, like I always done. Now, you goin' to help me, or what?"

Boyd made a big show of stepping to the horses' heads. He grabbed their halters and jerked them into motion, all the time watching Matt. His gaze flicked between Matt and that opening in the woods.

Matt poised on the balls of his feet, unsure of what to do. Then he walked quickly into the opening, squinting his eyes to adjust them to the darker forest interior. There was something lying on the ground, right off the path.

"Matt, come out of there!" Boyd's voice held panic. He stepped to the path opening, blocking even more light from the scene Matt was viewing. But Matt recognized it for what it was.

It was a dead Indian. A bloody, naked, dead Indian.

Scalped, shot in the back, and dead.

Matt bent over. Blood had dripped down the Indian's back from the bullet wound and the scalping. It stopped in a straight line at the waist, where the edge of the Indian's breach cloth would have been.

"Gawd, Boyd." Matt stood quietly, still staring at the body. "Boyd, you killed him, sure as anything. Killed him for what he had with him, the clothes on his back."

"It was self defense!" Boyd almost screamed the words. "He come at me, and I didn't have no choice. Lucky I had my gun with me, or I —"

"Don't lie to me!" Matt surveyed the scene once more, then turned and walked quickly out into the light, passing Boyd. He stood by the wagon, staring down the trail. Twigs snapped as Boyd approached him from behind.

"It was self defense," Boyd muttered. "He must have turned, just as I shot. Besides, all those other times I bought the stuff from people. Either Indians, or white men I met on the road. I promise you, Matt, I never done this before."

"Boyd, how could you do that? Killed that Indian, and he didn't do anything to you."

"But he did, Matt! Why, I was just settin' up my camp, and he come screaming out at me, swingin' his knife an' all. Come running right at me. Then, I guess he changed his mind, and turned, right when I pulled the trigger. That's what happened, Matt. You've got to believe me."

Matt remembered what Shelby had said about another murdered Indian, the day Russell stopped by the fort on the way home from Philadelphia. He turned to look squarely at Boyd. "You killed that Indian north of the fort, didn't you?" he said. "Shelby said he was shot in the back!"

"Now, I . . . No, I didn't! I was just minding my own business, an' . . . good Gawd!"

He turned toward the fire where black smoke boiled up from the skillet. "Damn' them eggs!" He jerked the spattering skillet from the fire, and peered at the blackened eggs from arm's length. "They's sure stomped on and fried good. Glad you didn't want 'em sunny side up or something. Made you four, that enough?"

Matt said nothing. He fastened the harnesses to the whiffletrees, and held out a tin plate. Boyd put the flattened, burnt eggs on it, then broke more eggs into the spattering grease. He looked questioningly at Matt, then beamed.

"Yep, sure was surprised. Figured you'd stay at the fort. Glad to have your company, though. Mighty glad."

Matt started to say something, but Boyd continued.

"You know, it do get lonely, driving these beasts all over God's creation. I get to know some good people and all, like you and ol' Evan Shelby. But that driving gets awful dull. One of these days, maybe I'll settle down. That's why I trade in them Indian things, you know, for my old age."

He fixed his own eggs, finished them off in big gulps, and put away his cooking utensils. He grabbed a leather water bag from under the tarp, chugged from it, and offered it to Matt.

"How far you going, Matt?" he said. "You can tie your horse to the wagon and ride up with me."

Matt drank and handed him back the water. "I'm not going north, Burton. I'm taking this wagon back to Shelby's fort. You want to come along, you can. If not, you'll have to get your wagon back later."

Burton Boyd stood there a minute and Matt eyed his short, muscular build. Matt had beaten Archelam Grubbs, and he was a lot bigger than this man. He'd rather not have to beat Boyd up. But if he had to . . .

"Why, that's . . . that's thievery! I'd have the sheriff after you so fast it'd make your head spin!"

Matt tied his horse to the wagon and climbed up into

the seat. He picked up the whip and looked back. Boyd was still standing there.

"You coming? I'll take you back to Royal Oak. And you're wrong. This isn't thievery, this here is our supplies order. It's the one you didn't bring before, when you decided to run from the Indians."

"Why, God dang you, I thought you was my friend! I give you my eggs and everything! I . . ."

He stared for another few seconds, then sort of slumped. He walked up to the front of the wagon and stepped up into it.

"But what'll I tell them other customers?" he said. "They ain't goin' to like this one bit."

"You can tell them some kid beat you up," Matt said.

Boyd thought about that for a minute. "Maybe I'll just tell them I got hijacked by some bandits. That's what happened. Boy, you sure are a pistol, now ain't you?"

They drove the three miles back to Royal Oak in less than an hour. Boyd fumed all the way and jumped off the wagon as Matt drove the team into the fort. Matt stopped the horses and stared at the unusual sight in front of him.

A number of saddled horses were tied to various posts. Several militia men, identified by their dyed and fringed hunting shirts, stood in groups talking. Major Campbell stood with one group and waved Matt over when he spotted him.

"Matt, this is Lieutenant John Cox. He came in right after you left yesterday."

"Pleased to meet you." Matt shook the young man's hand.

"Cox is the one I was waiting for. He has two dozen men just off duty and I've assigned them to range about Reedy Creek and Moccasin Gap and warn the forts about any Indians."

"Well, I'm sure pleased to meet you," Matt said. "Everybody down there's in a panic."

Major Campbell turned to Cox. "We can only give you a hundred rounds of ammunition. That's only four for each man, and that's a disgrace, but it's all we can do."

"Yessir. We'll be careful with it. We'll kill as many of those damned Indians as we can. Matt, you killed any yet?"

"Yes."

"Well, I haven't. I've done other kinds of hunting, but I bet none of it'd compare with hunting Indians."

Hunting Indians? Matt paused. He looked at Cox, then away. The man was actually looking forward to killing Indians, like they were so many deer, or bears. He shuddered. Why, he still had nightmares about the ones he'd killed himself, and he'd been forced to do it. Yet some white men, like Cox, actually thought of them as animals. Like that stranger Struthers told about that last night at his inn, the one who killed and scalped an Indian boy just because he'd walked too close to his campsite. Or Burton Boyd, killing Indians just for the things they carried. Matt shook his head, slowly, and turned his attention back to the wagon.

Major Campbell sent his sergeant for the ammunition. He noticed the wagon. "Well, hello. What's this?"

"That's our supplies," Matt said. "Boyd was saving it back for us. When you leaving, Lieutenant?"

"Right now. Shelby's fort isn't much out of our way. We'll ride part way with you."

Matt walked over to Boyd, who was acting like he was checking the tailgate latch. "You come with us, you don't have to explain anything," Matt whispered. "I guarantee I'm taking this load. You complain and Campbell will string you up by the ears for being a coward. Or maybe for shooting Indians in the back."

Boyd glowered at him and walked around the wagon. He stood there for a few seconds, got up in the seat, took the reins, and stared straight ahead. Matt climbed up next to him.

"Well, we sure thank you for your help," Matt said to Campbell.

Burton Boyd flicked the reins, pulled his team around, and headed out the fort gate. The eight men Campbell had promised for the Shelby and Bledsoe forts followed, then Cox's people lined up behind them. A half dozen trotted around the wagon and took the lead.

They neared Shelby's fort on the second afternoon. Five miles out, Lieutenant Cox and his men said goodbye and turned west toward Moccasin Gap. The four men going to Bledsoe's little station went with them, and Matt's wagon and the other four militia men continued south.

When they entered the fort, Matt saw people everywhere, some he didn't even recognize. Darass Hutchins came over.

"We got big problems," he said. "Looks like the Chero-kee have joined the fight."

"What's happened?"

"Taylor and Shoat were out hunting yesterday and run across Archelam Grubbs and his wife. They'd cut every one of that man's fingers off, killed them both and set their cabin on fire. God, can you imagine somebody cutting all your fingers off?"

"Yes, I can," Matt mumbled. "At least in this case. Where's Naomi? She all right?"

"She's all right, but she won't stop crying."

"Two dozen militia men followed me to the fort," Matt said. "They're on their way to Medicine Gap. Maybe they'll find those Indians."

He approached Naomi's blockhouse, and heard her cry-ing inside. As he paused to consider what to do, a loud scream came from outside the fort walls. He froze. A sentry on the platform waved for the gate to be opened. Captain Shelby's Negro girl Tizzie stood there, staring sky-ward, screaming her lungs out.

"Oh, my God, my God! They's out there! The Indians got me and tied me up an' . . . Oh, dear Jesus!"

Matt ran to her and shook her shoulders. "Tizzie, snap out of it!"

"Oh, Lord God, he'p me, dear Jesus . . . " She cried and her body shook. Others gathered around, saying nothing. Matt still heard Naomi crying in the blockhouse.

"Mr. Matt . . . Oh, God! They grabbed me right outside

the gate, drug me way off somewheres over that way. Wanted to know how many guns we had here, how many people. Oh, dear Lord!"

She pointed south. The Holston's south branch was that way, about ten miles. The Cherokees had probably followed the river up.

"Tizzie, snap out of it!"

"Mr. Matt, they . . . they was taking me somewhere, then seen li'l Jimmy come walking by. They tied me up and chased after him. I got untied and got away. I din't tell 'em nothin', I swear it! I din't tell 'em nothin' atall!"

"You'll be all right," Matt said. "There, now. How many were there?"

"They was a lot of 'em! Two dozen're more. They even had women with 'em, like they was travelin' someplace to stay. The leader, he was a big one. Looked almost white. He talked good, like a white man."

Chief Logan!

Matt stood back and stared at the gate, then turned to Darass Hutchins and the others. "The Cherokee killed the Grubbs, but this is somethin' else," he said. "This is the Mingo and the Shawnee!"

"I never heard of no war party taking women with it," Darass said.

"I seen 'em!" Tizzie said. "I swear I did! They was two women and they had a li'l girl with 'em. And she looked white too, had yeller hair."

Matt felt light-headed. He looked into Tizzie's frightened face and shook her.

"You sure? God, this is important! You sure it was blond? Yellow?"

"I ain't lyin'! I ain't lyin'! She was eight, nine years old. Just a little thing. Oh, God, I was jus' takin' a walk, mindin' my own bus'ness. Don't hit me, now!"

Matt grabbed a wagon wheel for support. It had to be Mandy. God, after four years, he'd found her! He got his rifle from the wagon seat and stalked toward the gate.

"Where you going, Matt?" Darass asked. "Say, you can't go out there by yourself!"

Darass turned to one of the newly-come militia men standing there. "Go get those militia what come with Matt. Hurry, now!"

Matt led his horse out the gate to the south, then mounted and turned down the trail. Silence. Even the birds were quiet. A breeze picked up in the tall trees, then fell off, leaving an eerie stillness. Matt felt his rifle's cold iron barrel in his hands.

CHAPTER 32

Matt heard the fort gate swing open and closed behind him. Muffled hoofs retreated to the north. Someone was going off to catch Cox's troops.

He prodded his horse and leaned over to study the path. It was covered with hoof and moccasin prints. The settlers took this trail in from their farms, and most wore moccasins. How could he know which prints belonged to the Indians? Why . . . why, of course! The Indians went in the opposite direction! He looked back and saw their tracks clearly.

Tizzie said they'd tied her to a tree. He alternated glancing at the trail and the trees ahead. Before long the tracks went right, off the trail. Bare footprints skidded across moccasin prints. Someone was being dragged. Then the skidding stopped. Had they hit Tizzie to force her to stop struggling? He remembered his own capture, his attempt to leave a trail, Black Beard's brandished tomahawk. It wouldn't take much to convince Tizzie to walk right.

Ahead, a rope fragment lay at the base of a maple tree. The forest floor was disturbed all around it where the Indians had milled about while Tizzie was questioned. She'd said they tied her up and chased after a boy walking toward the fort. A trail of disturbed leaves went off at an angle. Had they caught him?

Matt backtracked to the trail and stared down it, away from the fort. More tracks. A lot more. The main group had waited there while two or three had gone ahead and found Tizzie. Now, they'd all gone back toward the river.

With the little blond girl on horseback. He didn't see her smaller footprints.

Matt mounted and followed the tracks. Mandy would be almost nine years old now. Why on earth would they take her to war with them? A blond girl and two women, Tizzie said. It had to be Mandy. What chance was there that it was not? How many blond girls could the Indians have kidnapped? The women were probably there to care for her, but why was *she* there? Why was —

A shot. His horse slumped. Matt scrambled away as it fell, barely getting his leg out from under it. The horse breathed rattling noises and kicked its back legs out convulsively.

The shot had come from the other side of the animal. Sweat popped out on Matt's face and he wiped it away. A lone Indian had been left as a sentry. That meant Chief Logan and the rest were camped ahead. The Holston's south branch was only two or three miles away now. That had to be where they were.

Matt looked behind him, away from the horse. The tree-covered land sloped toward a creek. He backed down it on hands and knees, keeping the horse between him and the Indian guard, wishing he could put the kicking horse out of its misery. Below the sentry's line of sight he slid sideways down to the creek, then jogged downstream toward the river. He bounded over the logs and rocks like a deer as he had practiced at the Indian village.

Soon he stood where the creek flowed into the Holston's south branch, a mile below where the fort path met the river. He'd hunted the area many times, delivered goods there, knew the layout like the back of his hand.

The Indian tracks were there. They'd forded the creek on their way southwest.

Matt looked west, toward Reedy Creek, where Logan had massacred that family and left the little boy for dead. The creek hit the river only a few miles in that direction. Moccasin Gap was less than ten miles north of there. Logan had come down the Clinch and through Moccasin Gap, terrorized the population, then come up the Holston's south branch to Sapling Grove.

Now he was heading back.

With Mandy. God, it must be Mandy.

There were no Indians in sight, but certainly they'd stopped close by. A sobering thought hit him. What would he do when he found them? Storm the camp with his lone rifle? He'd kill one Indian and get shot for his trouble. That sure didn't make sense.

Then he knew what he had to do.

Matt laid his rifle behind a tree and covered it with leaves. He stepped onto the path and cupped his hands to his mouth, leaned back and let out a powerful yell.

"Yaieee!"

It vibrated through the trees, echoed back. He waited a minute, did it again.

"Yaieee!"

He heard the echo and waited. Nothing. A breeze blew from behind and the river lapped against a fallen tree trunk. But that was all he heard. He brought his cupped hands to his mouth again.

"Logan! Logan, I want to talk with you! I know you can hear me!"

Nothing. He took long strides forward. Twigs snapped, dead leaves crackled underfoot, but he didn't care.

"Logan! I know you got my sister. How come you brought her? She could get killed out here, Logan!"

The sun shined off something ahead. A gun? Indian jewelry? A bright leaf twisting on a branch? He strode toward it.

"You remember me, Logan? You ought to, you saved my life. Remember up in the Shawnee town where they burned my friend Jacob at the stake? You told them I wasn't with him when he killed that man. Remember that?"

Still no sound. Why wouldn't Logan answer?

"Logan, I want my sister back. She's my sister, and I want her back!"

The snort of a horse someplace, nothing more. He squinted, could not see through the trees.

"I been trying to get a home for us, Logan, trying real hard. I trapped some pelts to do it, but the Shawnee stole them. They done it twice. I been trying, Logan!"

A shot. He spun around and fell to the ground. The sentry behind him lowered his smoking weapon. Only then did Matt feel the searing pain in his left shoulder. He gritted his teeth and groaned, trying to force the pain away.

The sentry yipped and dropped his gun. He drew his tomahawk from his belt and sprang forward, raising it above his head. Matt reached for his own knife knowing he couldn't get up before the Indian struck him.

"Mattah!" From the trees.

The sentry stopped and stared in the direction the voice had sounded. More Indian words, shouted as if they were orders. Matt made out some of them and knew Logan was telling the Indian to spare him. The Indian stuck his tomahawk back into his belt, looking puzzled. Matt struggled to get up, but the pain washed over him like a hard rain. He squeezed his eyes closed and lay still, waiting for it to go away. He glanced up ahead but saw nothing save trees.

"Logan, I know you're there. I just heard you, for God's sake!"

Still nothing. The sentry stood back, arms folded, watching Matt. The breeze picked up again, and quivered the leaves next to Matt's head. He lay on his right side, left arm flung uselessly in front of him. The silence lengthened while he took long, slow breaths, trying to conserve his strength, to control the pain.

"Logan! Let me see Mandy. You can kill me then. In fact, if I can't see Mandy, will you just tell this feller here to go ahead and kill me? Just get me out of my misery, 'cause I can't stand it no more, not knowing if Mandy is all right!"

No sounds came from the Indians. Matt tensed his muscles to get up, but fell back and lay there, floating in the pain, fighting to stay conscious.

Logan yelled something Matt couldn't understand. He heard a noise behind him and turned his head to see the sentry squatting down next to him. Matt squeezed his eyes closed again, wondering if the tomahawk would hurt much. Or maybe the Indian would slit his throat instead. It didn't matter.

He felt pressure under his right shoulder. Not metal, but human flesh.

His shoulder was being lifted from the ground. Matt tucked his knees under him, and the Indian pushed him up onto them, into a kneeling position. The Indian stepped back.

Matt stared at the trees that hid Logan and the rest. Low limbs fluttered, then separated. Someone was coming out.

Two squaws appeared, their doeskin dresses blending into the background. They came out slowly and stopped at the edge of the trees.

Logan's voice sounded again and the women moved toward Matt. Only now did he see they were holding the hands of a little girl between them, a girl who was pulling back. She looked up at the women, whimpering softly. They tugged and she followed, a step behind.

Blond hair. About nine years old.

"Mandy! Oh, my God, it's you!"

She stopped again and was pulled forward. Matt sat as quietly as he could, so as not to distress her any more. They came to within fifteen feet, ten feet, five. They stopped, let go of the girl's hands, stepped back a half pace.

It *was* Mandy! Her yellow hair was braided down her back, just like Mama had done it. She looked at him with wide, bright blue eyes. Her lips quivered, as if she was trying to hold back tears.

"Don't cry, Mandy! Oh, Mandy, you remember me?"

She turned her head slowly, looked back at the women, turned back to him. Her mouth was open.

"Remember how we used to play, Mandy? When you was just a little bitty thing? You weren't more'n four or five years old. You remember?"

The girl stared at him with raised eyebrows. She looked back at the two women. They smiled and motioned her forward. But she stood stark still, as if rooted in place.

"Oh, Mandy, you look just like I remember you when . . ." The images came tumbling back. They were in the woods and he heard a turkey gobble. Matt didn't have his gun. He'd knelt down and looked into her face, just like he was doing now, told her to go back to the cabin to get it. Then there was the fire, and his daddy lying there in the front yard, his mama and sister gone . . .

"Oh, God, I'm sorry!" He reached out for Mandy and she jumped back and squealed. The pain in his shoulder stabbed him and he fell forward. He moved his legs quickly to catch his balance and the little girl screamed again.

"Mandy, I won't hurt you!"

She pivoted and yelled something to the women, something he couldn't understand.

She screamed again and ran back and hugged one of

them while Matt struggled to get up. He lost his balance and bumped his wounded arm against a tree, groaned as pain shot through his whole body. Mandy and the two women backed away toward the trees, Mandy crying hysterically and the women trying to calm her, then she jerked away and ran into the forest, the women after her.

They were gone.

All that was left were her screams.

No, there was one other sound. It started as a vibration he felt through his feet. Then he heard it. A low rumbling from behind the Indians. It sounded something like the buffalo stampede he and Bledsoe had been in, but not as loud.

Then he knew what it was. It was Lieutenant Cox and his company, coming to kill the Indians.

And Mandy.

CHAPTER 33

Matt staggered to keep his balance. Pain clutched his entire body, shot barbs into his brain. He gasped, reached out with his good hand and waited for the world to stop swirling. He focused his eyes and stared toward where Mandy had disappeared. Nothing. No movement, no sound. But beyond the Indians he heard the soldiers coming. Surely the Indians could hear them.

"Logan! There's soldiers coming. You got to get Mandy out of here! You hear me?"

He heard Cox's men more distinctly. Their yips and yells, their horses' hooves. The ground trembled under his feet like he'd remembered it doing with the buffaloes on the Cumberland River.

"We'll fight!"

It was Logan!

"Logan, you can't do that! You got women with you. You got Mandy! You got to . . . you got to get across the river! I'll try to keep the soldiers over here. Go on, now!"

No answer. There was sound of movement in the trees,

as if the Indians were shifting positions, preparing to protect themselves from the other side.

"Logan! You killed enough people! I know how you felt when they killed your brother and sister. Indians killed my own mama and daddy, too, I know how you felt. But you got even! That boy on Reedy Creek, the one you tomahawked and left for dead? Well, he finally died. Isn't that enough? Haven't you got even yet?"

Matt dropped to his knees and sat back on his heels, mind working frantically. Tizzie said there were maybe two dozen Indians. That's how many men Cox had. As stubborn as both were, they'd probably just keep fighting until they were all dead, Mandy included. And she hadn't done anything at all to deserve that. Nothing at all!

A plan formed in his mind. He didn't like it. It meant he had to lie, go against his own people. But Mandy was his own people, too. And the Indians? Well, he guessed they weren't villains. Just opponents.

"Logan, Cox has sixty men. Sixty warriors! They'll ride right through you, mash you flatter'n a pancake. What would that prove, if you was dead? All of you?"

Still silence. Maybe Logan was listening.

"Logan! You love Mandy, too. Don't you want her to live? Look . . . there's more soldiers at the fort, some you don't know about. They come down with me from Royal Oak. There's maybe twenty, thirty of them. I . . . I bet they'll be coming down the trail behind me, and you'll get shot at from both sides. You'll all be killed. And for what?"

Matt watched the thicket ahead. The breeze picked up

a little, made goose bumps on his arms and the back of his neck. The sentry stood next to him, awaiting orders.

Was that movement? Yes . . . yes, it was! The limbs quivered again and a horse poked its head out and walked into the little clearing by the creek. Logan sat tall and straight on its back. He rode to the creek's edge and paused, turned to look toward Matt.

Other horses followed, bunching up behind Logan. Matt just sat there, leaning back on his heels, watching. The Indians were sitting tall, wearing their jewelry and finery as they passed him one by one. Not like they were going off to a war, but maybe going to a ceremony someplace.

Mandy rode behind one of the women near the end of the procession. She suddenly jumped down from her mount and ran ahead, stopping by Logan's horse. She hugged her arms around Logan's leg and turned her face to Matt, but showed no recognition, only curiosity. Matt knew she had no idea who he was. Logan bent low and picked her up, placing her on the horse behind him.

And then Matt saw himself, in his mind's eye, a little younger than she. He saw his own daddy stop plowing in the field down by Turner Creek, and bend over to unhitch the harness from the plow. He ran to his daddy as he snapped the lines to the harness to keep them from dragging through the woods to the house. Matt hugged his dirt-encrusted legs, and smelled the sweat of honest work. His father straightened and placed a calloused hand on Matt's shoulder, and for several moments they stood there, as one, while a cooling breeze drifted over the plowed land to bring the odor of moist, fresh earth and, from somewhere, the sweet scent of honeysuckle. His daddy lifted him, hands under his arm-pits, and placed him on the back of the plow horse. He touched the horse's rump, and the huge beast lumbered to-ward the house, bobbing his head all the way.

And the enormity of what he was seeing, of Logan and Mandy's relationship, struck him.

These Indians were Mandy's people now.

They were her family, not him. Their group was her home, wherever they went. In a camp some place, up in the Indian towns, it didn't matter where.

She was home.

All this time, he'd been looking for a home for himself and Mandy, a physical place. And it kept escaping him. His mama and daddy's farm, Noah's — why, they were never his own home. He'd thought of them as home because of the people that lived on them, not because of the land! That's why he didn't want to go back to farm his own family's place, even after he knew the sheriff wasn't after him.

The two dozen Indian horses turned and followed sin-gle file down the creek and into the Holston's south branch. They waded across the river and disappeared into the trees. But the water kicked up by the horses still swirled in little whirlpools, leaving a wide path of stepping stones for Lieu-tenant Cox to see. His troops crashed through the trees off to the right, and Matt prayed the water would smooth out before they got there.

Let Mandy go home!

Home. His need had been a child's need. A physical

place of comfort. An island of protection. But that protection had come from the people, not the land. He'd tried twice to buy his home. The Indians had stopped him both times. Well, they couldn't stop him again. Not now. Knowing what he knew, no one could take that from him. Not ever again.

Horses burst through the trees and stopped in front of him. Cox sat on his mount, rifle in hand.

"Where'd they go?" Cox said. Then he must have seen the blood on Matt's hunting shirt. "God, what happened to you?"

"Got shot," Matt said. "They must of been sixty, seventy Indians, all told. Guess I was lucky I only took one bullet."

"Sixty or seventy? But they said that Negro gal saw only a handful."

"Well, I guess that's all that took her. The rest must have stayed back. Hid someplace, waiting to kill whoever come after them. Anyway, they've all gone. They shot me and took off across the river. They're done out of the whole area by now."

Cox stood in his stirrups and gazed out over the river. The Indians had cleared the trees, and there was no movement there. Matt stared at the water. The current had erased their path across it.

Cox studied the river a long time, as if trying to make his mind up about something. His troops gathered about him, their horses snorting from their dash, apparently ready to continue on. Finally he sat back down.

"Well, we got to get you back to the fort. You got a horse?"

"They shot it."

Cox twisted around in the saddle. "Morgan, help him up behind you. Careful now, he's hurting."

Soon Matt was sitting behind Morgan, good arm around his waist. Cox spurred his horse up the trail toward Shelby's fort, and the rest followed.

Matt turned one last time to look across the river. Mandy was gone. But Logan would love and protect her, he'd proven that. He'd taken her to be part of his family, just like Daniel Boone had said they did sometimes. White renegades had killed Logan's brother and sister, and he'd gotten even. But he still protected Mandy like she was real family.

A tear streamed down Matt's cheek. He brushed it away with his good hand, and looked ahead toward the fort.

CHAPTER 34

MATT RUBBED HIS BANDAGED SHOULDER AND SHUDDERED. It still hurt, even after two weeks of healing. But he'd be able to travel with it if he were careful.

Bledsoe was limping over by the forge, watching the blacksmith finish off a hinge. It seemed like Shelby's fort had become a town, with tradesmen doing work that would help the rest build their farms when the Indian problems were solved.

"I'll be right back," he said to Naomi. "Here, hold the reins." She nodded and touched his arm and he walked over to Bledsoe.

"Well, hello!" Bledsoe said. "How's your wing?"

"Doing all right. Hurts a little, but I'd expect that. Just thought I'd say goodbye."

"Hate to see you go, I surely do."

Bledsoe looked ill at ease, like he wanted to say something else. "Good news about Shelby and his boys," he said, finally. "They showed those Indians what's what, didn't they? Should be back in a week or so."

"Sure was good news," Matt said.

Good news the fighting was finally over, he told himself. Good news that, maybe, both sides had their fill of killing for a while. Maybe now they could tend their wounds, and realize that neither side knows everything about what is right and just. Maybe, for once, they could finally see that the other side was human, too, and had the same needs: for love, for family, for home.

Matt stepped in Naomi's direction. "Well, see you around. Horses are at the gate, raring to go."

"I'll walk over with you," Bledsoe said. He fell in step with Matt, looked over at him and grinned. "Damn, hard to believe. You goin' to the Clinch to settle down. Marrying that Grubbs girl! I figured pigs'd fly first, 'fore you'd tie the knot. 'Course, I wasn't much older when I done it."

Matt laughed. "Guess I been wanting to ever since I first seen her," he said.

"Well, I guess there's good land over on the Clinch. They say there is."

"There sure is," Matt said. He paused. "I was way up high looking over it not long ago, and it was the purtiest sight you could ever see. Little farms no bigger'n your thumbnail, strung all along the valley. And it's some of the best land there is. Why, the corn shoots up like it's magic, and there's plenty of deer and bear for meat right there. It's what I been dreaming about all my life, Tony."

"I guess that's what we all want," Bledsoe said. "Someplace to put down stakes, raise a family. But there's a lot to be said for the huntin' part, too. Out beyond the mountains in that Can-tuc-kee land. That's what I dream about."

"I'll always remember it," Matt said.

" 'Course the Indians're too unsettled now to go out there. But later . . . well, later on, maybe you and me can go back and get us some more pelts."

"Well, there is that," Matt said. "But I already had enough of that kind of life to last me. It's good to remember, but . . . well, I got my eyes on some of the best corn-growing land you ever seen. I want to stay there and take care of it."

They were quiet again, walking slowly. Matt looked toward the gate and saw Naomi standing with the horses, with Mrs. Shelby and her boys. He remembered that first day she'd served food when he was cutting the trees for the fort, the times he'd seen her on her farm. His heart had ached when he was away from her.

"Matt, how's that Ryborn woman doing? That was a sad case, her getting scalped."

"Doing fine, I guess. Naomi and I got to help her get her corn in, soon as we get there. It'll be a big problem all along the Clinch, getting the crops in with the Indians still out there."

They reached Naomi and the horses, and Matt checked the snugness of her cinch. The saddle was on one of Shelby's horses, borrowed at Mrs. Shelby's insistence. The three packhorses were also his. Matt walked back and checked their loads of flour, a little ammunition, salt, other necessities, half of what had been on Boyd's wagon. It was enough to help Fort Preston out a little.

Matt heard something behind him and turned.

"You ready to go?"

"If you are, Naomi. Take your time, though, if you need more."

"No, I'm ready." She hugged Mrs. Shelby, then did the same with the Shelby boys. They looked embarrassed.

Matt went to Mrs. Shelby and hugged her too. "Well, thanks for all your help. You and Evan have been . . . well, like family to me."

Her eyes teared, and she kissed him. "Oh, Matt, you *are* family, you know that! You need anything at all, you come back and get it. You just think of this as your home. And Matt . . . you got a wonderful girl there. You treasure her all your life, or you'll hear from me!"

He hugged her again, and let go. He helped Naomi up into the saddle and took one more glance around. The gate swung open and Matt led the horses out and turned right.

They'd stay at Fort Preston until things were safer, then homestead that land Virginia would let them have. That beautiful land he'd seen on the Clinch River. He didn't have those pelts to buy tools and supplies, of course, or more land. But that was all right. With hard work, things would work out.

He walked along for a while, then paused and turned back toward the east.

There . . . there over those hills, Noah was buried. He'd thought about him many times, about what they'd shared. The clearing they'd done, the harvesting, the hard work that was now a part of Matt. The smell of sap freed

by an ax, of cool earth freed by a plow. They pulled him to the land, where he could scratch the surface and plant and work and then see straight rows of tall corn, brown and rattling in the wind.

Matt smiled up at Naomi, turned back to the west and tugged the reins to get the horse moving. He reached into the neck of his shirt and pulled out a leather thong until the little whittled bird with the folded wings appeared at its end. He looked at it, knew he could make a better one now.

Maybe when his left arm healed and he had the time some evening in front of the fire with Naomi, he'd whittle that other bird he'd meant to do before. This one would have its wings spread, ready to take off. Why, it might be as good as what Noah would have done.

Matt stuffed the little bird back under his shirt and strode toward the Clinch.

THE END

STONES OF ABRAXAS

K. OSBORN SULLIVAN

David Stanhope is an average twelve-year-old. His two best friends are geeks. Both his older sister and his dodge ball obsessed gym coach seem to despise him. And his parents are dragging him to a broken down old cabin in the woods for summer vacation.

But there's a secret lurking in David's attic. It takes David and his sister Amanda to the magical world of Abraxas where a centuries-old Black Magician is bent on destroying them. Will David and Amanda be able to survive and return to their own world?

And why is the dragon afraid of a compass? Can a centaur wear a tool belt? What about the huge talking frogs, hungry vampires, a harpy who cheats at cards and Lucy the Moat Monster?

Maybe David isn't so average after all.

ISBN#1932815767
Bronze Imprint
US $9.99 / CDN $13.95
July 2006
www.kosbornsullivan.com

THE WITCH OF AGNESI

ROBERT SPILLER

Bonnie Pinkwater is a teacher, a good one. She cares about her students. So when Peyton Newlin, a thirteen-year-old math genius, disappears, Bonnie starts nosing around.

One by one, students who were competing with the young genius start turning up dead and Bonnie suspects Peyton may be narrowing the field. Then Peyton himself turns up murdered. Bonnie's investigation ratchets up.

What she discovers is a coven of witches, a teenage comic book magnate, a skinhead Neanderthal with violent propensities, an abusive father, an amorous science teacher, and a mistranslated medieval mathematics manuscript. Somehow, all the pieces have intersected at the tragically brief life of her math protégé.

As the body count mounts, Bonnie realizes she may have bitten off more than she can chew. Because whoever is eliminating her beloved students, has now decided East Plains, Colorado would be better off without one aging math teacher.

ISBN#1932815724
Bronze Imprint
US $9.99 / CDN $13.95
Mystery
August 2006

HORSE PASSAGES
JENNIFER MACAIRE

Voyagers from earth have not only found haven on a far-away planet, but vast herds of horses that seem to vanish as if by magic. In reality the horses are able to open passages through time and travel from planet to planet. Settlers on the Home Planet learn to tame these horses and accompany them on their journeys, following the herds through the universe. Their life, their existence, is idyllic but for the scourge of the alien Raiders, who stalk and capture the herders and their horses.

Twins Carl and Meagan Cadet are the youngest herders in the Federation. Though they savor their privacy and the bond with their horses, they eventually join forces with the rowdy Jeffries brothers. Just as they are learning to live and travel together, however, tragedy strikes.

No one has ever escaped the Raiders. But when Luke Jeffries and Meagan, long ago orphaned by the cruel and barbaric aliens, find themselves slaves on a mining planet, they know they must try. Yet to do so, they must first discover the key to unlock the mystery of the marvelous Horse Passages.

ISBN#1932815120
ISBN#9781932815122
Bronze Imprint
US $9.99 / CDN $13.95
Available Now
www.jennifermacaire.com

Secrets

F.M. McPherson

Mike Jaeger is a typical teenager. Well, sort of. He's got some problems, mental problems specifically. Maybe a few more than most. But at least he's human.

Or not.

At the ripe old age of sixteen, Mike begins to awaken to a new self. A self that remembers forty thousand years of war with humans.

Mike and his father are clones, as was every ancestor back to the First Brother, the homonid who saw his Pack-sister, his future mate, raped and tortured by humans. Sharing empathically in her fate, First Brother vows revenge on humans, and for that is cast out of the Pack. Every descendant since remembers the events vividly, for emotional memories are inscribed in their very DNA.

But Mike doesn't know his hallucinations are memories, or that the shadows in his mind are Pack-brothers. And his father can't bring himself to tell Mike what's happening to him. Mike only knows he has one good, true friend, Dave.

And Dave, too, has a secret.

ISBN#1932815309
ISBN #9781932815306
Bronze Imprint
US $9.99 / CDN $13.95
Available Now
www.fmmcpherson.com

The Secret of
SHABAZ

JENNIFER MACAIRE

ONCE UPON A TIME, there was a brave and noble unicorn whose name was Shabaz. So wondrous was this beast, so loyal and devoted to his mistress, that he gave up his horn to a powerful magic to save her and her infant daughter from the evil and terrible Dark Lord, a necromancer. He travels through time with his precious cargo, and Birchspring, a warrior elf, to a place they believe will be safe.

TWO HUNDRED YEARS have passed. Tania, a servant lass, toils in the stable of the once mighty Castle Storm. An orphan, Tania has only her Grandfather Birchspring, and the tired old war horse she tends. Her life is hard and dull with drudgery.

Until Tania hears that a new Dark Lord has risen, and threatens the centuries of peace the countryside has enjoyed. It is not all she learns. "Grandfather" Birchspring can no longer contain the secret of Tania's heritage. The tired old war horse can no longer maintain his masquerade. Together, the three cannot sit idly by while the evil force that destroyed Tania's mother returns to finish what he once started. Ill equipped, with only great heart and noble purpose, they ride to war. BUT IT IS MORE than battle they encounter. And it is only the force of love that will endure. Love, and the unicorn's final, precious gift. . . .

ISBN#1932815090
Bronze Imprint
US $12.99 / CDN $17.99
Available Now
www.jennifermacaire.com

For more information

about other great titles from

Medallion Press, visit

www.medallionpress.com